PRAISE FOR SIR

"Mitchell's wonderful novel *Everywhere to Hide* took me on a heart-stopping ride, and I read it in one day. I'd heard of face blindness before, but the novel brought home how hard it would be in every avenue of life—especially if a killer is after you! Mitchell's deft hand with characterization and the twisty plot made this a compelling read I couldn't put down. Highly recommended!"

—Colleen Coble, *USA TODAY* bestselling author of *One Little Lie* and the Lavender Tides series

"Fans of Terri Blackstock will love this fast-paced tale with a surprising, disconcerting finale."

—*Publishers Weekly*, for *State of Lies*

"Mitchell does a marvelous job of creating and maintaining an atmosphere seething with peril and perplexity."

—All About Romance, for *State of Lies*

"In *State of Lies*, Siri Mitchell has penned a page turner that I literally couldn't put down. I confess I kept reading when I should've been writing my own novel. My heart breaks with Georgia Brennan as she suffers blow after blow when a past she didn't even know she had catches up with her. Readers will applaud her resilience and determination to solve the mystery and save the lives of the people she loves—even when the face of the boogeyman turns out to be someone she never expected. Don't miss this thrilling ride!"

—Kelly Irvin, bestselling author of *Tell Her No Lies* and *Over the Line*

"In *State of Lies*, Siri Mitchell has created a story that will suck you in and not let go. With twists and turns, international intrigue, and danger galore, this book reads like a psychological thriller mixed with healthy doses of suspense. It's also wonderfully written with an attention to detail that had me seeing my former haunts in Arlington, Virginia."

—Cara Putman, author of the Hidden Justice series

EVERYWHERE TO HIDE

Other Books by Siri Mitchell

State of Lies

Kissing Adrien

Chateau of Echoes

Something Beyond the Sky

The Cubicle Next Door

Moon over Tokyo

A Constant Heart

Love's Pursuit

She Walks in Beauty

A Heart Most Worthy

The Messenger

The Ruins of Lace

Unrivaled

Love Comes Calling

The Miracle Thief

Like a Flower in Bloom

Flirtation Walk

EVERYWHERE TO HIDE

SIRI MITCHELL

THOMAS NELSON
Since 1798

Everywhere to Hide

Published in Nashville, Tennessee, by Thomas Nelson. Thomas Nelson is a registered trademark of HarperCollins Christian Publishing, Inc.

Interior design by Phoebe Wetherbee

Thomas Nelson titles may be purchased in bulk for educational, business, fund-raising, or sales promotional use. For information, please email SpecialMarkets@ThomasNelson.com.

Library of Congress Cataloging-in-Publication Data

Names: Mitchell, Siri L., 1969- author.
Title: Everywhere to hide / Siri Mitchell.
Description: Nashville, Tennessee : Thomas Nelson, [2020] | Summary: "Siri Mitchell's latest thriller asks: Who do you trust when you can't even trust yourself?"-- Provided by publisher.
Identifiers: LCCN 2020018841 (print) | LCCN 2020018842 (ebook) | ISBN 9780785228646 (paperback) | ISBN 9780785228653 (epub) | ISBN 9780785228660 (audio download)
Subjects: LCSH: Psychological fiction. | GSAFD: Suspense fiction. | Christian fiction.
Classification: LCC PS3613.I866 E94 2020 (print) | LCC PS3613.I866 (ebook) | DDC 813/.6--dc23
LC record available at https://lccn.loc.gov/2020018841
LC ebook record available at https://lccn.loc.gov/2020018842

Printed in the United States of America

20 21 22 23 24 LSC 5 4 3 2 1

To the class of 2020

"We live in an age of deception. Words and appearances mislead. Con artists prey on the unwary. The halls of power are choked with hypocrites, and the markets teem with frauds. Every stranger is a potential enemy, and one steps out the door at one's peril. In this world of swindlers, one must rely on one's wits to survive. How, then, to guard against the duplicity that seems to lurk behind every smiling face? Look to your kin, keep your possessions close, and trust no one."

—Translators' Introduction, *The Book of Swindles: Selections from a Late Ming Collection*

⏩ CHAPTER 1 ⏪

JULY
ARLINGTON, VIRGINIA

I was just ten steps away from the Blue Dog|RINO Coffee Shop where I worked when a hand closed tightly around my forearm. I flinched as my heart raced. Though I'd pulled my hair into a ponytail, a gust of wind grabbed the free ends, looped my hair around my neck, and then cinched it.

The hand tightened, jerking me off course as a wind-driven cardboard box tumbled past. Then it let go. "Sorry. Didn't want you to get hit." The man to whom the voice belonged headed toward the Virginia Square metro station, bowing into the wind.

I hated myself because I couldn't bring myself to hate him. He could have no idea he'd left me there on the sidewalk trembling. That his grasp had resurrected memories I preferred stay dormant.

As I leaned into the wind, I took a deep breath. Reminded myself that I was safe, that I'd left my ex-boyfriend on the other side of the river. That he had no hold on me. Not here. Not now.

⏩⏪

Every hiss of the espresso maker that morning amplified my anxiety. Every jangle of the bell on the door made me jump. I was well into my eight-hour shift before my nerves calmed. And it was several hours after that when my ex finally receded from my thoughts.

A hurricane was spinning somewhere out in the Atlantic. As always, the DC region was spared the worst of the storm. No hurricane-force winds, no rain. But fast-moving clouds, muggy humidity, and the gusts of tropical storm–strength winds reminded us of what we were missing. As our wind spun in concert with the hurricane, the door to the shop by turns wouldn't shut. Or became almost impossible to open. When I took my break, I popped a couple of ibuprofens to relieve the pressure building in my head.

My cell phone rang as I was heading back to the floor, and I pulled it out of my pocket. Not recognizing the area code, I let it roll to voicemail, but it added to the dread that had been pooling in my stomach since my encounter with the stranger.

I shoved my phone back into my pocket, determined to ignore it.

Corrine jabbed me with her elbow as I tried to pass her on my way to the register. "Hey! Your boyfriend's here."

"What?" My head whipped out to the tables where she had gestured. My heart stopped for a moment. But then I saw the man had red hair, not blond. He was wearing a pair of basketball shorts and a T-shirt, both things my ex wouldn't have been caught dead in. I forced my lips into a smile as I replied, "I don't have a boyfriend."

As we looked at him, though, the man raised a hand in our direction.

Corrine laughed. "I think he'd like to audition. Oh!" She jabbed me again. "Look at him wink!" As always, her dark curls were spun up into a bun on top of her head. Her short-sleeve T-shirt revealed the "Nevertheless" tattoo on her inner left arm and the "Persist" tattoo on her right. The blue apron she wore was the twin of mine.

But I didn't have a boyfriend. Didn't want one. Never again.

I stepped away from her so our other coworker, Ty, could open the fridge beneath the counter. Corrine and me? We always found our rhythm as we worked together. Ty and me? We were forever bumping into each other.

I tried to continue on my way, but Corrine wasn't done with me. "Ooh—Whitney!" Her voice carried over the light jazz playing in the background.

As I turned, she flapped her hand at me and then tilted her head toward the entrance as a man walked through the door. "Here comes Mustache Man. Can you leave him for me? Just for today?"

It was the joke that every man who walked into the shop fell in love with me. I didn't think it was very funny. But I was the newest barista and it was worth playing along, so I traded places with her and started pulling shots so she could take Mustache Man's order. Why not? It was the little things that made shift work bearable.

By the time things slowed down at the espresso maker, the guy by the window was gone. But Mustache Man lingered. He was a relatively recent regular customer. We never had to ask for a name for his drink because he always ordered a green tea. Iced. Once he got it, he'd sit at the bar by the mobile-order area, angled sideways so his back was to the wall. He'd sip that tea like he hoped it would last for the rest of the day.

Now that he had his order and was sitting at the bar, Corrine traded places with me again. From there, she would be able to talk to him.

I went on taking orders, juggling the long line of in-person customers with the never-ending queue of mobile orders. The printer was sprouting labels like politicians sprouted horns.

Our coworker Amber came in about half an hour before I clocked out.

I called to her. "Hey—Amber! Can you take over here so I can—"

She turned her shoulders toward me, pointed to her name tag. *Maddie*.

"Sorry. I caught you out of the corner of my eye and—" She had long, straight hair just like Amber did, and they both tended to wear bright colors.

As I grabbed a cookie from the pastry case and bagged it for a customer, I glanced at my watch. After my shifts ended, I met up with high school students at the library for my other job: college-test coach. I had ten minutes to make it from the Blue Dog to Central Library. With summer vacation in high gear, Mondays were my busiest coaching day. I had back-to-back students from two to eight.

When I wasn't working at the coffee shop or the library, I was studying for the bar exam I'd be taking at the end of the month. I'd already graduated from law school, across the river in DC, from one of the most prestigious programs in the country. But my degree wouldn't mean anything if I didn't pass the bar.

In my favor, I'd been one of the top students in my class, and the exam was pass/fail. Although most of my peers were taking private courses to prepare, I couldn't afford it. My solution was to check out books from the law-school library on a rotating basis and work through as many of them as I could. I was already on my second round.

When I wasn't working or studying?

Sleep. In very short doses.

Maddie and I tag-teamed the counter and the pastry case for a while. Then I moved down to the espresso machine and helped fill some of the mobile orders that were waiting.

An iced latte.

A brewed coffee.

I recognized one of our regular mobile orders: a large soy mocha with just one pump of chocolate syrup. No whip.

Honestly, why bother making it a mocha at all?

I took a peek at my watch: 1:40.

Five more minutes until my shift was over.

I tore off a label that was coming out of the printer, stuck it to the side of a cup, and added it to the others waiting to be made.

Maddie was dealing with a food order, so I went to the register and helped the next person in line. And then the next. By that time, my shift was long over. I called out my good-bye and stiff-armed the swinging door that led from the front area to the back room. Then I pocketed my magnetic name tag, drew the apron off over my head, and looped it over a hook on the wall. I opened my locker and grabbed my backpack, plunging my hand inside to search for my phone. I used it to clock out, and then accessed an app to unlock the scooter I'd have to take to the library.

I let myself out into the hall, making sure the secure door shut behind me, and decided to leave through the back door; I didn't want to get trapped into doing anything else out on the floor.

The door was difficult to open. The tropical storm had transformed the alley into a wind tunnel, funneling the muggy air from one side of the block to the other. I raised a hand to pull my hair off my face and turned into the wind to keep it there, quickly turning my ponytail into a bun. As I stepped away from the door, I was surprised to see someone sprawled on the pavement in front of me.

He was lying face up. A red puddle had formed a halo around his head.

He wasn't—was he—he wasn't—was he *dead*?

As I stood there trying to process what I was seeing, the wind sent a recycling crate skidding across the cracked pavement.

I jumped.

I glanced up the alley, then down. Nothing was there. Nothing but the wind. And a dead man staring up at the cloud-streaked sky.

Behind me, I heard something scrabble across the low, flat roof.

I pivoted and glanced up. Saw a form silhouetted against the sky. Shock gave way to panic as I realized he had a gun in his hand. As I realized that *he* had also seen *me*.

I should have lunged toward the door.

But a familiar numbness was spreading over me. The prickle on my scalp, the sudden dryness in my mouth. I was living my nightmares all over again.

As I had done too often in the past, I reverted to form. I froze.

Please. Please. Please.

My thoughts latched onto that one word and refused to let it go.

If I could just punch my code into the keypad, I could slip back inside and pull the door shut behind me.

But I couldn't do anything at all.

My fingers wouldn't work.

Please. Please. Please.

I willed them to function, but they had long ago learned that in a dangerous situation, the best thing to do was nothing. Any movement, any action on my part had always made things worse.

And so I just stood there as my thoughts stuttered.

Fragmented.

And then a garbage truck came rumbling around the corner.

▸▸ CHAPTER 2 ◂◂

The truck shuddered to a halt. The horn blasted. A head appeared from the window. "Hey! Can you tell that guy to move it?"

I didn't answer because I was trying to remember the code for the keypad at the door and because the person lying in the alley was dead. His head was leaking a puddle of blood.

I tried to delete the image of the body by closing my eyes.

It didn't work.

When I opened them, I realized I was kneeling in the alley beside the dead man.

How had I gotten there?

I put a hand to the pavement and pushed myself to standing. Took a tottering step toward the door. The man with the gun might still be up there on the roof. I had to get back inside.

I put a finger to the keypad, but I still couldn't remember the code.

I can't remember the code!

I put a trembling hand to my forehead. Closed my eyes. Took a deep breath.

Opened them.

Come on, Whitney!

3357.

Relief collapsed my shoulders and forced the air from my lungs. But it was premature. My fingers still wouldn't work.

Come on, come on, come on!

One of the garbage collectors had hopped down from the truck and gone up to the victim. "Hey! Hey, man, you can't just—" He swore. "Miss! Miss? This guy is *dead*!"

I turned around just in time to see him throw up.

I tried to refocus on the keypad, but my heart was pumping so hard, so fast, that my vision was pulsating. I blinked hard.

"Miss?"

I didn't want to turn around again because I'd have to look at the body. And I didn't want to go to the corner and shout for help because what if it gave the shooter a better angle to kill me too? Most of all I didn't want to just stand there, out in the open, trying to punch in the code.

The garbage collector swore. "This is *messed up*! I'm calling the cops. Hey, you! Hey! Miss!" I heard him, but I didn't turn around because I'd finally solved my problem. I was going to walk past the truck to the end of the alley and around to the front of the building to get back inside the shop. That way it wouldn't matter if my fingers didn't work.

I don't remember doing it, but I must have because suddenly I was tugging on the heavy glass door at the front of the shop. The wind pressed against it, trying to stop me, but I battled back. It abruptly gave up, as if in surrender, and I flung the door open, stepping from the tempest into a pool of still, cool air.

"Whit?" Corrine called my name from behind the counter. "What are you doing here? I thought you left."

"I did. I—"

"You okay?"

A couple of the customers waiting for drinks turned toward me. One of them gasped.

Someone came up behind me and put a hand to my shoulder.

I whirled around, striking the arm away.

"Hey!"

I blinked. Recognized the cowry shell necklace of Ty. "S-s-sorry."

He put down the wet cloth he was holding. "Did you fall or something? You've got blood on your head."

"I do?" I put my fingertips to my forehead. When I brought them down, they were stained red.

Ty wrapped an arm around me. "You okay?" He led me to an empty table. "Come over here. Sit down."

I sat.

The people at the table next to me got up and moved away.

I tried to focus. Tried to push words from my brain to my mouth, but nothing happened.

"I'll go get the first-aid kit." Ty tried to leave but I wouldn't let him.

I grabbed hold of his T-shirt. "Not mine."

"What?"

"Not mine. The blood. It's not mine." And then, finally, I found the words I wanted to say. "Call the police."

▸▸▸◂◂◂

It didn't take them long to arrive.

They fanned out into all of the stores on the block. As one of the officers escorted me back to the alley, I saw they'd left police cars at either end; the squad lights flashed a silent warning. With a garbage truck, two police cars, an ambulance, and a whole crew of investigators, the alley was hosting more traffic than the major thoroughfare on the other side of the block.

The garbage collectors were not pleased. They tried to argue that they were behind on their schedule and they hadn't really seen anything anyway.

The police didn't care.

We were the only leads they had.

As one of the officers grappled with the crime tape, trying to wrestle it from the wind and thread it from the door handle of the shop next door and out to the dumpsters at the opposite side of the alley, another knelt beside the body.

A man introduced himself. He leaned toward me, past one of the investigators, extending his hand. A gust of wind tossed me a whiff of his woodsy cologne. He squeezed my hand more than he shook it. "Hey. Leo Baroni. I'm a detective with the police department."

There was a hint of New Jersey in his accent. And in spite of the humidity, Detective Baroni was wearing a suit jacket. The inner elbows were creased, as if he'd been wearing it for a while.

His black hair had decided to break free from the gel he'd run through it. It spilled back onto his forehead from both sides of his part.

He gestured me over to the wall of the building where the wind couldn't reach, then took a notepad and a pen from his jacket pocket and began to question me.

"You said you came out of the door at 1:51?"

I nodded.

"That's very precise."

"I'd just clocked out. And I didn't want to be late for my—" My coaching appointment! My heart skipped a long beat and then tried to make up for it in double time. I pulled my phone from my backpack, thumbed it open, and pulled up my schedule. "Sorry. I just—I'm late for work."

"You just told me you were coming off your shift."

"At this job. I'm late for my other job. If you could just—" Hand shaking, I held up my phone as I tried to text my student. He'd be thrilled at not having to study with me. His parents? I'd have to deal with them later.

"So you clocked out and . . . ?"

"Just a second." I sent the text. Slid my phone into my back pocket. "Sorry?"

"You said you came out the door at 1:51. I noted that was very precise—"

"I'd just clocked out. That's how I remember what time it was. I left by the back door." I gestured behind me.

Beyond us, out in the alley, someone was taking pictures. Someone else was investigating a patch of stringy weeds that had grown up beside the dumpsters.

"So you came out that door and then what did—"

A text pinged my phone. It was my student.

Could you just tell my parents we had a session?

At a hundred dollars an hour?

No.

I couldn't. I wouldn't. Even though, in this area, my fee was a bargain.

"Ma'am?"

"I'm sorry. Um—" I tried to remember what he'd asked. Tried not to remember the man who was lying there in the alley with blood pooling around his head.

Behind us, the door cracked open. Corrine poked her head out.

The detective raised a finger. "Hold on." He leaned around me. "Hey!" He raised his voice to be heard over the wind. "Don't open that door. Please go back inside!"

Corrine ignored him. "You okay, Whit? Just wanted to check on you."

"Please shut the door. *Now.*"

"I'm fine, Corrine." Maybe not right that second, but I would be. I had to be. I didn't have time not to be.

The detective shook his head as he resumed his questioning. "You came out the door and then what?"

"I don't know." I went out the door and then what? "I saw that man. The victim. He was lying there on the pavement. I think he was already dead."

"Did you hear a gunshot?"

"No." I was trying hard to keep the detective's shoulder between me and the dead man so I wouldn't have to see him. "Is this going to take long?" I needed to get to the library.

The detective shifted.

I could see the body again. The photographer was taking pictures of it from every possible angle.

"Did you hear anything as you opened the door?"

"No." I heard nothing. I saw everything.

"Right. Okay. So you were—where were you standing?"

I walked back to the door and then took a few steps away from it toward the alley. "I was right here." As I stood there speaking, the door opened again.

The detective stepped past me and pulled it all the way open.

My manager came out.

"When I said I didn't want anyone opening this door, I meant it. Could you please just—"

"I'm the manager of this store. I wanted to know if—"

"After I'm done with Ms. Garrison, I'd like to talk to you. But I'll come around through the front." He gestured her back through the door. "There's been a murder. The shooter might have been one of your customers. The victim might have been one of your customers. Either one of them might have come into the alley through this door. That means there could be evidence somewhere in that hall. There might even be some on the door. And every time someone opens it, that evidence gets compromised. So please. Go back inside and tell the others to just stay away."

The manager hesitated for a long moment and then retreated, letting the door swing shut behind her.

The detective sighed. "Okay." We retreated back to the shelter of the wall. "So you come out the door, you stop right there"—he pointed—"and you're facing which way?"

"My back was to the door."

He made some notes. "Okay. Then what happens?"

"Nothing. Nothing was happening. The man was just lying there." With a hole in his head, staring up at the sky.

A car tried to drive into the alley. The policeman controlling access waved him off. Told him to turn around.

Out by the dumpster, one of the investigators squatted. Examined something on the ground.

"And what did you do?"

"I wanted to get back inside. But the door had shut. And then I heard something on the roof. I looked up and there was a man there. I think he was holding a gun. He pointed it at me."

"And then what happened?"

"That's when the garbage truck came around the corner." I pointed left, out toward the end of the alley.

The detective wrote some more. "What happened after that?"

"The man on the roof disappeared."

"Did you notice anything about him?"

"Besides that he was a man?"

"Anything."

I shook my head. He was a man. He was holding a gun. I was almost certain it was a gun.

"What was he wearing?"

I closed my eyes. Tried to recall. "A jacket? Dark. I couldn't see him below the waist."

"What did he do with the gun?"

"He put it into his jacket."

"Jacket?" He underlined something in his notebook. "Into the pocket?" He patted the outside pocket of his own jacket.

"Inside pocket."

"*Inside* jacket pocket. What kind of jacket?"

"Suit jacket."

The investigators were moving closer. One of them was inspecting the gutter beside us.

"Color?" the detective asked.

"Um. Sorry. What? Color of what?"

"The suit."

"I don't know. I don't remember. It was a dark color."

"And that was it?"

"That was it. He disappeared."

He made a few more notes. "Any idea who he was? Had you seen him before?"

"I don't know. I don't think so."

We exchanged contact information. He asked me to wait inside the coffee shop until he could work up a statement for me to sign.

As I turned to go, I nearly ran into one of the investigators. She was holding a Blue Dog coffee cup. Our tagline . . . *and other fantastical beasts*, written in cursive, ringed the bottom edge of the cup.

As I held on to her arm for balance, I saw the label.

It was one I'd put on that cup about half an hour before.

Joe
Soy mocha
One pump
No whip

I walked back to the detective. Caught his attention.

He turned away from the wind as he bent to talk to me. "Think of something else?"

"I know who the victim is."

"But you said before that you didn't recognize him."

"I didn't. I don't. But that cup?" I pointed to the investigator who was bagging it. "I gave that cup to that man just before I got off work."

He reached past me and gestured to the woman. Took the bag from her.

I pointed to the label.

The detective read it. "Joe?"

"He came in every day around one thirty. For a mobile order."

"So you *did* know him?"

"I don't know anything about him except that he usually ordered a soy mocha. One pump. No whip."

He gave the bag back, pulled out his notebook, and made a few more notes. "So we've got a couple of men with the garbage truck who might have seen a guy running down the sidewalk right before they turned into the alley and who may or may not have heard a gunshot when they were on the other side of the street. They were right in the middle of a debate about whether the Nats are going to make it into the playoffs, so they can't say for sure." He flipped the notebook shut. "And then there's you. You saw the killer and you knew the victim. At least we have you."

That was the moment I was dreading. The moment I finally had to tell him. "Not really. You don't really have me at all."

⏩ CHAPTER 3 ⏪

The detective took me around the block and into the coffee shop. It was mostly deserted. A police officer seemed to be wrapping up an interview with a pair of customers.

We sat at an empty table. The manager brought us some water. By that point, I was long past late for the library. I had already stood up my second student and I'd texted the third and fourth to let them know I wasn't coming.

The detective opened up his notepad and took out his pen. "Do you mind if we go over this again? You're the only one who saw the murderer and you just told me you can't be a witness?"

"Not in the traditional way."

"We don't have the victim's wallet. We don't have his phone. Don't have any identification for him at all. All we have is you and a coffee cup."

"I know, and I wish—"

"And now you're saying *all* we have is the coffee cup?"

The contrast between the mugginess outside and the coolness of air-conditioning had been refreshing at first. Not anymore. I pulled one of my hands up into the sleeve of my red blouse and then tucked it underneath my other arm.

"Is that what you're saying?"

"No."

"No?"

I shook my head.

"Then what are you saying? I need to understand. Are you asking for a lawyer?"

I smiled; I couldn't help myself. If all went well during my bar exam, then I would be able to do a half-decent job of representing myself. Even though, of course, no smart lawyer would do that. "No. Back in the alley, when I told you that you didn't have me, what I meant was, it's not that I didn't see the killer or know the victim—it's that I can't remember them."

He sat back. "Oh. Don't worry. That's not unusual. Murder is traumatic. It might come back to you in pieces, in flashes of memory. Or it could replay in an endless loop. The mind is funny that way."

"That's what I've been trying to say. My mind is particularly funny."

"In what way?"

"I can't remember faces. I have face blindness."

"I don't know what that is. What does that mean?"

"My brain can't process faces."

"So maybe we work with a forensic artist to sketch an image of the shooter. That's fine."

He wasn't listening to me, so he didn't understand. But that was typical. "That won't help. It's as if the software that stores facial recognition inside my brain has been deleted."

"So what you're saying is what, exactly?"

"I can't remember the face of the killer because it was never stored in my brain in the first place. I can tell you the killer wore a suit jacket, but I will never be able to tell you what his face looked like."

"Ever?"

"Never."

"If we can come up with a suspect, would a lineup help jog a memory?"

"*There is no memory.*" Hysteria fought its way up into my throat. I took a deep breath as I tried to think of another way to explain. I put my hand up and held it in front of my eyes so that it obscured his face from my view. "This is what it's like when I look at you. I know that your hair is black. I can see that you're wearing a blue suit jacket and a white shirt." He had square shoulders and several chest hairs peeking through his open collar. "But I can't tell you anything about your face."

"Ever? But what if you were to look right at me and I asked you, 'What color are my eyes?'"

"Always. This is always how it is. It's how it always has been. And that's all I would be able to tell anyone, ever."

"So what you're telling me is that you would never be able to recognize the shooter."

Finally! "Yes."

▶▶▶◀◀◀

He asked me a dozen more questions about the condition, and I gave him the same answer to every one.

I can't remember faces.

One of the investigators came in. The detective excused himself for a moment to join her. As they talked, he gestured once or twice at me. I didn't have to strain to hear their conversation.

"But she said she saw the shooter." The investigator seemed exasperated.

"I know. And she did. It's just that she can't remember."

False. I *could* remember. I could remember everything. The only thing I couldn't remember was the face of the killer. I hadn't told anyone at work about my condition, but just then I felt like standing on the chair and announcing it so everyone could hear. But even if I did, I knew it wouldn't matter. I'd still be the weirdo. It was better just to let people talk and get it over with.

The detective was still speaking. "She says she has face blindness."

"Face blindness? Is that a thing?"

"It's a thing."

Their conversation went on like that for a while. I finally dug around in my backpack for my phone and sent a text to my dad, asking how his day was.

He texted back, *I'm thriving.*

Thriving? That didn't sound like my dad. As I was puzzling over it, he sent another text.

You

I eyed the single word with suspicion. No complete sentence? No punctuation? I felt like asking him for his identification. Maybe he was following my advice and taking one of the social media classes down at the community center back home.

I texted back, *Fine.* Except for the murder. *Busy day.*

Chance of rain anytime soon?

After a fall and winter that had featured nonstop rain, the Pacific Northwest was now in danger of becoming a tinderbox.

He texted me a cactus emoji.

What was going on? In the space of two hours, my whole world had turned upside down. I'd stumbled into a murder and my father had discovered emojis.

The detective came back. "Ms. Garrison? I'd like you to watch the footage from the security camera with me."

"Sure. Yes. Of course."

"See if anything—I mean, I know you won't recognize anybody, but maybe you'll see something that will help you remember. Something that's not a face. I'll take anything that will help us identify the victim. Or the killer. The manager said she'd meet me in the office?"

"It's behind there." I pointed to the swinging door behind the counter.

He took a step forward. Paused. "How do we get back there?" The work area was completely enclosed by the counter.

"There's another door. In the back hall. But you said you didn't want anyone using the hall earlier."

"It's fine now. We've gone over it."

I led him back to the door. Punched in the code.

The manager was at her desk. She stood when she saw us.

"I'll set everything up here." She gestured to her desk and then leaned close to me. "The sooner the police can solve this, the sooner business gets back to normal."

As I put my things into a locker, she sat down in front of her computer. By the time I joined them, she had brought up some footage and maximized it to fill the screen.

It was from after the shooting. Police officers and detectives walked in and out of view. One of them knelt and picked up something in the alley. Put it into some sort of bag.

The image froze and then disappeared as the manager tinkered with the program. Then more footage appeared. "This is the start of the shift, when the first barista came in at four this morning." She vacated the chair.

The detective sat down. Turned to me. "You said the shooting happened when?"

"At 1:51." I stopped myself. "Actually, at some point before 1:51. That's when I came out the door."

"Can we fast-forward?" he asked the manager. "I'm just looking, at the moment, to see who used that door. Besides Ms. Garrison."

She leaned over and pointed to a button. Then she straightened and headed toward the swinging door that led to the counter area. "I'm going out on the floor. Let me know if you need anything else."

After the manager left, I watched over the detective's shoulder as he reviewed the footage.

The camera was positioned right above the door. Its fish-eye view captured the keypad and a narrow band of the alley. Its purpose seemed to be to identify who was coming and going through the back door.

At 1:43, the door opened into the frame and a man appeared. The camera caught the top of his head. The door retreated as he stepped into full view. As he walked into the alley, the wind flattened his hair against his skull. Holding a hand up in front of his eyes, he turned to his left, to his right. Then he took a drink from his cup. Seemed to look at his watch. Took another drink. Turned to look over his shoulder and then down the alley again. Took a drink. Turned his face up to the camera.

The detective paused the footage. Pulled out his phone. Called someone. "Hey." He listened a moment before speaking. "Can you send someone to check out the roof again? Take another look?" He paused again. "Yeah. Thanks. And we need to see if anyone else had a camera in the alley or along the street out in front. Go down to the metro station, see if we can get their footage too." He spoke for a few more moments and then hung up. "You good?" he asked me.

I nodded.

"Okay. I want you to explain to me exactly what you can see and what you can't. For instance—" He rewound the footage to the place where the victim turned his face full-on to the camera. "What can you see here?"

"The man—the victim—he turned around. Before, he was facing the dumpster across the alley. Now he's facing the camera."

"So you know where his face is."

"Generally speaking, a person's head is on top of their shoulders."

"I'm not trying to take a cheap shot here. I'm trying to understand what you can and can't see. It's important. The longer it takes to solve this, the greater the chance the shooter gets away with it."

"I'm sorry." I sighed. "I apologize. Face blindness has a continuum. Some of us are more affected than others. Here's how it works with me. When I look at someone, I can tell if they're a child or an adult. I have trouble distinguishing adult-size age unless I can see someone as they walk or I get an up-close look at their hands or their neck. Or their hair. But people can color their hair. Is a balding man with dark hair a young man or is he just vain? I would need other clues in order to tell you."

"What kind of clues?"

"Clothes. Shoes. Those aren't always accurate, but they can usually get me safely to one side of sixty or the other. Unless it's a woman having a midlife crisis. Or one trying to keep up with a teenage daughter. In that case, knees are a dead giveaway. If I can hear someone speak, that usually helps me too."

"If you can't see faces, then how do you know what he's facing? Where he's looking?"

"I'm not blind. Which direction are his feet pointing? I can tell if I'm looking at someone from the back or from the front. And in that footage, I saw him turn around."

"So it's only faces."

"Which is probably why the condition is called face blindness." That was a smart-aleck thing to say, but it really wasn't as difficult as people wanted to make it. "If you think of me intentionally blurring out the faces of people I see in order to protect their identities, then that would be an accurate way to think about it."

"Okay. So you see that he turned toward the camera. What else?"

"Can you play it back again?"

He rewound it a few seconds and then let the footage play.

I gave a running commentary as I watched. "He turns away from the dumpster. Pauses to look at his watch. Now he's facing the door. It seems like he's about to turn away again, but he looks up instead."

The detective paused the footage. "How do you know that if you can't really see his eyes?"

I shrugged. "I mean—" There were multiple ways. "The angle of his shoulders? The shift in the tilt of his hairline?"

"Okay."

"Why? Is there anything wrong with any of that?"

"It's windy."

"It is," I answered cautiously because I couldn't figure out where he was trying to go with that information.

"He was looking up and down the alley, he was checking his watch."

"Sipping his coffee. Maybe he was waiting for someone."

"Right. That's what I'm thinking. So why did he look up all of a sudden?"

"Is that rhetorical? Because if it was, I would ask in return, 'Why do any of us do anything?'"

"He was surveying the place. There was no reason for him to look up. Not when he was clearly intending to repeat his pattern. Up the alley, down the alley, turn and check the door. But he did glance up. I'm thinking he must have heard something."

He let the footage play on.

Immediately after looking up toward the roof, at 1:46, Joe took an abrupt step backward and then seemed to wilt. His knees buckled and he fell to the ground as his coffee cup hit the pavement and rolled away.

At 1:51, I came out.

I watched myself, on the screen, as I lurched over to the body and knelt beside it. I put a hand to his shoulder. Shook him. Put a hand to the pavement and braced myself so I could shake him again.

I remembered none of that.

Then I turned around and looked up as I put a hand to my forehead. When I drew it away, I left behind streaks of blood.

I stood.

Stared down at my hands for a moment.

And then my fingers pulsed wide as my head sank into my shoulders.

"You screamed."

"What?"

"You screamed." The detective pointed to the footage. "You were screaming."

I didn't remember any of that. None of it. I remembered nothing. I couldn't even recognize myself. And I hadn't even heard myself scream.

▸▸ CHAPTER 4 ◂◂

The detective pushed away from the desk, strode to the door that led out to the hall. "I'll just be a minute."

Not willing to be left behind, I followed him out into the alley where he was standing in the middle of the pavement, hand shielding his eyes as he tilted his head toward the roof. He walked over to the stain on the asphalt where the victim had been shot. Turned to look up, over his shoulder, at the roof.

I was still standing in the doorway.

He shook his head as he came toward me. "The roof is the only place the shooter could have been. And there's no way to get up there from the alley." He gestured for me to go back inside, ahead of him.

I punched in the code for the back-room door.

He sat back down in front of the computer and started the footage again at 1:50.

At 1:51, the door swung open. It was me. I recognized my shirt. As I paused to spin my hair into a bun, the door swung out of view.

It felt extremely odd to be watching myself. I'd been completely unaware of the camera.

He let the footage keep rolling. I could feel my heart slam against my chest as I watched. My vision was going hazy. A sweat broke out above my lip. I stepped away from the detective. "I'm sorry. I just—" I gestured toward the footage. "I need a minute."

"Hmm?" He turned around to face me. "Sorry. Sure. Can I get you something? Water?"

"Thanks. No. Just give me a minute." I concentrated on breathing. Tried to blink away the memory of the murder.

The detective was watching the footage again.

I angled my head so I didn't have to look right at it.

"Do customers normally leave by the back door?"

"No. But the bathroom is down the same hall. And people use that all the time."

"You say the victim was a regular customer. Did he always use the alley door?"

I shrugged. "I don't know. I have no idea."

"I don't mean to pressure you. If you don't know, you don't know. It's not a problem. This isn't a test; there's no right answer."

"I just wish I could be more helpful."

"Well, tell me this. Do *you* normally leave by the back door?"

"Sometimes. When I want to avoid someone out on the floor."

"Who would you want to avoid?"

"Customers, if they had issues with their order. Why give them another chance to yell at you? Or my coworkers, if I'm afraid they might want me to do 'one last thing' on my way out the door."

"Sure. I get it. So how often would you say you use the back door? Every other day? Every third day?"

"Once or twice a week."

"And the victim was your customer for how long?"

How long had I been making those mochas? "Since I've been working here, I guess. I started in May."

"So during all those times you left by that door, did you ever see him in the alley?"

"Not that I know of. I rarely see anyone out there. But like I said, I don't always leave by the back door."

"Do people come *in* that way?"

"Only if you have the code. Or if someone opens it for you. We get morning deliveries through the back door." I hadn't opened for a few weeks and I didn't really want to ever again.

He started up the footage again and watched it through the shooting. I averted my eyes.

"I'd be interested in knowing if anyone left the shop from the main entrance right before or right after our victim left by the back. You have a security camera inside the store too?"

I didn't think so, but I got the manager and she brought up footage of the floor from several different angles. I hadn't even known there were security cameras inside the store. "You never know what's going to happen," she pointed out. "And if something ever does, then I've got the cameras on my side." She wound one of them back to one o'clock.

That camera was posted behind the counter, but it was pointed toward the door. Most of the shop floor was within its view.

At 1:34, the door opened. The detective straightened. "There he is. That's our victim."

He slowed down the progression.

Joe went straight to the mobile-order counter. Seemed to look at his watch. He turned back toward the front door, and then he walked away from it, around the front counter, and disappeared from view.

"Where's he going?"

The manager answered, "The back hall. It's the only way he could have disappeared from the camera."

"Okay." The detective started the footage again. Several minutes later, Joe came back into view. He went back to the mobile-order counter and picked up his coffee. Seemed to look at his watch again. Then he walked toward the back hall, out of the footage.

The manager's phone rang. She stepped out to take the call.

The detective paused the video. "So he picked up his coffee and made a beeline for the back door. Although he looked at his watch first."

"Maybe he was worried about the time."

"Maybe. Okay. Let's go through it again. This time we'll look at who else comes in or goes out."

He went back to 1:10. Paused it. "We've got—" He counted underneath his breath. "Fifteen people before our victim comes in. Seven sitting down and eight in line." He resumed the footage and slowed the speed.

"Okay. One goes out." The video kept playing. "Three go out together. Joe comes in." He stood at the counter for a moment and then left the footage. "Two come in. Joe comes back. Another goes out."

It was Mustache Man.

"He comes in most days."

"What's that?"

"The guy with the mustache. The one who just left. He's a regular too."

"Okay. Two come in. One goes out. What's our line doing?" He slowed the footage and counted the people waiting to order.

About the time Joe walked out the back door, someone had approached the pastry case and then backed off and left. Several other people got up from tables and left as well. If the detective was looking for the shooter among the customers, there were several possibilities.

"Could be one of those who left at the end," he muttered. "And I'd like to know more about that man with the mustache. Especially if he's a regular. Maybe he saw something. Does he come at the same time every day?"

"Generally. After noon. Before my shift ends."

"You have my number. Can you call me next time you see him? The only people we were able to interview were those still in the shop after it happened. Which by definition . . ."

I finished his thought. "Makes them not the killer."

The detective had me wait while he wrote up my statement. The last time I'd given the police a statement was just before I'd moved to Arlington. I'd spoken to the police in DC—haltingly, awkwardly, pushing my words past a swollen lip. Blinking back tears from a blackened eye. Trying to ease the pain from a rib that I assumed was broken.

As that memory surfaced, I tried my best to block it.

I took out my phone instead. Replied to the students who had texted me back.

Then I clicked through to the latest edition of a financial news digest I subscribed to.

As I read the latest headlines, I felt an eyebrow rise in surprise. A bill that I had worked on when I'd interned on the Hill, a bill that had finally made it out of committee several months before, had died on the House floor. I clicked through to the article to read the names of the dissenters. Four of the representatives who had voted for the bill in committee, including the congressman I had interned with, had ultimately decided to vote against it.

How could that be?

The bill would have strengthened some of the most important financial oversight measures that had been put in place after the Great Recession of 2008. And those four representatives had been the loudest voices supporting those measures.

I was still puzzling over the failure of the bill when Detective Baroni approached. He offered me the statement. "Read it over. If it's accurate, go ahead and sign."

I read it.

"Any corrections?"

"Here." I pointed to a box on the form.

He picked it up. Read the box. "Age?"

"Twenty-*eight*, not twenty."

"I thought that's what you'd said, but it didn't sound right."

There seemed to be an assumed correlation between height and age with some people.

"Sorry." He corrected it and handed it back to me along with his pen. "Sign it for me?"

I signed.

"You're good on my end. Any questions on yours?"

"Just one." And it was really starting to worry me. "The killer saw my face. He knows who I am. I don't have any idea who he is. That scares me."

"He's probably miles from Arlington by now."

"But what if you're wrong? What if he hasn't disappeared? What if he tries to find me?"

He sat down across from me. "Crime seems irrational, but people who commit them have their own logic. That shooter knows you saw him. He won't want to have anything to do with you, won't want to be anywhere near you, because he won't want to be identified. We know you have face blindness, but he doesn't. In his mind, he gets away with this by making sure he can never be identified. You don't have to be afraid, don't have to go into hiding, because chances are, he already has."

I followed his argument; it was logical; it made sense.

I wanted to believe him. I really did. But I couldn't convince myself to do it.

▸▸ CHAPTER 5 ◂◂

After the detective left, I stayed at the Blue Dog. I canceled the rest of my students because I was afraid to go back outside.

I shifted to the table farthest from the windows, sat in a chair with my back to the wall. Then I spent some time calling parents to reschedule all the coaching sessions I'd missed. When I was done, I pulled my study guide from my backpack and did some review for the bar exam. But eventually, I didn't have any excuses left to stay. And I needed a study guide that was at my apartment.

If Corrine had still been working, I might have convinced her to walk outside with me to the scooters. Instead, I told myself that there was nothing to worry about, that the street out front was busy enough, that there were plenty of people walking to and from the metro, that nothing bad was going to happen. Still, after scanning the sidewalk, I jogged over to the scooters, quickly unlocked one with the app on my phone, and wasted no time as I started toward home.

▸▸▸◂◂◂

My new basement apartment was located in a part of Arlington I couldn't have afforded even to visit. As I headed away from Virginia Square, the modern high-rise apartment buildings gave way to older retail buildings and restaurants, which tapered off to several-story duplexes and townhomes and then into a century-old residential neighborhood. As the buildings shrank, the trees got older and taller. The sidewalks became more uneven, the streets more serpentine.

The cars changed from Priuses and Subarus to Teslas and Audis.

The gusty winds had mellowed into a stiff breeze. It carried with it the cloying scent of some kind of flower. Fallen crepe myrtle petals had drifted across the streets, accumulating in piles, clogging the sewer drains.

I was still getting used to not having to look over my shoulder for my ex all the time. After I'd gathered my courage and finally broken up with him, he'd shown up everywhere, trying to apologize, begging me to give him another chance.

At school.

At work.

At my tiny studio apartment across the river in the warrens of DC.

I'd tried to ignore him at first. It wasn't easy. He called, he texted, he sent flowers. But I wasn't open to persuasion. I had proof that he had cheated on me; he couldn't gaslight me anymore. I had a picture from his *other* Instagram account—the one someone had finally shown me—of him with another woman.

Of course, he insisted that it hadn't meant anything. He told me he deserved a second chance. So I tried to reason with him. He'd cheated on me, so clearly he wasn't happy with me. At that point, I didn't mind labeling myself as the villain. I just wanted out. It was an awful, heart-shattering end to what I had once thought was a beautiful beginning. The best day of my life and the worst were both thanks to him.

I'd never met anyone like him. He was smart, charming, charismatic. And I'd felt so lucky that the person he wanted to be with was me. I actually tried to reason him out of a relationship at first. I'd made every argument I could think of: the difference in our ages, the fact that I was still a student, and the reality that we came from two different worlds. But he never took no for an answer. That was how he'd come up with his innovative made-in-America secure-server solution to cybersecurity. By not taking no for an answer, he'd done what most people had considered impossible. He'd sourced all of his components and materials in-country. It wasn't that difficult for him to argue me around to seeing myself from his point of view.

It was his appeal to reason that had seduced me. He'd done it by laying down actual answers to all of my questions.

Why do you like me? *Why* do you want to be with me?

He said I was brilliant. I was passionate. I was committed to making the world a better place. Why wouldn't he want to be with me? If anyone was lucky in our relationship, it was him.

Eventually, I didn't have any arguments; I gave in to what my heart had wanted all along.

Growing up, I heard people say all the time what a beautiful girl I was. Though I could never see myself the way they did, I understood that to them, beauty was important. To my ex's credit, he never, not once, used my beauty as one of the arguments for why we should be together. He'd already figured out it wouldn't have worked with me.

One of the joys of our relationship, early on, was that we could debate anything. To the lawyer in me it was stimulating. Exhilarating.

When I was still new to dating him, I'd been left breathless once or twice by the sheer audacity of his arguments. He could take a point I made in support of a position and send it back to me as an argument against it.

The machinations of his mind were dazzling.

But that wasn't his only attraction. I melted at the way he was so thoughtful. The way he always asked about my day before telling me about his. The way he brought me flowers randomly, spontaneously, just because. I loved the way he towered over me, the way he always leaned into me. And the way he always seemed to be waiting for me. It seemed so protective.

And manipulative.

Only I didn't see it that way at first. It took me sixteen months and three weeks. Two black eyes and—finally, after our breakup—one restraining order to see him as he really was.

The first few weeks after I'd moved from DC to Virginia, my senses were still attuned to him. I thought I saw his slick-haired, preppy-clothed frame everywhere. I could have sworn I heard his confident voice. Recognized his laugh. I even woke up sometimes at night thinking I'd felt the fan of his breath on my neck.

But we were done.

As categorically as a lawyer could, I'd broken things off. I left him just as surely as I left all the little gifts he'd given me. I put them in a pile on his kitchen counter, keeping only a small cactus, an aloe plant, and a planted palm. They were his, but I didn't figure he'd notice. The diamond tennis bracelet, the smartwatch I'd never really liked, the cashmere sweaters, the calfskin boots, the luxury handbags—I left them all behind.

He understood my background. He knew I didn't have the money to spend on myself. I'd protested every gift he gave me, but he always replied the same: "It's all in the details. I know you're brilliant and it's what's inside you that counts. But if you look the part of a successful, high-powered lawyer, then it will be easier for other people to see you that way too. You don't want to give them any reason to discount you."

In hindsight it was a bunch of BS. He gave me all those things for another reason entirely, but he was right. He was absolutely right. Especially in the world of the DC elite.

If I had sold those gifts on Craigslist I might have made a couple thousand dollars. I could have used that money. But I couldn't bring myself to do it. Maybe I was leading with my heart instead of my brain, but he'd taken enough of my past from me. I didn't want him to have anything to do with my future.

I scootered past brick colonials and sprawling Arts and Crafts bungalows.

Past a school.

More houses.

I heard the thump of tires as a car pulled up next to me at a stop sign, baking me for a moment in the heat from its engine. Then it rolled through the intersection, leaving me behind.

I let it. I'd rather have a car ahead of me than behind me. I waited until the air had cleared of the exhaust, until the dust and pollen had come to rest. Then I pressed down on the throttle and glided on.

At the end of the block, where a modern, angular concrete-and-glass home stuck out like a pariah, I turned onto a narrow curving street. The houses along it didn't have garages and, for reasons that weren't apparent to me, most of the residents ignored their driveways. Fortunately, my side was mostly clear.

Behind me, I heard another car coming, wheels churning over scattered gravel that had been left behind after a road repair project.

I pulled my elbows in, moving away from the middle of the street toward the sidewalk.

I threw a glance over my shoulder.

The car was coming up fast.

There was a pothole right in front of me. I slowed, made a sharp turn to the right, and tried to navigate the thin strip of road between the pothole and the curb. I'd have to turn left—hard—to avoid running myself into a parked car.

As I scootered around the pothole, the car flew past me so closely that its tire thumped into the pothole and the side mirror caught the scooter's handlebar.

It pulled me along for a moment.

The sudden momentum was dizzying. I put a hand to the side mirror and tried to lever myself away.

Didn't work.

"Hey!" I bent, taking one hand off the handlebar in an attempt to pound on the window.

The car jerked in my direction, throwing me off balance.

On instinct, I pressed my foot on the back wheel to brake.

The wheels scraped against the pavement, making everything worse.

If I didn't break free soon, I was going to get dragged into a parked car.

But we were going too fast for me to risk jumping off.

I squatted, lowering my center of gravity, and tried to rock myself free.

That didn't work either.

The car sped up. As it did, it hit another pothole, shaking me free.

The sudden abandonment of our game of tug-of-war left me reeling. I lost my balance. I put a foot to the pavement, then jogged a few steps.

By that time, the car was already turning the corner at the end of the street.

I walked beside the scooter for several long minutes, taking deep breaths between sobs, chanting a shaky mantra. "It's okay. You're okay. You're alright."

⏩ CHAPTER 6 ⏪

Riding a scooter was not the safest form of transportation, and I'd had close calls before, but never *that* close. Had the driver not seen me? But how was that possible? How could a person wearing a red blouse not be visible? If I hadn't swerved toward the sidewalk to avoid that pothole, the car would have hit me!

All I wanted was to get inside. To be safe.

I left the scooter at a wide spot in the sidewalk. If someone scootered away with it before I had to work in the morning, then I would just use my app to find another.

I walked down the sidewalk and then up the long driveway toward the house. The blue iris that lined the drive in June had melted during a series of summer thunderstorms, then were overtaken by hordes of orange daylilies. At the top of the driveway, I ignored the paver stones that wrapped around the side of the house and took the herringbone brick path that led to the front door. I walked up the front steps and rang the bell.

Though my rent was rock bottom and the utilities and Wi-Fi were free, it came with a stipulation. I was supposed to check in daily with the eighty-year-old owner. She lived upstairs in the main part of the house.

A month before I moved in, she had a heart attack. The basement apartment was a compromise with her children. They kept asking her to sell the house and move into a retirement community; she kept refusing. I was the buffer that permitted civil conversations.

"Whitney Garrison! You're home early!" Mrs. Harper always greeted me with enthusiasm, as if she'd been waiting all day for me to return. "Come in, come in!" She opened the door wide as she pushed a pair of purple tortoiseshell readers from her nose up into her hair. "Come in and tell me about your day." She said the words as she walked from the front hall into her living room.

The walls were covered with framed damask fabric panels in cream, peach, and pale blue. A gleaming chandelier hung from the center of the ceiling.

A grand piano sat in front of the room's bay window, and a set of skirted furniture clustered around the brick fireplace.

When I first moved in, I told her I'd taken piano lessons once upon a time, and she told me to use her piano whenever I wanted. Her children were living out somewhere in Loudoun County. Her grandchildren much too busy to visit. And her hands? They'd betrayed her. She held them out for me to see. Beneath her sparkling rings, arthritis had bent and twisted what once had been long, elegant fingers.

In spite of her invitation, I hadn't yet used the piano. I didn't have time.

I shed my backpack and sat down in a swivel chair as she perched on a love seat. My hands were still trembling, so I tucked them under my thighs. I gave her the short version of my day, leaving out the part about the murder. And the part about almost being hit by a car.

Due to her heart condition, I was not, under any circumstances, to distress her.

She told me about her day. Her daughter, Jess, the one who'd been a champion swimmer at the country club, had called. Besides that? She'd been out and about running errands and had gone to the club to work out. She didn't mind water aerobics so much—she'd signed up because you could only do it in summer when the pool was open—but she'd be happy to get back to her Pilates. Her conversation moved on to her friends.

I'd never met Doris or Helen or Irene, but I knew almost everything about them. Whose husbands had died. Whose children lived in the area and whose lived away. They all liked to travel together. At the end of the next week, they were headed to Bermuda. As she talked, I found myself thinking about the shooting, and a longing for my apartment crept over me. After about ten minutes, I couldn't help myself. I stood. Grabbed my backpack. Smiled. "I'd better get back to studying."

She stood as well. "Forgive me! I shouldn't keep you."

The kitchen had a back door, which opened onto the deck. It was a quicker route to my basement than going out the front door and around. I might have used the interior stairs that led from the front hall down to the basement, but in deference to my privacy, she never used them herself. Her folding step stool leaned against the door and her collection of reusable grocery bags hung from its knob.

She walked to the back door with me.

As I went out, she called me back. "I almost forgot! I have a package for you."

For me? "I haven't ordered anything." I didn't have the money to.

"Maybe someone ordered it for you. Birthday present?"

"My birthday's in the fall."

"Well. Surprises are always nice, aren't they?"

It had to be from my father. He was the only one who knew where I lived. Was that why he'd been so strange when we were texting? Maybe he was waiting for some sort of reaction to the package.

"Can you wait for a minute? I'll go get it."

I really didn't want to wait. I just wanted to get to my apartment, close the door, and lock it behind me. Maybe I'd even study in bed. But she had already disappeared. She soon came back, hand at her hip. "I thought I put it on the front table, but I can't find it now. I don't know where I put it."

I told her not to worry. "It's nothing I've been waiting for. Just let me know when you find it and I'll come back up to get it."

I continued on my way, crossing the deck, then went down into the yard to access my apartment. It would have been convenient if the steps down to the basement met the steps that led up to the deck, but they were at opposite ends. I'd worn a trail in the grass going back and forth.

Shadows were creeping toward the house from the trees that lined the property. The space under the deck was already a dark void.

I hurried past.

My basement door was at the bottom of a concrete stairwell. I'd placed a big terra-cotta planter filled with impatiens on the retaining wall beneath the deck. Mrs. Harper had won it at a garden club meeting and passed it on to me. The plants liked the cooler air that pooled there in the shade. But now the planter rested, shattered, at the bottom of the stairwell.

I glanced over my shoulder out into the backyard.

Daylilies and giant hostas waved back at me.

How had the planter fallen? The wind had been fierce earlier in the day, but not against that wall. It was too well protected by the deck.

Slipping off my backpack, I knelt and pulled the terra-cotta pieces from the dirt and the flowers. I stacked them inside the half of the planter that was still intact and pushed it toward the wall. I'd dump it in the garbage on my way to work the next morning.

But what to do about the impatiens? With their roots exposed, they'd soon die.

I fished a scoop-shaped shard out of the remains and used it to dig a hole in the dirt beneath the deck. I placed the impatiens in it and then covered their roots. They'd be safe there, and sheltered, until I could find something else to put them in.

I brushed the dirt from my hands, then picked up my backpack and let myself in the door. Turning on the light, I stepped into what Mrs. Harper called the rec room.

Despite the heat of July it was unpleasantly, humidly chill. With its faux beams and wet bar with accompanying spindle-backed oak bar stools, it was a time capsule from the midnineties. There was still a green leather wood-framed couch beneath one of the windows and some ghostly marks pressed into the carpet where several chairs used to be. What some people might have preferred to disguise with throw rugs, posters, or tapestries, I had decided to ignore. Mostly because I couldn't afford to do otherwise. But also because it reminded me of a picture I'd once seen of a ski chalet in Switzerland.

I'd always wanted to visit Switzerland.

I moved the plants I kept on the bar top. When I left in the mornings, I made sure they sat squarely in the ray of sun that slanted in through one of the high, narrow basement windows. When I came home at night, I grouped them beneath a grow light I'd picked up at a bargain. It was the one luxury I'd allowed myself since I'd moved in.

My ex had only used the aloe vera, palm, and cactus as decorating props. He paid a plant whisperer to come in every week and take care of them, so I hadn't felt guilty when I took them with me.

Since then, I'd added a start from Mrs. Harper's hoya and one from her jade plant.

Some people had cats. Some had dogs. I had plants. Which were just as demanding as any other life form. If I was being honest, they gave me structure and purpose . . . as well as peaceful vibes and clean air. But more importantly, I recognized them.

Every single one.

The aloe, with its long, prickled, fleshy spears, was different from the jade with its shiny, rounded, plump leaves. The palm was the opposite of the cactus. They required nothing of me that I couldn't give. And in return for my attention, they thrived.

Okay. Maybe not the hoya. The hoya grew best with a regimen of benign neglect.

They say every child, even those born into the same family, has his own unique requirements. Plants do too.

I ran a fingertip along the leaves of the palm. It came away dusty. I wet a paper towel and used it to wipe down the leaves.

Even though I hadn't eaten lunch, I wasn't that hungry. But I was exhausted. And shaky. I walked over to the bar where I kept milk, eggs, and cheese in the mini fridge beneath the counter. I made my nightly two-egg omelet on a hot plate and added some toast. Then I grabbed an apple from a plastic bag filled with them and hauled my study books out of my backpack along with a new pack of index cards.

As I dove into my study guide, Mrs. Harper phoned. "I was wondering if you might be able to help me, Whitney."

I helped her with something almost every night. Sometimes it was a lightbulb that needed to be changed. Sometimes it was an investigation of some strange noise. She was always very appreciative. "You sure made that look easy!" she would say as she patted my forearm when she let me out the back door. "I'll see you tomorrow."

I decided *that*, in fact, was the reason for the phone calls and little tasks. If I didn't say, "See you tomorrow," in return, she'd repeat the phrase.

See you tomorrow.

I didn't mind. I'd done the same when I was a kid. I'd placed an inordinate amount of faith in the fact that if my mother said she'd see me in the morning, then she would. If I were Mrs. Harper, if I'd had a heart attack, I probably would have pressed for assurance that I'd see another sunrise too.

As I hung up, I glanced out the window of the back door.

The concrete stairwell was already shrouded in twilight. Who knew what was out there in the shadows?

I tried to reason myself out of the prickling of panic that had spread up my arms.

What's out there? Birds, squirrels, rabbits.

My argument wasn't very convincing.

I'd played along with Mrs. Harper since the night I moved in. But I didn't feel like playing tonight.

My phone rang again.

I jumped and then stretched across the bar to pick it up. To make it stop ringing.

It was Mrs. Harper. "Whitney? Are you coming?"

"Sorry. I just— Yes. Can you turn on the deck light for me?"

I waited until the light slanted through the boards of the deck before I left my apartment. And when I did, I had my phone in my hand, ready to make an emergency call if I needed to. Detective Baroni had insisted that everything would be alright, but it didn't feel that way. Not yet.

That night Mrs. Harper's task involved her television. It didn't take long to fix. And then I had to go back outside.

"See you tomorrow?"

I was so absorbed in steeling myself to open the kitchen door that I almost forgot to say my part.

"Whitney?"

"What? Sorry. Yes. I'll see you tomorrow, Mrs. Harper."

▸▸▸◂◂◂

I tried to study that night, I really did, but I kept hearing things.

I put my pen down several times and turned toward the door to listen.

Nothing.

I decided it was just nerves.

But as I had done when I'd first moved in—still traumatized by my ex, still anticipating him around every corner—I moved my books down to the far end of the bar and I angled my stool so I was facing the door and the windows that sat high on the outside wall.

It didn't help.

I could have sworn I saw things moving at the top of the steps. I blinked once. Twice.

I had to get a grip. Had to shake off the shooting and the scooter incident. I told myself—again—that it was probably just squirrels.

But I got up and let the mini blinds down over the windows on the door, and then I found my cell phone. All I'd wanted earlier was to get to my apartment and be alone. Now? I desperately wanted company, someone to talk to. I needed something to keep my thoughts from the murder. I called my dad.

"Whit." I could almost hear him clamp down his smile by biting the inside corner of his cheek. "I must be some hot property. Can't get enough of me?"

"Never. I just—I just wanted to say hi."

There was a long pause on the other end. "Is everything okay?"

"Fine. Everything's fine. I was just thinking maybe I could come out for a few days at Christmas maybe."

"Oh. Christmas? Let's talk. Maybe when it gets a little closer. We can figure it out."

He was always saying he wished I lived closer, and now he wasn't sure about seeing me at Christmas? "Sure. Yeah. Well, I'll talk to you soon then?"

"Hmm?"

"Talk to you soon?"

"Yes. Of course. Yes. Great talking to you. You just keep living the dream." He paused. "So proud of you."

"Are you okay, Dad?"

"What? Fine. Yes. Yes, I'm fine. Just distracted. Sorry. I'm fine."

He hung up, leaving me staring at my phone, certain in the knowledge that everything was not fine. And that something was most definitely going on.

▶▶ CHAPTER 7 ◀◀

Living the dream. That's what my father always told me I was doing.

To him it must have seemed like it.

I was only hoping that one day I could. But I would have to pass the bar first. And then I'd have to get a job—a high-paying one—at one of the big firms downtown. My ex had lined up a job for me at one of them. At the time, I'd thought it was sweet. Now I understood it to be just another way he'd tried to control me. Not that the firm wouldn't have wanted me. It was more that I didn't want to owe him anything.

But I still didn't have a job, and I was worried.

Though I had several interviews in June, none of them worked out. I did, however, have an interview tomorrow afternoon at a firm that had a practice area in international economic law. I got out the notes I'd taken on the firm and the list of things I wanted to mention in the interview.

I definitely needed to highlight the internship I'd done for the congressman who chaired the House Financial Services Committee.

Since I couldn't recall faces, I took notes on everything. People I'd met, things I'd done. My ex used to call my notes *The Life and Times of Whitney Garrison*, volumes 1–101. But detailing conversations and events sometimes helped me remember things about the people involved. So I dug out my journal from the year before and flipped through bullet points to find my notes on the cryptocurrency meetings I'd sat in on.

The attendees had been a mix of people from the Federal Reserve, the Federal Deposit Insurance Corporation, and the FBI, as well as from blockchain companies, Silicon Valley, and Wall Street. Representatives from nongovernmental organizations and the World Bank had been in attendance too.

Everyone was interested in cryptocurrency. It wasn't clear yet, however, whose interests would best be served once the government got around to regulating it, mostly because so few people outside the relatively small, impassioned cryptocommunity actually understood it.

When I was little, my father always made me wash my hands after I touched cash. Coins or bills, it didn't matter. "You never know where it's been," he would say. That's the advantage of cryptocurrency; you never have to touch it, and you always know where it's been. Every cryptocoin carries identification papers. Every exchange is attached to the coin as a permanent record.

As I sat in those congressional hearings, my curiosity about the technology had turned into a growing passion. As I listened to representatives from NGOs and the World Bank talk about how cryptocurrency allowed citizens of third-world countries to participate in the global economy, I thought about how much it could do for America's own underclass. How it could be used to address some of the biggest problems in our society.

I mined a few of the observations from my journal for the interview, noted a few more things I wanted to make sure I mentioned, then slipped those notes into my attaché. After that, I took a few minutes to write down in my current journal what had happened in the alley behind the coffee shop. If I put it down in enough detail, maybe my mind wouldn't feel the need to keep replaying everything.

I wouldn't have to keep remembering the pool of blood congealing underneath the victim's head. Or how his hands had begun to turn a terrible shade of gray.

I swallowed the bile that had risen in my throat and decided to start with my memories of the detective instead. I guessed he was probably in his midthirties. He'd been efficient but not pushy. Effective but considerate. Professional but reassuring. That hair, I'd recognize anywhere. It was black and he'd combed some gel through it in an attempt to keep it off his face. Despite that effort, his bangs kept falling off both sides of his widow's peak. He'd been taller than me, but that didn't take much height. The top of my head probably would have glanced off his chin.

What else would help me remember him?

The cologne he wore. It reminded me of the woods back home. Clean, fresh. Green.

He was nothing like my ex. Unlike the stereotypical hipster tech mogul, my ex had been polished to a shine. His hair was sleek; when he combed it back from his forehead, it stayed. His clothing was always styled. Precise. Even his casual wear had edges. His cologne had been a feral-smelling musk.

But I didn't have to think of him anymore.

He was gone and I wasn't going back.

I steered my thoughts toward the victim.

First impression: the wind. It had been relentless, pushing his hair away from his face, prying one side of his jacket loose and lifting it away from his body.

He'd been wearing a suit. But that wasn't unusual. Not in DC.

White shirt.

Brown shoes.

Striped socks. Green, yellow, and dark pink.

And he had a hole in his head.

His suit jacket had been flapping in the wind. And the hole . . . I didn't like thinking about that hole. Didn't like thinking about his coffee cup either.

Less than an hour before I found him, I had made him that drink.

Joe.

Who were you, Joe?

He'd come in every afternoon. I remembered his drink but had no memory of him.

I shifted my focus to the killer, closing my eyes as I tried to remember how he looked. He'd been wearing a dark suit jacket. Had I seen anything else?

I'd clocked out, put my apron on the hook. Took my backpack from the locker. Went out the back door. Joe was lying on the ground.

Maybe the detective was right. Maybe my memories were going to come back to me in pieces, like a puzzle. Already, images of the alley played in my mind like a slideshow every time I blinked.

I shut the journal and put my pen down.

I didn't want to remember any more.

For the first time since I'd moved in, I went to bed before midnight. I closed my bedroom door, locking it, before I clicked off the ceiling light and slipped beneath my blankets.

It was dark—pitch black—down in that basement. But it seemed to me that I could still see Joe lying in the alley, blood puddling around his head.

I punched my pillow into a more comfortable shape and turned over.

Closed my eyes.

Immediately the specter of the killer appeared. I blinked in an effort to clear him from my mind.

It was replaced by an image of Joe with a hole in his head, his hair ruffling in the wind.

I turned over to my other side. Stared into the dark. Thought of all the study questions I hadn't gotten through in my race to lock myself into my bedroom. When I closed my eyes again, trying to ignore the guilt, I saw that congealing puddle of blood.

I sat up.

Threw off my covers.

If I wasn't going to be able to sleep, then I should study. At least that would take care of the guilt. Everyone at law school, all of my professors, would have told me I had no reason to worry about the bar. I was going to pass; how could I not pass?

But I also knew, from life experience, that the unexpected seemed to happen on a completely predictable schedule.

Exhibit A: Joe.

Easing up on studying had always felt like tempting fate. So I studied and then studied some more.

I threw the light switch, unlocked my door.

Eased it open.

Listened for a long moment.

Then I gave myself a pep talk. I was twenty-eight. Much too old to be afraid of the dark.

I raced to the bar, grabbed my book and study materials, ran back down the hall to my bedroom, and locked the door again. Then I burrowed into bed and flipped through the pages of my study guide.

One review question always led to another. And then to five or six more.

At least it kept thoughts of the shooting at bay.

I could study twelve hours a day and still not study enough, because I couldn't afford to fail the exam. Literally. Between the money I spent trying to pay down my credit card debt and the money I put toward my student loans, I didn't have enough money left to stay in the area without the salary that a job in one of DC's prestigious firms could supply. So whatever life plan I came up with, it could only work if I passed the bar my first time.

If I didn't?

Panic wrapped its steely fingers around my throat.

If I didn't pass?

That wasn't an option.

But reason insisted upon being heard. *What if I don't pass?*

I would pass. I just had to study. I'd been studying; I would study more.

But what if it doesn't work? What if I can't do it? What if I don't pass?

I would pass.

And then what will I do?

I would do what the vast majority of law students who passed the bar did: work for a few years in a big law firm as an associate in order to make enough money to pay off my student loans. Those first few years were a necessary stop on the road to a career in law.

So although working for a big firm, even in international trade and finance, wasn't really what I wanted to do, it was something I had to do. A pit stop before I could get on with the pursuit of my dream. Was I looking forward to it? No. I was looking beyond it.

But that assumed I passed the bar.

My throat constricted again.

I forced myself to swallow. Made my fingers pick up my pen.

If I didn't pass, I would find a job doing something different.

Doing what? What do I know how to do?

I could go into business for myself.

I don't know how to do anything but study. And help other people study. And if I didn't pass, that meant I would be a failure at the thing I was best at doing.

Despair pressed its chill palms against my chest. But I wasn't going to fail.

I couldn't.

CHAPTER 8

As I parked my scooter in front of the Blue Dog the next morning, a crowd of reporters swarmed in front of the door.

I wasn't worried about anyone trying to interview me. How would any of them know that I was the one who'd discovered the body? I was, however, worried about breaking through the circus in order to get to work. If I hadn't vowed never to use the back entrance again, I would have done it.

As I stood there trying to figure out a way through the crowd, I waved at Ruth.

She stood out by the metro station every day in her bright yellow reflective vest selling copies of a newspaper written by the homeless in the region. She was a former drug addict who was trying to get her life back on track.

When I'd first started at the coffee shop, the trauma I'd experienced in leaving my ex must have shown on my face. As I walked past her that first day, she'd reached out and touched my arm.

"Hey," she said gently. "It's going to be okay. It's all going to be okay. When Ruth tells you it's going to be okay, it's going to be okay."

I still couldn't think about that, about the hope she'd given me that first morning, without tears welling in my eyes.

A few steps ahead of me was someone I also recognized as a regular at the Blue Dog. Her name was Kim. I'd never really talked to her before, but she always ordered a cappuccino with extra foam. I'd once heard her tell someone that she'd been injured in an explosion in Afghanistan. She had a prosthetic leg and came by every other day or so dressed in workout gear.

She appeared to have given up trying to get into the shop, as had many other potential customers. Normally there was a steady stream of people flowing from the mouth of the nearby metro station into the shop. That morning, however, they all seemed to be swerving away.

As she turned from the shop, I reached out and tapped her on the arm. "Maybe we can get through together." I'd ditched my normal backpack for a more professional-looking attaché. My rolled-up interview suit, blouse, and shoes were stowed inside. Wielding the attaché like a shield, I plowed my way into the crowd.

She followed.

One of the reporters stopped me and shoved a microphone into my face. "Are you a regular customer? Did you see the shooting?"

I chose to answer the first question. "No."

▸▸▸◂◂◂

It was dead until about lunch and then customers started flocking in. I worked the espresso machine for a while and then I switched with Corrine. As I took her place at the counter, a boy stepped up to order. Headphones collared his neck and shaggy hair curled out from his baseball cap. He was chewing at the edge of his thumb as he stood there. He seemed like an undergrad. Tall, but angular in the way of boys who hadn't quite yet grown into men. He came by between 1:00 and 1:30 every afternoon.

He lingered this time, letting the line build behind him as he asked me what I was doing over the weekend. Because his family had this great house in Delaware out past Millsboro, kind of near Rehoboth but not really and not ever very crowded and he was maybe thinking that—

Ty ambled over. He was a grad student at one of the nearby

universities. He had a slow way of moving that made it seem like he'd just rolled out of bed. The scent of Ivory soap always wafted from him like cologne. His standard uniform was a cowry shell necklace, some sort of concert T-shirt, and a pair of Vans. He nudged me aside.

As I slid a cup from the stack and marked it for the order, Ty took the boy's loyalty card and hijacked the conversation. "I know what you're thinking, man. 'She's really pretty. She always smiles at me. I think she likes me.' Here's the thing"—he leaned toward the boy—"it's not you. It's the money. She's paid to be nice. To you. To everyone. We clear here?" He handed the guy back his coffee card.

The boy took it, jammed it into the pocket of his shorts, and slunk away toward the far end of the counter.

"Awww." Corrine leaned away from the espresso machine, pointing her finger at Ty. "Meanie."

Ty snorted.

I thanked him for saving me.

He ignored my gratitude. It wasn't the first time he'd had to rescue me from overeager customers.

"I didn't do anything to encourage him. I honestly didn't."

"You never do." He pulled an empty plate out of the pastry case and headed toward the swinging door that led from the counter area into the back room. "It's part of the charm." That last part he said under his breath as he disappeared through the door.

At the end of my shift, Corrine dumped two mobile orders that had been waiting for pickup for over half an hour.

She shook her head as she did it. "Why would you go to the trouble to order yourself"—she paused and took a look at one of the labels—"an iced coconut milk latte, or a"—she read the other label—"soy mocha, one pump, no whip, if you weren't going to bother to pick it up?" She snorted as she poured them down the sink. "At least they paid for them."

It took a few minutes for the information to click.

Soy mocha.

That was Joe's drink.

I went to the trash can and tipped it toward me so I could see inside. I removed the two cups on top. I read the label of the first one.

Joe.
Soy mocha.
One pump.
No whip.

A chill went up my spine.

How could Joe have ordered himself a drink?

She started pulling another shot. "Hey—aren't you on your way out?"

"What?"

"Your shift's over. And don't you have that interview today?"

Interview! "Yes. Bye." I tossed the cups back into the trash. If I didn't move it, I was going to be late.

▸▸▸◂◂◂

After I clocked out, I changed from jeans and a shirt into my interview clothes. They came courtesy of a consignment shop. The charcoal-gray jacket and skirt and the white silk blouse were understated and classic. My black heels were tipped in rubber so they wouldn't click when I walked. I washed my hands with the flower-scented soap, hoping it might seem like perfume. After side-parting my hair, I spun it into a sleek, low bun.

My ex had always told me that people underestimated me. "They focus on that face and don't even see the intelligence behind it." What did it say about him that he was always encouraging me to show more of my body and less of my brain?

What did it say about me that I went along with him?

I shoved my shame to the back of my mind. I needed to put the best version of myself forward. The law firm didn't need to know I'd been terrifically stupid in all the ways that really mattered.

After rolling up my work clothes, I left them in a locker; I'd come back for them later. As I walked to the front of the shop, Corrine whistled. "You go, girl! Break a leg."

I waved and then thumbed open Google Maps and checked the traffic before I brought up my ride-sharing app. Jammed on both of the closest bridges. I entered the address of the law firm.

Forty minutes. But I knew I could make it there by metro in twenty-five.

I was going to have to. Otherwise, I'd be late. I pulled up the metro schedule on my phone. There was a train headed to DC in three minutes. Taking my metro card from my wallet, I left the store, hurrying to the metro entrance.

"Looking good!" Ruth shouted as I approached.

A man coming out of the metro bumped into her as he came off the escalator and rounded the corner.

The newspapers tumbled from her arms.

He kept on going.

"Hey!" I shouted as I bent to help her collect them.

He didn't even pause in his step.

"Bless you," Ruth said. "I can do this. Do it ten times a day, seems like. Don't worry about me."

I handed her the newspapers I'd collected.

Over to my right, a man wearing a dark suit and a green tie walked out of the convenience store and headed in our direction. His hair was slicked back from his forehead.

I walked over to the stairs that led down into the station.

By the time I hit the bottom step, the man had begun to close the distance between us. There was nothing about him that was overtly sinister, but he made me uneasy.

My metro card nearly slipped from my suddenly sweaty grasp.

I told myself he was just like me. That he was only hoping to catch the next train.

In front of me, a pack of tourists clogged the tunnel. They were trying to figure out how the ticket machines worked.

I looked back over my shoulder.

He was only a few steps behind me now.

Sliding around the tourists and their backpacks—zigging right and zagging left—I cut through the crowd.

The man got stuck in the middle of it.

But then I ran right into a group of people who had clumped around the ticket readers. They kept trying to put their hard passes through the paper-card slots.

A line was bunching behind them.

I gave a glance over my shoulder again.

The man had freed himself from the tourists in the tunnel and was heading in my direction.

I considered jumping the turnstile, but there was an actual metro attendant in the information booth. I could get fined.

As the man approached, I angled away from him along the edges of the tourist crowd. From my position I could see down onto the metro tracks. The floor lights lining the platform began to blink. The train was approaching.

And so was the man.

"Excuse me. Pardon me." I was counting on the tourists being polite.

Sure enough, they began to move out of my way. With a little deft maneuvering, I reached the turnstiles. "Can I show you how to do it?" I asked one of the tourists, holding my card aloft.

They parted like magic.

As I reached the ticket reader, several opportunists had already pushed forward to fill the gaps behind me. "You just—" I laid my card atop the reader and the turnstile withdrew. I ran through and then raced down the escalator.

The train glided to a stop.

I hit the platform. Glanced over my shoulder.

The man appeared at the top of the escalator. He jogged down, taking the steps two at a time.

The train's doors hadn't yet opened.

I ran toward the nearest one.

The man reached the bottom of the escalator.

The doors still hadn't opened.

He pivoted from the escalator, walking toward me.

I retreated down the platform, heading toward the next train door, and then the next, positioning waiting people between us.

By the time I reached the next door, the doors still hadn't opened.

Inside, impatient passengers were checking their watches and shifting attachés from one hand to another. On the platform, clusters had formed on both sides of the doors.

Open, open, open!

The tourists, seeing they had a chance at catching the train, poured down the escalator like a waterfall, pooling at its base and then spreading out to engulf the platform.

The man was still moving in my direction.

I left the door I was waiting in front of and moved toward the next.

A hiss. A long pause. The doors opened.

I jogged the last few steps and joined the several people waiting on the far side of the door.

The man paused. Swiveled toward the door he'd just walked past. Turned back toward my door.

Was he looking at me?

I tried to keep my head down, hiding behind the woman in front of me as we shuffled forward. But I also tried to keep an eye on the man.

Just as he got on, I backed up, bumping into the woman behind me. "Sorry!"

The doors shut.

The train pulled out, slowly picking up speed, fanning the scent of hot electrical wires and stale dust as it left me behind.

▸▸▸◂◂◂

I trembled.

The tips of my ears were burning. My hands were icy cold.

Memories of the day before assaulted me as panic squeezed the air out of my lungs.

My head began to spin.

I stepped away from the edge of the platform. Took a few deep breaths.

It's okay. You're okay. You're alright.

I could deal with the memories later. The most important thing was to get to my interview. I pulled up Google Maps. Traffic was even worse now across the bridges.

According to the digital display above the platform, the next train was due in three minutes. I could still make it on time.

I waited beneath the elevator by one of its cement piers, trying to stay out of sight.

The platform began to repopulate.

The sign flashed a two-minute delay for my train.

A minute later, a train pulled in on the opposite side. And then, finally, a train pulled in on mine.

I got on as quickly as I could.

As we pulled away from the station, a man walked down the platform on the other side, face turned toward my train. He was wearing a dark suit. His hair was slicked back from his forehead. As I passed, he touched his forehead in a one-finger salute.

⏩ CHAPTER 9 ⏪

I had almost convinced myself that it was the same man. That he must have gotten off at the next station and hopped a train coming back in my direction. But then I realized he was wearing a red tie.

It was a different man.

A different man who was probably just trying to catch the eye of a pretty girl.

A cold sweat broke out on my brow.

I let out a sigh of relief, tried to slow my breathing as I forced myself to focus on the interview. I repeated the facts I'd learned about the firm.

Established in 1911.

Home to seven former congressmen and one former congresswoman.

First DC-area law firm to name a woman as a partner.

⏩⏪

I made it to the Metro Center station, jogged up two blocks and over one, and entered the lobby of the law firm exactly on time.

"Ms. Garrison?" The receptionist called my name before I even had the chance to sit down.

I smiled. Transferred my attaché to my other hand so I could wipe my sweat-drenched palm on my skirt. "Hi." As I followed her down the hall, I tried to get my breathing under control. Glanced down to make sure my white silk blouse wasn't stuck to my chest.

We took an elevator up toward the top of the building and then she led me down a long, carpeted, tastefully decorated hall.

She knocked on a door at the end and waited for an answer. Then she opened it and gestured me through.

It was an office that looked out on the grassy triangle of a city park.

There was a modern sculpture in the corner, a round lacquered conference table positioned in front of the window, and a black angular desk by the far wall. Bold, colorful canvases hung on the walls. The impression was both dramatic and understated. It spoke of power, influence, and wealth.

The woman behind the desk rose and gestured to the table. Then she approached, hand extended. "Ms. Garrison? I'm Sydney Buckingham, assistant director, international trade."

We sat at the table across from each other. She began the interview with the dreaded, "So tell me about yourself."

The question was much too broad. But that, I supposed, was the appeal from an interviewer's perspective. Half of its value resulted from what the interviewee chose to say. Talking about my family's blue-collar background might earn me points in the specialties of social justice and advocacy, but it would do nothing for me here, in the practice area of international economic law at one of the most prestigious firms in the nation. In environments like this one I had learned that connections mattered. The right connections mattered even more. So I began to tell her about my internship on the Hill instead.

She cut me off. "With Congressman Thorpe's office, right? Financial Services Committee? I thought I recognized you. I was there."

Face blindness strikes again. "I'm sorry. I didn't—"

"Not that you would have remembered me. But I was at several of those committee hearings. When Congress finally starts taking notice of cryptocurrency, our firm keeps track of what Congress is noticing."

I heaved an inward sigh of relief.

"It must have been fascinating interning up there during that semester. Tell me about it."

What could I say that wouldn't take four hours to explain? "The first problem is to define cryptocurrency. It doesn't exist in a cash format. So can we really call it money, or is it more like property? Should it be regulated like cash or as an investment, like real estate? And can you actually possess something that only exists in digital form? After that? There are just so many stakeholders. Banks and Wall Street. Sovereign nations and tech companies. Should cryptoaccounts be insured by the FDIC as if they were traditional bank accounts? Should they be allowed to trade in traditional financial markets? Should the Federal Reserve have any jurisdiction? And what role does Congress play in legislating currencies that, by definition, aren't linked to any nation?"

"Sounds like a summary of the hearing agenda. But that was last year. Give me your read on the latest developments."

"In a word? China. Once they said they were all in on blockchain technology, everything changed." The blockchain allowed total transparency in digital assets. Whether that asset was a cryptocoin or a property record, instead of waiting for financial statements to be released, or having to access a property assessor's website, everyone could see transactions, both past and present, in real time. The record of the asset was constantly available for anyone with permission to see it. No need to guess whether money had been laundered to pay for a real estate transaction. And there was no middleman. The trail the asset had made through the digital landscape couldn't be hidden. It was permanently attached and constantly exposed for everyone to see.

"Everything changed for whom?"

"For everyone. To develop the technology, they created a pilot zone in one of their provinces and they partnered with a cryptocurrency exchange."

She was nodding. "We were following that experiment. Tell me why it was significant."

"Whoever sets the rules for the technology will control it. Unless someone steps up to challenge China, they'll be to the cryptoworld what Microsoft was to the computer world. They'll set the pace, they'll create the standards, and they'll impose the rules."

"So separate the blockchain technology from its cryptocurrency application. Tell me your thoughts about cryptocurrency specifically."

She was asking me the equivalent of separating the cash in my wallet from the paper it was printed on. Or the money on my credit card statement from the plastic card itself. Paper could be used for hundreds of purposes, from books to toilet paper, and so could plastic cards. We used them to carry loyalty points from our favorite stores as well as to gain entry to places like parking garages and hotel rooms. "There are obvious benefits to cryptocurrencies." And those benefits were exactly why I was interested in this field of law. "Since it's not minted by any nation, since no nation can claim it, it's apolitical. And because cryptocurrencies carry their records with them on their blockchain, it could put an end to dark money in politics. Everyone could see exactly where a politician's money has come from."

Imagine living in a world where money wasn't tied to economic policy, where governments wouldn't be able to manipulate its value. Foreign aid couldn't be hijacked by dictators when spending stipulations or contracts were attached, by the blockchain, to their disbursement. Citizens wouldn't be punished by the mess their leaders made of the economy or by runaway inflation as they were several years ago in Venezuela. Imagine all the fraud, waste, and abuse that could be eliminated if federal money was forced to be put to the use for which it was intended. The advantage of cryptocurrency was that all sorts of strings could be attached to it. Or none at all.

I kept talking. "I'd like to think that, aside from the few highly publicized scandals, new players in third-world countries who don't have access to banks could be brought into the international economy. Bank accounts aren't needed for cryptocurrencies. Cryptoaccounts can be established and managed through cell phones. All those new players would mean new markets. New markets would bring prosperity to areas that haven't seen development before."

"Drawbacks?"

I blew out a deep breath. The pros and cons of cryptocurrencies had been something my ex-boyfriend and I had often debated. He had definite opinions as a cybersecurity expert who'd made a fortune heading the start-up of the moment and then licensing the technology to a federal agency. He loved to remind me that even a blockchain could be hacked, and supposedly unalterable digital information had been known to be changed.

But cryptocurrency was something I believed was worth the growing pains. And so had Congressman Thorpe, the chair of the House Financial Services Committee. As an outsider in the world of DC politics, I'd been happy to accept the help of my boyfriend in getting me an internship in his father's office. While dating him, I'd become the ultimate insider. "There are several drawbacks. Crypto is more than money because of the information that can be encrypted on its supporting blockchain."

"Am I hearing a *but*?"

"But not everyone is interested in world peace and prosperity." That's what my ex had always argued. He'd laid it down like a trump card at every hint I'd given of my growing passion for the topic. Thing is, he was right. "If the benefit is that money could finally flow to those who need it, then the drawback is that it could simply be redirected to those who already have it." And that was an age-old problem. "It goes back to the basic question of whether human nature is good or evil."

Some of the best, most intellectually stimulating conversations I'd ever had were at the Thorpes' legendary parties, arguing about those very things. Some of my biggest triumphs of the past year had been getting people who mattered, people who made policy, to think differently about cryptocurrency. To realize its vast potential to change just about everything.

Those triumphs, however, had always been challenged by my ex.

"You know she just said that because my father was listening," he'd say. Or, "You know, he's heard that a thousand times before. It's your pretty face he was responding to, not the idea."

When I thought back on all the times he'd said things like that, I wanted a do-over. I wanted to go back in time and stand up for myself. And beyond that? To punch him. Hit him. Kick him. I wanted to do to him all the things he'd done to me.

Which just made me hate myself even more.

"And why do you want to work for us?"

I blinked. Forced myself out of the past and into the present. I would not let him ruin anything else for me. "Coming out of law school, I know I have a lot to learn. I'd like to learn from the best. I'm building a career and I want to do it here, where I can have a chance to help influence policy."

"You know that being a junior associate requires a lot of sacrifice. Did you ever pull all-nighters during your degrees?"

"I tried to manage my time so that I didn't have to."

"You will here. I can guarantee it. Many times. But hard work is also rewarded."

That's what I had been hoping to hear. I'd traded my soul for my student loans. The quicker I could pay them off, the quicker I could start working on things that really mattered.

▸▸▸◂◂◂

I brought up my ride-sharing app before I left the building. When my car was a minute away, I started toward the building's revolving door. I waited outside, beneath the overhang, phone raised in the universal where-is-my-ride gesture.

A gray car with a ride-share sticker pulled up to the curb. I walked over. Knocked on the window.

The driver rolled down the window. Music poured from the radio. "Who are you here for?"

He leaned toward me, arm draped over the steering wheel. He was wearing a button-down shirt that was rolled at the sleeves. A gold watch circled his wrist. It looked like a Rolex—my time with my ex had taught me to recognize them—though it was probably a fake.

"You want to sit in front? That's fine."

"Who are you here for?" Behind him, another car pulled up to the curb.

"It's unlocked."

There was a duffel bag on the floor of the passenger seat. I saw something green inside of it.

The car behind him honked. Its rear bumper was sticking out in traffic; cars were stacking up behind him. The driver was gesturing in a sweeping motion. Clearly he wanted the driver I was talking with to leave.

I glanced at my phone to verify details. I'd been told to expect a gray car. The car in front of me was gray. My face blindness made differentiating things like vehicles difficult, but I didn't have any problems with license plates. I checked his. "Sorry. Wrong car."

"What?" He leaned over and turned down the radio.

"Wrong car. You must be here for someone else."

"Just cancel your ride. I can take you." He leaned over and opened the door. "Come on. Get in. Where do you want to go?"

He was way too aggressive; I was already backing away.

The driver behind him honked. That car was gray too.

I looked at my app to verify the license plate. It matched.

"Hey!" The driver of the first car was yelling at me. "Lady! Where you going?"

I put a knuckle to the passenger window of the other gray car.

The driver rolled it down.

I ignored the first driver, directing my attention to the new one. "Who are you here for?"

The driver shifted to look at the phone that was located in a holder attached to an air vent. "Whitney?"

Relief nearly buckled my knees. I got into the back seat. It was only as I fastened my seat belt that I realized my hands were shaking.

▶▶ CHAPTER 10 ◀◀

It took me a while, but by the time I got back across the river, to the library, I'd reasoned myself away from paranoia. I pushed thoughts of the shooting to the back of my mind and then willed them to stay there. As I walked toward the entrance to the library, I tried to focus my thoughts on my students.

I'd worked for one of the big test-prep companies until last year, when I decided to venture out on my own, in Arlington. In such a high-income, high-education county, everyone wanted their child to get ahead, and lots of people were willing to pay for it. It only took one student acing the test for word to spread. I might have been able to turn my coaching into a full-time position, but I would have been lacking benefits. After seeing the progression of the disease that ultimately killed my mother, I didn't want to be without medical insurance. If nothing else, my job at the Blue Dog provided that.

An advantage of my current setup: I didn't have any overhead. I just set myself up at a table in Central Library and waited for my students to come. On Saturdays, I held group sessions in one of the meeting rooms, where I took students through test-taking strategies.

Honestly, most of the benefit for my students came from just being there. If I assigned a test for homework, then students knew they actually had to take it before we met again because we were going to go over the results. In some cases, I was paid simply to sit at the table for three or four hours while a student took a practice test. If I was sitting there watching, then they couldn't do anything else. Couldn't weasel out of it. Couldn't check social media for "two minutes." And frankly, taking practice tests was the best way to study for taking the real test.

I did, of course, bring some value. I diagnosed areas of difficulty. I gave them practice problems. For which services I was paid quite well.

As I walked in and up to the second floor, I had a few minutes to spare. I scanned the room, looking for friends.

I saw Harold sitting in a carrel toward the back, by the windows that looked out on the tennis courts. Harold was retired. He spent his days at the library, reading. I knew him by his hat. It was a faded homburg that had a bright blue feather stuck in the band. I also knew him by his small, round, wire-rimmed glasses. I went over to say hi.

"Hey, Brown Eyes. You're sure dressed to the nines."

I smiled. "I had an interview."

"How'd it go?"

"I'm hopeful."

"Anyone would be lucky to hire you."

"Thanks for the vote of confidence." I smiled. Asked him what he was reading.

He held up the book. *The Jungle*. "I never read it when I was in school. I was supposed to. Sometimes I think about all the things I was supposed to do but never did. Finally made a list. *The Call of the Wild* comes next."

"That was one of my favorites." I glanced at my watch. "Have to go."

I saw Sunny as I staked out my table. She spent her days at the library and her nights on the streets. I recognized her because she always wore pants beneath her skirts. And purple sneakers. I lifted a hand. She waved.

I opened my phone and checked my schedule so I would know who to expect.

Brian.

He slouched into the chair across from me ten minutes late. "Sorry." His parents would still have to pay me for the full hour. I'd written that into my contract.

As if he'd changed his mind about his posture, he leaned forward and folded into himself instead.

"Do you have the test?" He was supposed to have taken a practice SAT since we'd met the week before.

He shook his head.

"Did you do the test?"

He nodded.

Terrific. I knew what his weaknesses were—they all had to do with reading comprehension—and we could work on those, but I really wanted to see that test. Then we'd know if any of the work we'd been doing had started to pay off.

"So you forgot it?"

"I didn't bring it."

"You didn't bring it, but you didn't forget it." I thought about that for a moment. "Does that mean you didn't bring it on purpose?" Never try to joust with a lawyer-in-training.

He nodded again.

"Why?"

"What's the point?" I could hardly hear him. And the library was relatively quiet.

"The point was to work smarter, not just harder. You don't want to waste your time—"

"I'm not going to get into college anyway."

"Why not?"

He shrugged. "I can't get into any college worth going to with a score of 1000."

"Hey." I reached out and shook his flannel-shirted forearm, trying to let him know I cared without violating the bro code. A teardrop fell onto the table in front of him.

"Brian?"

He pulled his arm from my grasp and swiped at his eye, then crossed his arms as he shifted away from me.

"Do you know what the average SAT score is?" I asked. "It's about 1050."

He scoffed. "That would get me into the University of Nowheresville, USA. If my parents didn't kill me first."

"But the point is, you already have 1000. And I think we can boost your score by at least 100 points. That would be well above average."

"Maybe in your family, but everyone in mine goes to Notre Dame. Or Cornell or Dartmouth."

"There are hundreds—thousands—of universities in the country."

"But only about ten really count."

"Is that what you think?"

"It's what my parents think."

"Your parents aren't the ones who will be going off to college next year."

"Yeah, but what are they going to say to their friends? What kind of magnet are they going to put on their car?"

I wanted to shake him.

He took a swipe at his eyes again. "All of this practice stuff I've been doing? It's not even helping. I did worse on the English and the reading than I did last time."

"If I could see the test, then I could help you figure out what—"

"No one can help me."

"With 1000, it's true: you're not getting into Dartmouth. But the number of people who get into Dartmouth is just a tiny portion of one percent of the population. Do you actually *want* to go to Dartmouth?"

"No."

Now we were getting somewhere. "Then where do you want to go?"

"It doesn't matter what I want. If I don't get into one of those 'reach' schools, then I won't be able to get into the right grad school, and if I don't get into the right grad school, then I might as well not even live. Because what's the point?" He stood up, rubbed a fist against his eye, and then grabbed his backpack.

"Sit down. Because I have something to say to you that I would never tell your parents. Do you want to hear it?"

He put a hand to the table, hesitated for a moment, and then sat back down.

"College is your choice, not theirs. You're the one who's going to be going there. You're the one who's going to have to do the work. I know your parents only want the absolute best for your future. That's why they're pushing so hard."

He lowered his backpack to the floor.

"And you've done some hard work too. So here's your homework for next week. I want you to find three schools that will take you with an 1100. And not just three schools that will take you, but three schools that you really want to attend. Can you do that?"

"Is that it?"

"That's it."

"'Kay."

"And one other thing."

He waited for me to speak.

"I also want you to tell me five things you like about each one. Got it?"

He nodded. "You want me to bring the test too?"

"Not really."

"Yeah. Okay. Yeah." His spine had started to straighten while I'd been speaking. His shoulders were relaxing.

I had the feeling he'd been sabotaging himself. Subconsciously, maybe he was trying to make sure he wouldn't disappoint his parents by ensuring, from the outset, that he wouldn't get into an Ivy. I'd seen it before. Ivies were a lot of pressure. Some students dealt with it by taking the possibility off the table. He probably wasn't going to get into one, even if he did his best on the test; I wasn't a magician. But if he could find a school he really wanted to get into, then maybe the motivation would convince him to stop throwing obstacles in front of himself.

I watched him as he jogged down the stairs to the ground floor.

Why did we put so much pressure on kids, requiring them to be perfect? And why couldn't I follow my own advice? Why did I force myself to keep reaching, keep pushing? Why could I not just admit to myself I didn't have it all? That I might not ever get it? And maybe that was okay?

As I sifted through my notes for my next student, someone slid into the empty seat across from me.

My heart thumped in my chest.

"Hi. Sorry. Do you mind if I ask you a question?" He was whispering.

The man wasn't holding a gun. He wasn't a killer. But he also wasn't Zach, my next appointment. Zach had long hair. The guy across from me didn't. And he was older. I could tell by the lines on his forehead.

"Uh—no." I paused. Swallowed. "That's fine. But I have a student coming."

"Great. Thanks." He was wearing a pair of chinos and a plaid button-down shirt. "You're a coach? For those college tests?"

I nodded.

"Could I get your contact information?" He pulled out a phone.

"I'm sorry?" I could hardly hear him.

He raised his phone. "Your number? I have a niece who's looking for someone and—"

"I'm not taking any more students right now. I'm sorry." I got asked that question at least once a week. I was booked up until the ACT test in September. After that, I was hoping to be employed as a lawyer somewhere.

"Is there anyone else you can recommend?"

I gave him the name of the test prep company I used to work for.

He entered it into his phone and then stood, lifted his phone. "Thanks." And then he left me as I swiped at the cold perspiration that had broken out above my lip and tried to slow the arrhythmic thumping of my heart.

▸▸ CHAPTER 11 ◂◂

After my last student, I scootered to the Blue Dog to pick up my things and then scootered home. The sun had already sunk behind the taller buildings; the streets were growing shadows. I left the scooter on the sidewalk and walked up to the house. Mrs. Harper's car wasn't in the driveway. I couldn't remember what she said she had planned for the day. I'd give her a call later, once I heard her come in upstairs.

With a glance or two over my shoulder, I walked around to the backyard and quickly let myself in. Leaving my backpack on the couch, I went into my bedroom and pulled a sweater on.

I soon heard the click of heels on the wooden floorboards above my head.

Mrs. Harper.

I grabbed an apple, dug a book out of my bag, and got ready to study.

Taking a bite, I went to close the mini blinds on the door to the apartment. As they slid down, one of the last rays of the setting sun backlit the window, highlighting the pollen smudges on the panes. I saw something I hadn't noticed before: a handprint.

A big one.

My heart rolled once.

Twice.

I put a hand up to the window. Forcing my trembling fingers apart, I held them up to the print.

The ghostly hand stretched way past mine.

I tried to swallow the bite of apple that I'd taken, but the jagged bits stuck in my throat. My mouth turned sour.

For the fourth time that day, I forced myself to stay calm. To be rational. Mrs. Harper had asked a cleaning crew to tidy up the apartment before I'd moved in. Maybe it had been one of them. Maybe it had happened when they'd cleaned the window and I just hadn't noticed it before.

Or maybe it was the lawn care company that took care of the yard. Maybe they were the ones who had knocked over my impatiens too.

I put a finger to the handprint and tried to smudge the edges. It didn't work.

It was on the outside.

I twisted the blinds shut, withdrew my hand, fisted it, and pulled it up into the sleeve of my sweater. I stepped away from the door and took refuge by the bar. But the longer I thought of that handprint, the bigger it seemed to get.

The thing about that door is that it wasn't any sturdier than the typical closet door. And the window was so close to the door handle that if anyone really wanted to get in, all they had to do was smash the window, reach in, and— I pivoted to the bar top, grabbed my phone with a trembling hand, and dialed Mrs. Harper.

"Whitney?"

"Hey. Hi. It's me. I was just wondering," my voice stalled. I swallowed and tried again. "When I came down last night, that planter of impatiens you gave me was knocked off the wall."

"I'm so sorry!"

"Do you know what happened?"

"Me? No."

"Was the landscape crew here yesterday?"

"No. They can't come until the weekend. I wonder if it was that awful wind we had. Or one of those foxes we've been seeing."

I hadn't thought of the foxes, but they were wary. They always stayed close to the back fence. I didn't want to worry Mrs. Harper with peeping Toms or would-be intruders though. I didn't want her to have another heart attack. "I'm sure it must have been."

"Oh! I've been looking all day for that package that came for you, but I still haven't been able to find it. And everything's a mess with all my packing. Don't tell my daughter. She'll think my memory's slipping."

The package. I'd forgotten about that. "Are you sure it was addressed to me?"

"That's what he said."

He? The hairs at the back of my neck began to rise. "Who said?" I'd made sure no one knew I lived here. I'd dumped my cell phone plan in favor of a no-contract option. I took advantage of free Wi-Fi wherever I could. Mrs. Harper paid all the utilities. I didn't have insurance on anything, except through work.

"He did."

"Who did?"

"The man who delivered it."

"He asked for me? Specifically?"

"Yes. You're the one it's addressed to."

Of course. He'd only been reading the address.

"He was a very nice young man."

"How so? How long did you talk to him?"

"I asked him to come in for a glass of water. It was so hot. And it seemed like he could have used something to drink."

"When was this?"

"Yesterday? No. It was the day before. Just before supper. Before you got home."

The day before yesterday had been a Sunday. "You invited him into the house?"

"He was very nice."

Her daughter most definitely would not have approved.

"You didn't tell him anything about me, did you?"

"I told him you were a nice young woman. Very kind."

"Did you tell him about our arrangement?"

"About how you take such good care of me? Of course I did!"

"And that I lived downstairs?"

"I don't know. Possibly? I may have mentioned it."

She probably had. "Let me come up and help you look for it. Can you leave the deck light on for me?"

I made sure the door was locked before I ran up to the house just as fast as I could.

Mrs. Harper was waiting for me at the kitchen door. She waved me through. "Quickly! Before the moths come in." They were already circling the deck light in frantic loops. Mrs. Harper was wringing her hands. "I'm so sorry I can't find it."

I helped her look for it. We scoured the living room and the kitchen for at least ten minutes. We checked the front hall. It wasn't there. It wasn't anywhere.

"I can't believe I lost it!"

"Did you sign for it?"

"Did I?" She paused for a moment. Put a finger to her lips. "I must have. That's why he didn't just leave it on the porch, isn't it?"

"Maybe it actually had to be *my* signature. Maybe he took it with him."

"I can't remember. He rang the bell. It was good timing. I'd just gotten home. I opened the door. He explained about the package. He asked if I had some water."

Wait a second. "He asked you for water? Or you asked him if he wanted some?"

"I did. Or he did. I don't quite remember how it went. But I asked him in."

"How long was he here?"

"Five minutes?"

"Do you remember what kind of van he drove?" He had to have been driving something. If it was a big brown van, then it had to be UPS. If it was white, then it was probably FedEx.

"I didn't see any van."

"What was he wearing?"

"Gray? Gray. A gray shirt. Or maybe it was a gray suit."

"Was it a uniform?"

"I don't know."

"Did you see where he went when he left?"

"I didn't." She was holding a hand to her chest. And her voice was tremulous. The whole incident was suspicious, but I didn't want her to get worked up over it. More than anything, she needed to stay calm.

"They'll probably just try to deliver it again. No worries. Let me know if you find it. Or if you need anything." I thanked her and raced back down to my apartment. Stepped over the spot where the planter had shattered.

That planter was bothering me even more.

It didn't take much imagination to picture what might have happened. Only one scenario made sense. That planter was heavy. And it had been tipped from the wall into the stairwell. How could that have happened? If someone had climbed over that wall to hide under the deck. And then crawled back out.

I made sure the door was locked behind me. I glanced over into my living area and made sure the small slit of a window above the leather couch was locked. I grabbed some tall books from the stack in my bedroom and leaned them up against the glass to block the view.

I locked myself in my windowless bedroom and then I called the detective.

▸▸ CHAPTER 12 ◂◂

"Whitney Garrison. From the coffee shop, right? You okay?"

As I sat on the floor between the bed and the wall, I explained to him about the mysterious package.

"So you're worried about what?"

"I'm worried about all of it. What if someone talked his way into Mrs. Harper's to check out the house? Take a look around?"

"That happens."

"Or what if . . ." I didn't quite know how to tell him what I felt. "What if it wasn't about Mrs. Harper? What if it was about me?"

"It *was* about you. It was your package."

"But don't you think it's suspicious that someone talked his way into the house, asking about me, and then didn't even leave the package?"

"When was this again?"

"Sunday afternoon. But with the murder in the alley and everything . . ." I let my words trail off.

"The victim was shot on Monday afternoon. It couldn't be the killer. I don't think the shooting and the package are related. Your landlady probably just misplaced it. Did you check the refrigerator? My grandmother used to find things in there all the time."

"There's nothing wrong with Mrs. Harper's mind." Though she was awfully vague about this visitor.

"Now, if the guy was poking around *your* place? That would give me pause."

"He did."

"He what?"

"I mean, someone did." I told him about the handprint and the planter.

"And this happened when?"

"The planter happened on Monday. I noticed the handprint just this evening."

He was silent for a moment. "I don't like it. I don't know if I can connect it with the shooting, but I really don't like it. Could be the guy with the package took a look at the house from the outside. Tried to peer through your door into the apartment. Remind me where you live?"

I gave him the name of the area.

"Hmm. Million-dollar homes. It sounds like the guy was casing the house."

That's what it had seemed like to me too. That was the logical conclusion. "The planter was knocked over the evening of the shooting."

"Still couldn't have been the killer, could it?"

"Couldn't it?"

"Happened before you got home, right?"

"Yes."

"He would have to be a psychic to know, in advance, that you would see him in the alley. And how would he have known where you lived? The timing's wrong."

Of course it was. It made me feel stupid. My law professors would have been disappointed.

"You want me to send someone out?"

"What would they do?"

"Look for evidence. Footprints. Fingerprints. But you said nobody broke in, right? And your landlady *invited* the guy into her house."

That was true.

"Might not have been the wisest move, but it's not a crime. Has anything been tampered with?"

We'd probably destroyed any evidence tearing the house apart during our search for that package. "Nothing in my apartment." Not that I'd noticed.

"Could *you* have made that handprint? At some point?"

"It wasn't my hand. It's too big."

"Let me send someone over."

If he did that, it would make me feel better, but what about Mrs. Harper? How would she feel about a police car pulling up to her house? Even if she didn't happen to notice, the neighbors definitely would. They noticed everything. They'd even called the police on me when I first moved in, before she had a chance to tell them I was living there. If Mrs. Harper asked me about the police showing up, then I'd have to tell her about the shooting at work and— "You know what—it's probably nothing. It's fine."

After I hung up with the detective, I called my dad. Mostly, I just wanted to hear someone else's voice. And I wanted to keep memories of the alley at bay for just a few more minutes.

"Sweetie. Hi."

"Hey, Dad. Just called to see how you were."

"Well—" He broke off for a moment. Said something I couldn't hear.

"What?"

"Sorry. I've been in and out these last few days. Kind of busy."

"Is everything okay?"

"What?"

Had he said that to me or someone else? I couldn't tell. "Are you okay?"

"Fine. Everything's fine. Sorry. I'm fine. You okay?"

"I'm good."

"Okay. Well. I've got to get going. Talk to you soon?"

"Wait! You didn't send me anything recently, did you?"

"Like what?"

"Anything. In a package?"

"Not since Christmas, back before you moved."

For the last few Christmases, he'd sent me a pound of special-roast coffee I really liked along with Sasquatch gifts. He got a kick out of them and always included a message about putting my lawyer skills to work on something truly important. But this year he'd given me a basket filled with self-care items: lotions, a foot scrub, massage oils, and a scented candle. All of which I had yet to use.

We talked for a while longer and then I hung up.

How long had it been since I'd been home? Too long. It had been the summer before last, for a quick three-day visit. But right then, I wanted, more than anything, to tell him what had been happening. To hear him tell me it would all work out, that it would be alright. But to do that? I would have to tell him everything I'd been trying so hard to hide.

▸▸▸◂◂◂

I tried to push away all the questions that swirled through my thoughts, tried to ignore the creepy feeling that someone was watching me, and concentrate instead on my studies. In spite of the fact that I was studying on my bed, I was doing a good job of it until my phone rang.

"This is Theresa Ripley. Brian's mother? I wanted to talk to you about your session today."

I nudged my study guide away and drew a blank index card from my stack so I could take notes if I needed to. "I'm happy to go over with you where he is on—"

"Did you tell him that college is *his* choice?"

Wasn't it? "We talked about finding schools he's interested in."

"Well, now he wants to go to *art school*! I didn't raise my son and drag him through high school just to have him go to art school!"

"The reason we were talking is because he's been really stressed and—"

"I know he's stressed! If he would just work a little bit harder, then maybe—"

"—I asked him to look at his college list a little differently."

"Wait, wait, wait. Are you saying my son's not smart?"

Danger! Whatever I said next needed to be worded very carefully. "I think your son is very smart. I just don't think this test—"

"You think he should be taking the ACT instead? Why didn't you tell me? I wouldn't have signed him up for the SAT."

"I mean that he's not likely to earn a score, from either test, that will get him into Dartmouth. Or Notre Dame."

"Then you need to give him more practice questions. You need to teach him more test-taking strategies. Or maybe I should reschedule the test. Do you think if he had another couple months he'd do better?"

"I think he's set to do as well as he can. I just need you to understand that the test isn't an accurate reflection of his intelligence. It's highlighting his weaknesses, not his strengths. And wouldn't you rather he be the top student at a nonelite school than a poor student at an elite one?"

"If he ever found out you were saying things like this to me, he would be so embarrassed!"

I'd heard *way* more embarrassing things about her. And her son was the one who had told them to me. "If we could just stop and stand back a minute and see what all of this pressure and stress is doing to students like him, then—"

"We're not paying you for perspective! If the test wasn't two weeks away, we'd drop you and go to someone else. But it is. And he likes you. Just, please. *Stop meddling.*"

I didn't want to meddle. I really didn't. But I'd made so many wrong choices that I didn't want any of my students to have to repeat them. If I hadn't blithely decided to go to an Ivy, then I wouldn't have just blindly followed everyone else along the presumed path to success; I wouldn't have applied directly to a master's program.

If I hadn't applied, then I wouldn't have accepted the offer to the most prestigious one in the most expensive city in the nation. And then I wouldn't have had to take out so many loans to afford the tuition.

I wouldn't have had to cobble together part-time jobs, wouldn't have had to go to school half-time. I wouldn't have maxed out a credit card paying for things like food and rent and books. I might not have met my all-time favorite professor, but then again, I wouldn't have followed her advice to apply to a top-ten law school.

If I hadn't been accepted to that law program, hadn't gone to every single corporate mixer I could, hoping to make the connections most of the students already seemed to have, then I wouldn't have met my ex. If I hadn't met him, then I wouldn't be carrying so many scars, both physical and emotional, out of that relationship. I wouldn't have to work my coaching job. I might have been able to afford a bar exam test prep program for myself. Most of all, I wouldn't have had to work at the coffee shop.

And if I hadn't been working at the coffee shop, then I wouldn't have walked into a murder. The situation I found myself in was directly attributable to a series of bad choices. It was, quite literally, all my fault. And the more I tried to recover from all of those choices, the more I realized I was trapped.

▸▸ CHAPTER 13 ◂◂

Later, as I was studying, Mrs. Harper needed one of the knobs on a kitchen cabinet tightened. I darted up through the dark, one more time, to help her. Sprinted back down.

My dad phoned.

"Dad? Has something happened?"

"What? Oh! No. Nothing like that. I'm sorry—I didn't mean to scare you. It's just that I forgot to tell you something earlier: one of your old classmates called."

An old classmate? "Which one?"

"Give me a second." In the background, there was a shuffling of papers. After a few moments he came back on. "I thought I had it, I thought he said, but I can't find it. Everything's a mess around here."

It was a he? "Did he say from which school?"

"I don't think so."

I told myself it was probably just someone from an alumni association looking for donations. "What did he want?"

"Your address."

"You didn't give it to him, did you?"

"Of course I did."

"Dad!"

"He seemed like a nice young man. You're a nice young woman. Just wanted to catch up. That's what he said."

"When was it that he called?"

"Yesterday."

"When? Was it in the afternoon?"

"Around lunchtime. I'd just eaten a sandwich."

It would have been around three o'clock in Virginia. I thanked him for letting me know and then hung up.

The problem was, I didn't know any nice young men. My ex didn't even fit into that category. And that made two nice young men who had asked about me in the past few days. I didn't like it. But once again, it was hard to see how it might be connected to the murder. Even if it had been the killer looking for me, trying to find my address, how would he have known my name? Or who my father was? And how would he have found his phone number?

It had to be an alumni association using an old number for me, didn't it? It was just a coincidence. It had to be. But I seemed to be turning into a coincidence magnet. It made me uneasy.

I turned back to my books and tried to study.

I was supposed to be treating the bar exam like a full-time job. Of a salaried employee. Most experts said I should be studying eight to ten hours a day, six days a week, for at least two and a half months prior to the exam.

I'd been studying, little by little, for the past year, although that had been in conjunction with my last year of law school and both of my jobs. But there was no point in mourning the time I'd lost to circumstance. The best remedy was to be efficient with the time I had.

So I tried to be.

But I couldn't stop thinking about Joe. Every time I closed my eyes, I saw him sprawled in the alley.

And I had so many questions. Who had Joe been? Why was he killed? Who was the shooter? And what about that mobile order he'd placed from the grave? It was just so odd.

And creepy.

How could a dead man order himself a coffee?

It felt like one of the logic puzzles on the LSAT, the test for entrance to law school.

Joe goes to a coffee shop every day and orders the same drink around 1:30. One day, Joe dies. The next day, he orders the same drink. Which one of the following must be true?

a. Joe didn't die.
b. Joe's ghost ordered the drink.
c. Joe is a time traveler.

I called Detective Baroni again. This time it rolled to voicemail.

"This is Whitney Garrison. From the Blue Dog? I'm sorry to keep calling, but I just remembered something strange that happened at work today. I'd like to talk to you about it." I might have told him on voicemail about Joe's order, but I couldn't even explain it to myself.

I didn't go to bed so much as I just finally gave up studying. I'd spent the night taking notes on the Uniform Commercial Code, but in the background, every brain cell felt as if it was still churning over the shooting, trying to tie together a string of odd happenings that refused to be connected. If I could just arrange my questions in a logical order, then they should lead to answers, but I couldn't see logic in any of it.

Bed provided no rest.

Every time the air conditioner clicked on, I jumped. Every time I rolled over to try to go back to sleep, I thought about Joe and his death. And that strange mobile order. It had to have been some sort of glitch, didn't it?

▸▸▸◂◂◂

The next morning at work, I decided to do some investigating.

Customers' data was absolutely private. I could get in trouble—I could get fired—for accessing Joe's account. But I wanted to understand what had happened.

After we'd cleared the first rush of customers, I went into the back room and scrolled through the mobile orders from Monday. Saw that Joe's had been placed at 1:20. Precisely. I scrolled back to the day before.

1:20.

And the day before that.

1:20.

It seemed odd that each of Joe's orders had been placed at exactly 1:20. Our mobile-order system didn't have an automatic capability. You could reorder a previous order, but you couldn't schedule an automatic order and you couldn't schedule one in advance. You had to place it, each time, yourself.

1:20. Exactly.

That really bothered me. I didn't know if I could place an order so consistently if I tried.

I took a look around. Peeked out the window on the back-room door and into the hallway. Glanced through the swinging door into the work area. Everyone else seemed otherwise occupied, so I dug deeper, accessing his profile.

There was an address on his account. The database required one. And there was a telephone number, obviously. Mobile ordering didn't work without a mobile phone. I sent a glance back toward the door again to make sure no one was coming in, and then I took a picture of the screen with my phone before I went back on the floor.

We got busy again midmorning. Nearly a dozen people came in at the same time. Ty pulled shots just as quickly as he could, but the orders still backed up.

One of the customers took advantage of the wait to strike up a conversation. He seemed a bit older than I was. He had blond hair and was wearing a suit and tie.

"So, I'm new in town. Just moved here."

"It's a great place to live. Lots to do."

"I heard there's some sort of games place around here? Bowling, karaoke? An arcade?"

"Punch Bowl. It's at the mall in Ballston." It was Corrine's favorite place to hang out. Ty had mentioned going there too.

"Have you ever been?"

I shook my head. Leaned away from the counter to see how Ty was progressing on the drinks.

"Want to go?"

I straightened. "I'm sorry?"

"Want to go with me? To Punch Bowl?"

"No." I used to give an explanation when I turned men down, but it was usually a wasted effort. They'd take it as a maybe instead of an outright rejection. I'd decided short and honest was better. It didn't leave room for ambiguity.

He reached into his suit jacket and pulled out a business card. Handed it to me. "It sounds like a lot of fun. Give me a call if you change your mind."

I smiled at him and then turned my attention to the next customer. Later, when they had all been served, I threw his card away.

When I went on my break, I brought up the picture I'd taken of Joe's account information and searched for the address.

347 Oakleaf Court in Fairfax.

But Google Maps couldn't find it.

It gave me Oak Leaf Drive in Mt. Vernon instead.

I left off the street name and put in just the number and the zip code.

It returned several choices: an auto mechanic at 347 Second Avenue in Fairfax, and a beauty salon at 12589 Broad Street, #347.

Sometimes I used fake addresses for online accounts. So I understood why Joe might have used one too. There was one possibility left to try. I brought up the picture I'd taken of his account, wrote his phone number on the back of one of my manager's business cards, and dialed it just to see what would happen. Maybe his voicemail message would provide some information.

But it never picked up.

As far as I knew, the police hadn't found Joe's phone, so I hadn't expected anyone to answer. But I hung up more puzzled than before.

Most people had some sort of voicemail greeting even if they rarely used voicemail anymore.

Something thudded against the swinging door.

I jumped. Moved so the desk was between me and the door.

It swung open and Ty came in, carrying a container of used coffee grounds.

As my heart caught in my chest, I slid the phone into my pocket and pretended to search for something on the storage shelves.

When Ty left, I brought up the picture of Joe's account information. In spite of the fact that Joe used the account every day, he'd never activated the most popular feature. In order to get a free drink on your birthday, you had to enter your birth month.

His was blank.

Clearly, he didn't have a problem making things up. He could have listed a fake month and taken advantage of the free coffee.

Why hadn't he?

And he'd never redeemed any of the points he'd earned as a regular customer either, though he'd amassed fifteen free drinks.

Why not?

It wasn't that he didn't want them; otherwise, he wouldn't have signed up for the card. It was that he didn't care about them. Somehow points weren't the reason he'd signed up.

But if he wasn't using the account to accumulate points, then what was he using it for?

That was the question.

And I couldn't figure out an answer.

As my shift ended, I glanced at the mobile-order area. Saw two orders waiting to be claimed. I walked over and turned them around so I could read the labels. A soy mocha with one pump. No whip. For Joe. Order placed twenty minutes before. I left it there.

The other order was a bag. Some sort of bakery item for Kate.

A woman approached. "Is that mine?"

"Kate?"

"That's me."

I handed it to her.

That left just the cup. A mocha. For Joe.

Again.

▸▸ CHAPTER 14 ◂◂

As I walked out of the coffee shop, I called Detective Baroni.

I couldn't stop myself from glancing up the street, from looking for someone, anyone, who was acting suspicious.

I shrank back against the building where a tree had thrown its shadow up against the wall. There were too many men wearing dark suits. Entirely too many. But they couldn't all be Joe's killer. Probably none of them were Joe's killer.

That's what I told myself.

The detective answered. I explained who I was.

"Sure. Right. You left a message for me. Something about work? I was just getting ready to call you. Can you be more specific?"

"I told you before that Joe came in every day for a coffee around 1:30?"

"Right. And?"

"He placed an order today."

There was a long pause. "Come again?"

"And he placed one yesterday too. The same order he placed the day of the shooting."

"Coffee addiction is real." He sighed. "Tell me what you know."

"So Joe placed a mobile order every day and—"

The detective interrupted. "Every day? Or just weekdays?"

"Weekdays."

"Okay. Important information. We still don't know who this guy is; we just know his name is Joe. But if he's only ordering on weekdays at one thirty—"

"One twenty. He placed the order every day at one twenty."

"Then chances are he works around here somewhere. And you say he's still placing orders? Even though he's dead?"

It sounded weird. I knew it did, but that's exactly what I was saying. "For the past two days. Soy mocha. One pump. No whip."

"Is there a way to do that? Can you pre-place orders? Maybe he just has a standing order and—"

I was already talking over him, cutting him off. "You place an order and the system gives you an approximate pickup time. You can't select a date or a time."

"So maybe someone's using Joe's card. Which is possible. We never found his wallet."

"If they're using his card, then why hasn't the order changed? And how would they access his account?"

"Soy mocha, no whip isn't a big seller?"

"It's not even a small seller."

"Okay. So let's just game this out. The killer takes Joe's wallet and by some odd coincidence orders the exact same thing Joe likes."

I was shaking my head even though I knew he couldn't see me. "I would buy that if he was ordering in-store using Joe's card, but it's a mobile order."

"Ah. From his phone. So maybe the killer stole his phone too."

"Along with his access code?" This was the environment where I thrived. I could out–devil's advocate just about anyone. Except my ex. Turns out he actually was the devil.

"Maybe Joe didn't use a security PIN. Is Joe locked in to always ordering that drink?"

"You can order whatever you want. But the program always suggests what you've previously ordered."

"Right!" The detective's voice was triumphant. "So our killer-thief *could* be ordering."

"Except that if he is, he hasn't come by to pick up the drinks."

"How do you know?"

"Because we've had to dump them the past two days."

He sighed. "So someone is ordering drinks they're not bothering to pick up using Joe's mobile account."

That's what it seemed like.

"Are you sure the orders come from him? How can you tell?"

"The label always prints out the name, the account number, and the drink."

There was a pause before the detective spoke again. "If he was ordering from his phone, does that mean there's a record of his phone number somewhere?"

I could have told him Joe's phone number, but I didn't want to get him in trouble for obtaining evidence illegally. His case shouldn't have to suffer for my curiosity. "The manager could probably tell you."

"Right. I'll give her a call. So we know the orders come from Joe's account. Do they have to come from a phone?"

"Or a computer."

"So it doesn't have to have anything to do with a card in his wallet." He paused for a moment and then continued. "But the person doing the ordering would have to have his phone or his computer."

"Or just access to his account."

"Sorry?"

"You wouldn't have to have Joe's actual phone. You could order from your phone. Or I could order from my computer. All you'd need is Joe's username and password."

"Right. Okay. So we've got someone ordering coffee on Joe's behalf."

"Someone who doesn't know that he's dead." That seemed like a salient point to me.

"It's strange. If you're sharing an account with someone, why don't they know that you're dead? We don't know much more about him than we did when you found him. Kind of waiting for someone to show up and claim him. He didn't have any identification. His fingerprints weren't in the system anywhere."

"Nobody's reported a missing person?"

"No. And we don't have that many homicides in Arlington. Four last year. Four the year before. Mostly crimes of passion, domestic violence. Joe doesn't fit." He was silent for a moment. Then he spoke again. "Any chance you can come in? We can talk this through down at the station?"

"I can't. I'm on my way to my other job. I'll have to refund a whole bunch of money that I don't have if I don't show up again. But I'll be done at four." A couple of my regular students were on vacation.

"Remind me where this job is?"

"Central Library."

"I'll meet you there."

"But—"

He'd already hung up.

I was jolted from my thoughts by a man who walked right into me.

The notebook he was carrying took flight and the papers that were tucked inside began to flutter away, end over end, down the sidewalk.

"Sorry. So sorry." He stooped to gather them. His arm was in a sling.

I bent to help him.

"I'm sorry. Thank you. Stupid arm. You wouldn't believe how many things you can't do with your arm in a sling—"

"It's no problem."

"I think I've probably discovered every single one. Thank you. Would you be able to do me a favor?"

"I, um—" I glanced around. The jolt had moved me away from the building, out of the shadow. I was feeling exposed. My mouth went dry.

He tried again. "Are you headed to the metro?"

"No." The word came out as a croak.

"I just wondered if—"

"Sorry." I handed him the papers I'd gathered and hurried toward a scooter.

⏵⏵⏵⏴⏴⏴

As I arrived at the library for my coaching sessions, I received an email from Ms. Buckingham at the law firm. I stepped aside, over to the wall by the outside book drop, to read it.

Ms. Garrison—

Delighted to meet you yesterday. Would love to schedule a follow-up interview. Does 1:30 next Monday work for you?

Yes! Yes, yes, and yes. I would make it work for me. I didn't want to get ahead of myself, but *if* the job worked out and *if* I passed the bar—I didn't want to tempt fate—then things were looking up.

As I was putting my phone away, I saw there was a voicemail message waiting for me. I pushed Play and held it up to my ear.

"Whitney, hi. This is Cade."

Of course it was Cade. I recognized his voice. He talked with the twangiest Southern twang I had ever heard, and he was the only person I knew who pronounced my name as if it were spelled H-witney. He'd worked on the Hill as Congressman Thorpe's tech wiz while I was there. He'd been so genuinely, so constantly nice. And he'd warned me several times about my ex, or tried to, but I'd always found a reason to excuse his bad behavior. Life would have turned out so much better if I had been attracted to Cade the way I suspected he'd been attracted to me.

He'd moved to Arlington before I had. He'd found a job at the FDIC. He'd also, in some roundabout way I never clearly understood, found me the apartment at Mrs. Harper's. And now and then, he'd check in with me at the coffee shop.

On the voicemail, there was the sound of traffic—of a horn honking—before he spoke again. The tone of his voice had dropped. "Can I meet you after your shift? Out behind the Blue Dog? About 1:45?" He blew out a deep breath. "I don't want to drag you into this, but you mentioned something once to me when we were on the Hill. I think it might be really important. So, um . . . yeah. Won't take long." There was another long pause. "Oh, and hey: if I miss you, I'll just come the day after. If we don't see each other then, I'll call you back. Probably better if you don't call me. See you tomorrow."

Tomorrow?

When was this? When had he left the message?

I checked the date stamp.

He'd called me Sunday.

The day before the shooting.

Despite the heat of the sun, despite the general mugginess of the day, a skin-prickling chill swept over me as I realized who the victim in the alley had been.

▸▸ CHAPTER 15 ◂◂

I called Detective Baroni and told him.

"Cade Burdell? Spell it for me."

I spelled it for him.

"So you're saying the victim wasn't Joe?"

"I don't know. I don't know who Joe is, I don't know what he has to do with any of this, but the victim was Cade Burdell."

"How do you know that? How are you so sure?"

"Because he left me a voicemail message." My voice caught. I pressed my back to the building's redbrick wall and slid down into a squat. Put my free hand to my forehead to keep passersby from seeing the tears that were leaking down my cheeks.

"You knew him?"

"Yeah."

"What did he say? On the message?"

"He wanted to meet me."

"When?"

"When I got off work." I swiped at a tear with the back of my hand.

"At the coffee shop?"

"Mm-hmm." I was afraid if I tried to speak, I was going to lose it.

"He wanted to meet you. At the coffee shop, after work. In the alley."

"Mmm."

"*You* were the person he was waiting for."

He'd been waiting for me out there and I hadn't even known. He'd died, practically at my feet, and I couldn't even recognize him.

"Hey, you okay?"

No. I wasn't. In a place filled with ladder-climbers and strivers, Cade had been uncommonly decent. I opened my mouth to answer, but a sob came out instead.

"Ms. Garrison?"

I bent myself double, resting my forehead against my knees.

"Whitney? What's going to happen now is that this whole investigation is going to accelerate. We know who he is."

Who he *was*. Cade was dead.

"Can you do me a favor? Do you still have that voicemail message?"

"Mm-hmm. Yeah."

"Can you play it for me? I really need to know what he said."

I pulled up the voicemail app, turned up the volume, put the phone on speaker, and pressed Play.

He had me replay it once. And then, after he'd listened the second time, he let out his breath in a whoosh. "Okay. That gives me a lot more to work with. Don't delete it. I'll still plan to meet you at the library. You can give me a better sense, then, of what he was talking about."

He hung up before I could tell him the most important thing. The conversation Cade had referenced? I had no idea what he meant.

▶▶▶◀◀◀

That afternoon, I was grateful for my students. I would have fallen apart if I'd been by myself. And my first one of the day required all my attention. I spent a large part of her session trying to talk her off a ledge.

"But the more practice tests I take, the worse I get!"

"When you feel confident in choosing your answer, are you sticking with it, Dani? That's what we talked about last week."

"Yes!"

"Because in that case, when you have that confidence, first instincts are usually right." There was a fallacy that initial answers are *always* right. I worked hard with my students to help them gauge the confidence they felt when making their initial choice. That was the better indicator.

"I stick with it until I start to think, 'But that other answer sounds right too.' And then I can't decide. And then I end up choosing the wrong one."

"So we'll focus more on test-taking strategies these last few weeks and less on the actual practice questions. It's okay. This happens."

"But why does it have to happen to me? Why am I studying so hard? It used to be I didn't know anything and I was a really good guesser." She raised both of her hands and bobbed her head, tucking her hair behind both ears. "Now, it's like I know more, but I guess worse!" Her voice was climbing.

"So here's the thing about this test: you're giving it too much power."

"Yeah. Because if I fail it, I don't get to go to school!"

"You'll get to go to school."

"But not my *dream school*!" She put her hands behind her neck and pulled her elbows together in front of her.

"Listen to me." I reached out across the table and offered her my hand.

She lowered her arms and then took hold of it.

When I spoke next, it was in an intentional whisper. Other library patrons were starting to turn in our direction. "This test doesn't get to say what kind of person you are. It doesn't get to tell you how kind you are. How intelligent you are. What a hard worker you are. You shouldn't give this test the chance to rule your life. It's not worth it."

"It is right now!"

"You know what will happen in about twenty-four months from now?"

"What?"

"No one, and I mean absolutely no one, will care what you got on this test. No one will even ask."

The panic eventually subsided and the rest of our session was productive.

There wasn't much time to think about Cade. It was my last student of the day who turned out to be the most challenging. He sat down, arms crossed. "I'm *not stupid*."

"I know you're not stupid, Henry."

He shoved his practice test at me. "This test says I am."

"Did you have enough time to finish all the questions?"

"No."

"Okay. So this test"—I put my hand on it—"this one right here says only one thing to me. It says that you don't know how to pace yourself. That's all it says. It doesn't measure how smart you are, it just measures how well you take the test. That's it. So you can do better if you give yourself the chance to finish it."

He didn't say anything.

"Right now, it's not about being smart or not, it's about spending less time on each question so you have more time at the end. More questions answered means more opportunities to gain points. So let's work on that, shall we?"

His mood lightened and toward the end of our session, I actually made him laugh. After he left, I gathered my things and then followed the path he'd taken through the tables to the stairs. But my legs felt as if they each weighed a hundred pounds. My backpack, as if it was filled with rocks.

Cade was dead.

He'd been out there in the alley, waiting for me, and now he was dead.

A man who had been studying some student artwork that was displayed in the lobby approached me as I came off the bottom step. "Ms. Garrison? Hey. It's Detective Baroni."

I took him into an empty meeting room.

He pulled his notebook from his pocket and set it on the table in front of us as I sat down. Then he reached over and pulled out the chair next to mine. Sat down beside me.

"I need to ask you about your friend Cade. How long had you known him?"

"A year and a half. I met him up on the Hill. In Congressman Thorpe's office."

"When did you last see him?"

"A couple weeks ago? He worked at the FDIC. He'd stop in once in a while to see me."

"So you'd kept up with him?"

"I'd kept in touch with him." But that wasn't quite right. "He'd kept in touch with me. That's the better way to put it."

"How closely?"

"He moved to Arlington before I did. When he found out I was moving across the river, he found my apartment for me. It was a friend of a friend of a friend connection."

"Were you close?"

"He was my friend. A really good guy. I don't even—" My breath hitched. I paused for a moment to compose myself. "I don't even know where he lived exactly. Somewhere in Ballston? We didn't hang out, but he was a friend at a time when I really needed one. He was one of those people you can count on."

"From what he said in his message, he was counting on you too. Can I hear it again?"

I brought the voicemail message up and played it so the detective could record it.

"Tell me what he was referencing when he said, 'I don't want to drag you into this.' What is 'this'?"

"I don't know. I really don't. I wish I did." Because he'd also said something about it being better if I didn't call him.

"He mentioned something you talked about when you were on the Hill together. Can you tell me what that was?"

I shook my head. "I have no idea. And it's been haunting me all afternoon. I might be able to tell you once I look at my journals."

"Journals? What journals?"

▸▸ CHAPTER 16 ◂◂

I told him about my habit of making notes every evening about the day's events and the people I met.

"Did you scooter here?"

I nodded.

"Then I'm your ride home tonight."

"You don't have to take me—"

"I want you to look through those journals. And I'd like to see that handprint you told me about earlier."

I didn't protest. Too many things had happened in recent days for me not to appreciate the company.

But when I headed toward the library's front doors, he steered me to the elevator instead, where he punched a button for the parking garage. At this time in the evening, the garage was nearly deserted. Except for the black SUV parked right next to the door. He beeped it open and then hustled me into it.

As we climbed the ramp to Quincy Street, I gave him my address and then I sat there, in the passenger's seat, clutching my backpack to my chest.

There was no other time in the past ten years when I'd so strongly, so desperately, wanted to go home. No other time that I could remember wishing I was eight or ten or twelve years old again. Before my mom got sick, before she died. But I was a big girl and I was living in the big world. I just needed to hold on a little harder, keep my head down a little longer. In a couple weeks, after Cade's murder was solved—in a couple months, after the bar exam—I'd be able to breathe again.

"We already found out most of what you told us about your friend. LinkedIn led us to the congressman's office and then to the FDIC. His social media posts told us where he's from, where he went to university. He tagged a bunch of pictures on Instagram, so that's given us a whole list of people to talk to. But what I still don't know, what I'd give anything to find out, is why he wanted to talk to you out in that alley."

"Hopefully I made a note of it. I talked to him every day. We geeked out on economics. I know I wrote down some of his ideas. They were interesting. He's a deep thinker." *Was* a deep thinker.

"Were any of those ideas interesting enough to get him killed?"

"I wouldn't have thought so. His training was in cybersecurity, but one of his interests was the economy. A lot of our conversations were about the fallout from the trade wars a few years ago." Cade especially had lamented how some of the markets once available to the nation were gone.

"You think we're looking for cloak-and-dagger economics?"

"Economics has real effects on real people." The words came out sharper than I had intended. "Those are the kind of things politicians care about. And you can't work around such powerful people without noticing who cares more about the money side of politics and who cares more about the people."

He held two fingers up. "Peace."

"Sorry. We talked a lot about the hearings we were organizing. Or which staffers were running around with their hair on fire and who to avoid. I just can't remember anything so important, any reason to talk about any of that, this long after the fact."

"Any possibility he might have confused a conversation he had with you with one he had with someone else? Was there anyone else he spoke with regularly?"

"I don't think so. Most people treated him like the tech guy. That's the relationship they had with him. 'Hey, Cade, my computer's not coming on. The printer isn't working. My conference call is in five minutes and I can't log in to the site.'" He might have talked like he was from the backwoods of the Deep South, but he was—had been—brilliant. And he had never turned down a cry for help.

But how did any of that fit in with his murder?

And why had he been holding Joe's cup?

I was tempted, as we drove, to let the detective know about the information I'd gotten from the "Joe" account. But I didn't want to get in trouble for accessing it and I didn't want to pass on tainted evidence. Detective Baroni had said he was going to talk to the manager about the account's phone number. He'd probably already been given that information. "Do you know yet how Cade is connected to Joe?"

"Hmm?" He was drumming his fingers against the steering wheel as we waited for a light to change.

"I was wondering about Joe."

"The coffee orders."

"Yeah."

He shook his head. "No idea on that one."

"I didn't mean to pry. It just feels like, from the message, that . . . It just seems like there's more that . . ." I didn't know how to put words to what I was feeling.

"It feels like there's something going on. I know."

That was it, exactly.

The detective continued speaking. "He used the word *better*."

Which, ironically, made me feel a lot worse. "And he said he didn't want to 'drag me into it.'"

"What's *it*? That's what I want to know. We figure that out and maybe that's the whole case."

I hoped so.

"That just leaves the roof."

"The roof?"

"Your normal murder isn't committed by a gunman in hiding. The shooter had to do some work. He had to figure out how to get up there. And he managed to do it without being captured on security footage. Then he had to wait. There's some planning involved there. And I really don't like it."

Neither did I. "Take a left here." As he followed my direction, I pointed out the corner up ahead. Told him which way to go.

As we turned onto Mrs. Harper's street, I asked him about the package delivery and also about the planter and the handprint on my door. "Can you see any connection?"

"I really can't. But with this new information about Cade? I want there to be."

My scalp began to tingle. It all felt too much like my last weeks in DC. I didn't want to have to look behind every corner again, didn't want to have to wonder if someone was out there somewhere, waiting for me. I thought I'd left all of that behind. It felt like a vise was tightening around my lungs as I pointed out Mrs. Harper's house.

"Am I in danger?"

"I wouldn't have thought so, but your friend's message is making me wonder. If I knew what it was he wanted to talk to you about, then I might know for certain. But I would say that until we figure this out, you're safer if you stay in crowds. With groups of people."

My breath caught.

"I'm just trying to let you know how serious this is. Rather, how serious it *might* be."

"I know it's serious. I also know that, killer or not, I'll have to pay my rent at the end of the month. I can't just stay in my apartment for the next few days until you work it out."

"Then we'll have to figure out how to gamble." He parked the car out front along the curb and turned off the ignition. "Can I download a GPS tracker onto your phone?"

"A what?"

"A GPS tracker. That way we'll always know where you are. Here's the thing: Cade Burdell worked with some very important people. That shooting wasn't typical. So if this is the worst-case scenario, then the killer would be a professional. He probably gets paid by the job. And this job isn't finished yet."

▸▸ CHAPTER 17 ◂◂

He asked if he could come in with me. "I'd like to at least see what the shooter saw if it really was him at your place. And maybe you could tell me if you see anything in your journal."

I explained about my lease and the requirement to check in with Mrs. Harper.

"That's fine. I'll just come with you."

"No. She'd want to know who you are, and if I said you were with the police then she'd start to worry, and that would defeat the whole purpose of trying to keep her from worrying."

He wouldn't take no for an answer. "Just tell her I'm a friend."

I gave in. Walked up the front steps. Rang the doorbell.

"Whitney! Come in!"

Was she looking more pale than normal?

I would have introduced Detective Baroni, but he stuck his hand out before I could say anything. "I'm Leo."

"It's so nice to meet a friend of Whitney's! Come in, come in."

My goal was to get him out of there as quickly as possible. "How are things today? Is there anything I can do for you? Anything you need?"

She flapped her hand at me. "No. I just can't find that package. I was hoping to have it for you. Who knows where I put it? I hate to think I lost something that was yours."

As we stood there talking, I saw the detective shift several times, changing positions slightly. If I were to guess, I'd say he was surveying the place.

"Don't worry about it, Mrs. Harper. I know it's nothing that I ordered, so I'm not out anything, am I?"

She tilted her head. "I suppose not." She walked into the kitchen, beckoning. "I brought half a cake back from bridge. Dolores made it but she didn't want the leftovers. Would you like some?"

"I had a big lunch."

She was already cutting a piece. "Then maybe you can have it later. Or maybe your friend would want some." She slid it onto a plate and then put some plastic wrap over it for me.

I thanked her. "Is there anything you need?" I opened the fridge as I asked the question, thinking maybe the detective had been right. Maybe Mrs. Harper had put the package in it.

It wasn't there.

"I'm fine. Don't give me another thought."

I told her good night and then we left through the kitchen.

I shook my head as we went down the stairs. "I'm thinking there probably was no package."

"Or if there was, maybe it was just a decoy. An excuse to get access to the property."

"Mrs. Harper might have another heart attack if I told her that. She's already worn herself out trying to find it."

He paused at the top of the stairs that led to my apartment. "You said the planter was where? Here?" He nodded toward the concrete ledge that separated the deck from the stairwell.

"Right there. It was clay. Big. And heavy."

"It fell the day of the shooting?"

I nodded.

He peered over the wall into the area beneath the deck. There were still leaves there, left over, I supposed, from last fall. When he walked down a few steps, I joined him.

"It wasn't anything a mouse or squirrel could have pushed over. I was thinking the only reason it would have fallen is if someone had been hiding up there."

"Right." He nodded. "And pushed it off the ledge as they went up. Or came down." He pulled his phone out of his pocket and thumbed something. The phone lit up, illuminating the space under the deck.

Somewhere down the street, a car door slammed.

Somewhere out in the backyard, a mourning dove cooed.

He climbed back up a few stairs and then leaned over the ledge, stretching his arm out to make the light shine farther. His bangs fell forward onto his forehead. "Few broken twigs. Someone might have been hiding there. Don't see any footprints though. Hard to tell."

As we walked back down the steps to the door, the detective held out his hand. "Key?"

I put my key into it.

He unlocked the door, switched on the light, and started to enter. But then he stopped. "What—!" He put his arm up, blocking the threshold, to stop me from walking in.

I leaned past his broad shoulders to peer around him. Gasped. My mouth fell open as I took in the scene before me. I swallowed air in deep gulps as I tried to talk.

Tried to think.

But I couldn't do any of that.

My plates and bowls had been shattered against the bar's counter. My forks and spoons had been bent and then thrown onto the rug.

My eggs had been taken from the carton and hurled against the wall—whites, yolks, and shells mixing in a pile of debris.

And my plants!

My plants had been torn from their pots.

I forced my way past him, ducking beneath his arm. I shed my backpack and went to kneel beside my cactus. It had been sliced open, its tender, fleshy pulp exposed.

Tears streamed down my cheeks. I tried to press it back together. The spines pricked my palms, but I didn't care.

I drew my hands away.

It fell apart.

I tried again, but it wouldn't stay.

The fresh green smell of crushed stems permeated the room.

I cried, openmouthed, at the abject cruelty.

I pushed myself up into a crouch, then stretched out a hand to gather the aloe vera, whose long leaves had been snapped off.

And then I saw my palm. The fronds had been stripped from the trunk and tossed on the floor. I gathered them up and stood, clutching the stack to my chest as I wept.

As the detective approached me, I held them out to him in mute appeal.

He took them from me and placed them on the bar.

As I tried to talk, sobs tore from my throat instead. I stood there, arms folded across my waist, trying to hold on to myself so I wouldn't fall apart.

"I'm so sorry, Whitney."

"I—I—"

He came over and put an arm around my shoulder, turning me away from the massacre on my living room floor.

I shook my head, or tried to. It was jerking to the rhythm of my sobs.

He drew me closer and then stood there with me as I cried.

▸▸▸◂◂◂

The detective reported the break-in.

I couldn't make myself move. Everything around me had been shattered and broken and slashed and crushed.

But I was frozen in place.

As he took pictures with his phone, I tried to get my brain to engage.

The pages of the study guide I'd checked out of the law library had been torn from the book and scattered about the room.

I stooped to pick one up.

Then another.

And another.

The police came. The detective let them in. Then he took me out into the yard and stood beside me, arm wrapped around my shoulders, as the team went in.

I felt safe there, at his side. With my ex, I'd felt caged when he put his arm around me. Absorbed, possessed. As if the gesture was more about him protecting what was his than it was about protecting me.

At the detective's direction, the handprint on the window was lifted.

Mrs. Harper came down. "Whitney? There's a police car parked out front. I came to see if—" She paused as her hand rose to her throat.

A police officer stepped out, hand up. "Ma'am? If I could ask you not to come any closer? We don't want to contaminate the crime scene."

"Crime scene?" Her other hand joined the first. "There's been a *crime*?"

"Are you a neighbor?"

I stepped away from the detective to take one of Mrs. Harper's hands in my own. It was cold. "She lives here. This is her house. This basement I live in is hers."

Her hand began to tremble. "There's been a crime? In *my* house?"

"We think it might be related to what happened to Ms. Garrison at work."

Her head swung toward me. "Something happened to Whitney at work?"

I should have told her. I should have told her everything. I took her by the arm and went back upstairs with her. Settled her in a chair and made some tea as I told her about the shooting. About finding Cade out in the alley.

But telling her gave me flashbacks.

I pulled the tea bag from the cup and mixed in several teaspoons of sugar before I gave it to her.

Her hand shook as she took it from me.

"Are you okay?"

"I'm fine. I'm really quite fine."

I don't know that she was, but as she drank the tea, a little color seeped back into her cheeks. Eventually I told myself I could believe her; she really would be fine. I joined the detective back downstairs in the basement.

After the police left, he helped me clean. We dumped all the broken dishes and bent utensils into garbage bags. We did what we could with the plants, trimming the damage and then soaking roots in water to get rid of any air they'd accumulated. With soil salvaged from the mess, we replanted them in my now-dented mixing bowls. Maybe, with enough time and care, they would start to grow again.

The basement felt different now. It was a crime scene. It had been denuded, stripped of all that had been vital. All that had been mine.

In the center of the living room, the detective stood, his posture erect. "The door was locked when we came in."

I nodded.

"I don't like this."

I didn't like it either.

My phone rang.

I jumped.

Leo took it from the counter where I'd set it and handed it to me.

It was Mrs. Harper.

I'd forgotten all about her. "Mrs. Harper? Are you okay? I'm so sorry about—"

"Can you come up? Right away? I'm in the bedroom."

▸▸ CHAPTER 18 ◂◂

I found her on the floor in her room. One of her legs was bent at an awk-ward angle and her folding step stool was lying next to her. "I'm just—I'm having a time—a hard time—" She blew out a breath of frustration. "I used to laugh at those commercials on TV, but I just can't seem to get up."

I wrapped an arm around her waist to support her, but she cried out when she tried to push to standing. "I was making sure all the windows were locked, but I missed a step as I came down."

I texted the detective and asked him to come up.

"I'm fine. I'll be fine." She said the words as if to negate my fears. But I didn't believe her. And what concerned me most was her hand. It was clutching her chest.

The detective came in through the door, took one look at her, and pulled out his phone. "I'm calling an ambulance."

▸▸▸◂◂◂

They wouldn't let me ride with Mrs. Harper, but the detective took me to the hospital so I could be with her. I called her daughter as we drove.

At the hospital, they whisked her away from us for X-rays. I stayed until her daughter came, and then the detective took me home.

I was still shaky from all that had happened, but my mind was hard at work. "I've been thinking about the break-in. Whether it was that package delivery guy or not, anybody who spent any time at all watching the house would know Mrs. Harper never used the basement apartment. Never entered or exited by that back door. They would know those spaces were mine."

He grunted.

"So whoever it was had either been looking for a way to get inside and up into the house undetected, or they had been looking for me." Waiting for me.

"Agreed."

"Can we say this person was the owner of the handprint?"

"And the one who knocked over the flowers? I really want to."

Inherent in his answer, however, was the obvious. We couldn't. Not until we had more information.

The detective stopped at Home Depot on the way back. I was happy to accompany him on his errands. I would have gone with him anywhere. It left less time for me to be alone, back at my apartment.

I followed him to the locks and fasteners section.

"Your lock was just begging for someone to pick it. Unless you have something more secure, it's as good as having nothing at all."

"Wait—we're here for me?"

He swiveled his head from a lock he was examining to me. "Yeah. I wouldn't sleep well knowing you're at risk. I don't know how you would manage to sleep at all. So I'm going to fix it."

It had been so long since someone had taken care of me that I might have broken down and cried right there between the keyed locks and the combination locks. I forced myself to pick up a package and start reading the fine print. Fine print was a specialty of mine.

"Whitney?"

"Hmm?" I was still blinking away tears.

"I don't suppose you have a drill?"

"What?"

"A drill? Do you have one?"

I shook my head. Sniffled.

"You alright?"

No. "I'm fine."

We went to the power tools aisle. He'd grabbed a box before I realized what he was doing. I put a hand to his to stop him. "Mrs. Harper might have one."

"Do we really want to spend time looking for it?"

No. We didn't.

He went over to the garden section and grabbed a few pots and a smallish bag of soil, piling it all into a cart.

My dad called while we were waiting to check out.

"I know it's late, but I need to give you a new address, sweetie."

New address? "For what?"

"For where I live."

I tried to make sense of what he was saying, but I couldn't do it. "Where you live?"

"I've sold the house."

"You've—what?"

"I've sold the house. I had to. Your mother lived for six months after she got diagnosed, but the medical bills we racked up? It's going on six years now that I've been paying interest on them."

My mind struggled to switch gears between the house and the bills. "I didn't know that."

"I didn't want you to. There was no need."

"I don't know what to say." Every time I talked to him, I knew where he was calling me from. I could picture him sitting in his chair in the family room, feet propped up on the coffee table. Without the house, without him living the life I'd once known, he didn't have any context.

"You couldn't say anything I haven't thought, but I can't hold on to it anymore. I tried. I took out a second mortgage on it when your mom got sick. But I just can't make the payments. I've declared bankruptcy."

What? "I'm sorry, Dad. You should have told me."

"I tried to do the honorable thing. I've tried to pay off that debt. I gave everything I had to get rid of it, but it wasn't enough. How long am I required to drag it around? If we're talking money-back guarantees, then I want my money back because it didn't work. In the end, your mother died anyway."

The memory of her reverberated between us for a few long moments. An echo of her laugh rose in my mind. And then I let her go. "When do you move?"

"Already did."

Already? I forced myself to breathe. Forced myself to let go of what I had no ability to save. "Do you like it?"

"Yeah. It's fine. Smaller. But then, it's just me. Closer to work. Just a couple blocks from that burger joint you always liked."

"The one that has fifty different flavors of shakes?"

"That's the one."

There was silence again. It stretched taut. Became brittle. I broke it. I wished him the best in his new place, wrote down the address, and then said good-bye.

Things happen. Or we make choices.

Either way, money comes into it eventually. My father's problem was that it took money for my mother to die. My problem? It took money for me to live. People might have castigated us both for not having money when we needed it. But I was starting to think that might not be the problem. The problem was that you could spend your life doing all the right things, and then something unexpected, something unforeseen, could wipe out all your resources. It wasn't anyone's fault and yet there was no recourse.

You have a modest but happy life. You have everything you ever wanted, the savings everyone said you need.

Then you don't.

It didn't seem right.

⏩ CHAPTER 19 ⏪

My mother died when I was getting my master's. It was a sudden diagnosis with a tragically steep descent to death. She was fine when I went home for Christmas. By the time spring semester was done, I was attending her funeral. She tried every treatment doctors thought might help—or might at least delay the inevitable.

She'd been our center, the one our family rotated around. I don't think my dad and I realized it until she was gone.

I talked to my father every day. It started, I think, because I needed to know he was still there. It continued because we were all we had left.

Until I started dating my ex.

All kinds of things went wrong when that happened. My relationship with my father was one of them. It's not that my ex didn't want me to talk to him; it's that he consumed me. First, by devouring anything that wasn't focused solely on him. And then, by devouring my soul.

Our dating began with a whirlwind of DC fundraisers and charity balls. It was either too early to call my father before we left for an event or too late to call after we returned. And even when the timing was right, it was inconvenient, because my ex needed me for something or wanted to go somewhere.

Can't you just call your father later?

I did at first. But then I fell out of the habit. And after several weeks, a month or two, I found there wasn't much to say. I hadn't told him I was dating anyone, and the longer I left it, the more awkward it had become to announce it. And then my ex decided we should move in together and I realized I needed to tell my father something. But I never actually made that call.

It was one more reason to hate myself. But since I'd broken things off with my ex, I talked to him every day.

The detective bought everything while I talked to my father. I followed him out to the car as I finished up the call.

"Hey." He paused, probably noticing I was trailing. He turned around to fall into step with me. "Everything okay?"

"It was just my dad."

"It can just be your dad and still everything can be not okay."

A corner of my mouth tipped up in appreciation. Emotional perception had not been one of my ex's strengths. At least, not in terms of my emotions. He was always extremely in touch with his.

"Yeah. He just sold the house."

"Sounds like it's time to celebrate. Houses can be hard to sell."

"I didn't even know he'd put it on the market."

He put his arm around my shoulders. Gave me a sympathetic squeeze.

I wanted to burrow right into him and stay there. But that was crazy. I'd only known him for a few days. I didn't want to embarrass him; he was just trying to be nice. But when he let me go, I was sorry. The warmth, the sympathy he'd provided, evaporated.

Once again, it was me, alone, against the world.

"When's the last time you saw your dad?"

"Summer before last. I've been hoping to go back again at Christmas." Even if it was just a couple days. Surely even a big law firm wouldn't begrudge a first-year associate Christmas Day. And, hopefully, Christmas Eve. I'd make my best argument. "My mom died six years ago. It's just the two of us." My throat was closing around a sob. "It was really tough on him." I swallowed it. Cleared my throat. "He's worked for the transit authority ever since he graduated from high school. He and my mom were so proud of me for getting into an Ivy."

"Any parent would be."

"But they had been planning on me going to the state school, half an hour down the road." In-state tuition was doable. I'd already lined up some scholarships from my father's union and some of the local community organizations. But most importantly, I'd only be a short drive away if I needed them. "It took some convincing for them to let me go to school on the other side of the country. They were terrified that someone would take advantage of my face blindness. It took a lot of trust on their part, a lot of promises on mine." And I kept them all until I met my ex. Then I'd broken every one. And everything they feared had happened. They'd been right; I'd been wrong. "Turns out the world is just as scary, just as terrible as they always feared it could be."

"I'm sorry."

"How do I tell him any of this? How do I tell him I am literally starving from debt, when he's so certain I'm already a success? How do I tell him I'm afraid I might not pass the bar exam? That really, the only thing for certain at the moment is that I live in someone's basement? Oh—and that I'm a barista, clocking an hourly wage. How do I tell him that?"

My ex would have told me to stop whining. Would have ordered me to change my emotions the way you order a dog to heel. But the detective only said, "He wouldn't care. You should tell him."

"I can't. I just can't." Why could I not stop talking? "I've lived my life trying not to disappoint anyone. I try to avoid everyone because they might feel bad when I don't recognize them. That way I won't hurt anyone's feelings."

He reached down and pulled his key fob from his pocket and beeped his car open.

"I just want to pass the bar. I just need to pass it." I said the words to myself more than I said them to him. And I needed to get a job. And figure out who had murdered Cade.

He put his hand to the small of my back as he helped me into the front seat, then he loaded the bags and we returned to Arlington.

As we drove, the weight of Cade's death increased. *I don't want to drag you into this, but you mentioned something once to me when we were on the Hill. I think it might be really important.* What had he meant? Once we got back to the apartment, I'd dig out the journal from my time on the Hill. We'd talked—often—but it was general conversation. Which representatives seemed like they were supportive of our congressman's work. Which would actually come through for him, on the record, when it mattered. Gossip we'd heard from other staffers. Predictions for the next election.

Even in the perilously partisan halls of Congress, none of that was particularly damning. And Congressman Thorpe had been a dream to work for compared to most. He was charming, relatively easygoing. One of the rare congressmen who was respected by politicians on both sides of the aisle.

But Cade had been worried about something. And now that worry had attached itself to me. I closed my eyes to try to clear my head.

Big mistake.

I saw my friend lying in the alley, with blood leaking out of his head.

The detective spoke. "So you're studying for the bar. You want to be a lawyer."

My eyes flew open. "That's the plan."

"Why?"

"Why what?"

"Why lawyer?"

"Because the barracuda is my favorite fish and I like eating small children for breakfast."

He laughed.

"It's because I want to do something I'm good at. I got tired of disappointing people who were counting on me to recognize them. Logic doesn't depend on gaining friends or influencing people. It doesn't depend on me either. It just is. And the measure of my success is only how well I can articulate it."

He said nothing.

"Why did you want to be a policeman?"

"It was the closest I could get to being a superhero without having to wear the spandex and the cape. It's not the best look for me."

I smiled. Just a tiny bit.

"So when do you take the exam?"

"At the end of the month."

"What are you going to do after?"

"Results don't get released until October. I'll have to keep myself busy until then."

"You worried?"

"Constantly."

"Is it really that difficult?"

"Difficult enough that I can't treat it as a sure thing." A tendril of worry wrapped around my heart and then spiraled down into my stomach.

If I did pass the bar, one thing I knew for certain: I wouldn't tell a prospective employer about my face blindness. There were no advantages in that for them. It's not classified as a disability. They wouldn't get extra points, extra anything if they hired me. I just had to convince someone to give me a chance—on my merits, in spite of that deficit. I had to be a lawyer. No backing out.

It's what I'd chosen. But money was power. If I wanted to get cryptocurrency into the hands of people who had neither, then at least I would learn how the system worked. After that maybe I would know more about how to change it. That's what I really wanted to work on. I reined in my anxiety. I had an interview on Monday. I would allow myself to worry about jobs then.

The detective stopped for some takeout on the way home.

I told him I couldn't eat anything. "Really, Detective Baroni. Don't worry about me."

"Cut it with the Detective Baroni. I know I'm a detective; you know I'm a detective. Just call me Leo."

I nodded.

"And I don't care whether you can eat or whether you can't. You're going to."

My brows peaked.

"That's what my grandmother would have said."

"I thought grandmothers were supposed to be nice."

"She was Italian."

Back at the apartment, after we'd eaten, Leo took his jacket off and rolled up his sleeves. I went to hang it up in my closet. The gesture was a reflex. My ex had been very particular about his clothes. But I'd forgotten that all my hangers were bent and twisted. I brought it back out and laid it over the couch.

Then I found my journal.

In the meantime, in the fast-falling twilight, Leo had gone to work pulling the old lock out of the door. My ex had always hired someone to do what he called "the dirty work" for him. Leo didn't seem to think twice about doing something that wasn't part of his job description. He opened the mini tool kit he'd bought, took the new lock out of the packaging, and laid out the parts on the floor by the door.

He seemed to know what he was doing. But he was stuck in the threshold between the humid air that had pooled in the stairwell and the cool air of the basement. Perspiration wet his brow. As he gripped a screwdriver, he pushed his bangs out of his face with the back of his hand.

I got him a glass of water. Set it beside him, on the carpet.

He set the screwdriver down and took a drink. "Thanks."

While he was finishing, I repotted my plants. Of all the things that had been destroyed, the plants were the most disturbing. It seemed, somehow, just a little too personal.

Leo came over to the bar to join me after he was done. He took up a plastic cup I was using as a watering can and poured some water into one of the pots.

As he was doing that, his phone rang. He walked over to the couch where his jacket was lying and pulled it from the pocket. "Detective Baroni." He listened for a moment. "Yeah. The Burdell case. That's right." He turned slightly toward me. Paused. Turned away.

What was happening?

"Sure. Yes." Another pause from Leo. He sat down on the couch. "So we're transferring it to you then? You're taking jurisdiction?" He gestured for me to come join him.

I walked over. Stood beside him.

"Can I ask why?" As he listened, he gestured with an open hand to the cushion beside him.

I sat.

"My notes? Sure. I don't have them with me now, but I can go over them with you." He paused again, listening. "I have her contact information, but I could just pass the phone to her if you want. I'm with her." He wrapped his palm around the speaking end of his phone and turned to me. "The case has been transferred to the FBI. We'll be working with them, but they're taking the lead."

"The FBI?"

"I'll explain later. But they want to talk to you." He offered me his phone.

I took it. "Hello?"

"Ms. Garrison? I'm an agent with the FBI. James Beyer. I'm taking the lead on the Burdell case. Are you the woman who found the body?"

"I am."

"Once I read Detective Baroni's report and your statement, I'll be caught up. And he'll be working with us until we identify the shooter, so I don't anticipate having to schedule to meet with you in person." His voice was low, calm, measured. In spite of my apprehension over the switching of roles, the agent projected authority and confidence. "Since I have you on the phone, can you tell me what you saw?"

Easily. Because I could see it every time I closed my eyes. I told him everything I remembered.

"And you knew the victim."

"I did. But I didn't realize it was him. He asked me to meet him in the alley."

"For what purpose?"

"I have no idea." But I hoped to. Just as soon as I could read through my journal. "We worked together on the Hill. He left a voicemail on my phone and I didn't listen to it until this afternoon. That's when I found out he was the victim. I have a journal from that time and I'll read through it tonight."

"But you were the one who found him in the alley?"

"Correct."

"And you didn't recognize him then?"

"No."

"Why not?"

"Because I can't."

▸▸ CHAPTER 20 ◂◂

I spent several minutes trying to explain face blindness to him. Leo finally took the phone from me.

"Hey. Detective Baroni here. It's like all those police reality shows when they block out the faces of everyone. When she looks at someone's face, she can't see it. Her brain doesn't map facial features. And if it can't map them, it doesn't store them. She could be talking to her own father and she might not even recognize him. Get it?" He offered the phone back to me.

In all the years I'd been gone from home, I'd never, not once, had anyone take on the burden of explaining what face blindness was and how it worked. I raised a brow as I took it from him.

He shrugged. "I did some research."

When I came back on the line, the agent apologized.

"Is there anything else I can tell you?" I was hoping we were almost done.

"If you didn't recognize the victim, then I'm assuming you can't recognize the shooter?"

"I never saw him."

"At all? Or you can't remember him?"

"I saw his silhouette against the sky. I could tell he had a gun; he was wearing a dark suit. Then he disappeared."

"Thanks for clarifying. I'd like to take a look at that journal you were talking about. If you can give it to the detective, he can pass it on to me."

I handed the phone back to Leo and they arranged to meet the following morning. After he hung up, he put the phone on the arm of the couch.

I pulled a knee up onto the cushion and pivoted to face him. "Why did the FBI take over the case?"

"He didn't tell me much. Just said that they'd been working with your friend on something at the FDIC."

I thought through the implications. "The FBI is serious."

He nodded. "Yep."

"It kind of takes all of this to a new level."

"It does."

"Does that mean you're done working on it?"

"I'll stay with it. Arlington police will be a cooperating agency. But he'll be the lead, not me."

His phone vibrated. He picked it up. Thumbed something open. "You mind if I stay for a while and answer some emails?"

I told him that was fine. As he went to work on his emails, I went to the bar and opened my journal. "Leo?"

"Hmm?" He looked up from his phone.

"Thanks."

"For what?"

"For that. For everything. All of it."

▸▸▸◂◂◂

I read through my notes from the Hill, scoured everything I'd written about Cade, looking for something that would make sense of the message he'd left me.

I couldn't find anything.

When I finally admitted defeat, I noted Leo was still on the couch where I'd left him.

"Hey." I offered him the journal. "Agent Beyer wants to see it. I couldn't find anything though. I read through it twice. There's nothing there."

He came over and took it from me. "And you've tried to remember conversations outside of those you noted."

I nodded. "When you work with someone, when you talk to them every day, it's not discrete conversations that you have with them. They all blend together. It's one long conversation." And in spite of that, I didn't know much about him. I knew his thoughts on economics and cybersecurity, certain politicians, and my ex, but what was his favorite color? When was his birthday? Did he have any pets? "I knew him narrowly. And you do understand that I live my life not really knowing who anyone is anyway."

He sat back down on the couch. "I do."

"Until now, I've always been able to presume that all the strangers around me—those I should know and those I've never met—are benign. That, in spite of my disorder, no one is actually out to get me even if it seems like it sometimes."

"Seems like a good way to approach it."

"I get out of bed every morning and I paste a smile on my face because chances are I'm going to mix people up. Or not recognize someone, for instance, that I work with all the time. Why? Because maybe she has a hairstyle and the same general form as another coworker. So I do the only thing I can: I smile. And I apologize. And I hope she doesn't hold it against me."

He nodded.

"I don't have friends, Leo. Not really." My ex had frozen them out or insulted them enough that they'd melted away. In the end, there'd only been him and me. And Cade. He'd stuck with me. "So the only person I can tell any of this to, the only person who would understand, is my dad. But if I told him, it would break his heart. And it already broke when my mother died." We'd been in daily contact, but we never talked about how we felt. About anything. I think we probably wanted so badly for the other to be fine that we couldn't risk knowing that they weren't. "Do you know what age I was when I figured all of this out? Seven. I was seven years old. I have been going through life smiling ever since, apologizing at every opportunity. But it's okay. Because, generally, people are forgiving. Most of the time, I can count on them to be nice."

He shifted, turning to face me more fully.

"But someone killed Cade. And he thought he was into something dangerous. Which is probably true if the FBI is involved. And now, apparently, maybe I'm involved too. We have to assume that, don't we, if he needed information that he thought I have? So I guess we assume that someone might be after me too?"

"We don't know for sure that—"

I held up a hand. "I just need to say this to someone. This is not okay." My hand began to tremble. I used it to scoop my hair back and push it behind my shoulder. "Because now, I have to assume that *everyone* is out to get me. And you know what? In that case, I would just rather not get out of bed in the morning."

He got up from the couch and came over to the bar. "We know who the victim is; we're trying our best to figure it all out. And now we have the FBI to help."

"I don't know what I'm supposed to do. How am I supposed to live?"

"Just hear me out. You're the only link we have to the murderer until we can figure something out from your friend's side—and we're trying to. The sooner we solve this, the sooner it's over."

The corners of my mouth started to wobble, but I had a lifetime of experience in controlling them. I swallowed. Forced them up and then into a smile. "Then I'm glad I can be of some help." I forced it wider. "But I still need to get some studying in tonight."

He folded his arms on the counter. Leaned into them. "I'd like to stay."

"Here?"

"Yeah."

Really? I felt the tension drain from me. He was staying! Maybe I wouldn't dream about Cade lying in the alley. Or be haunted by the thought of an unknown shooter hunting me down. "Okay." But how was he going to sleep? I had enough provisions for me and no one else. I had one pillow. One set of sheets. One blanket. One comforter. If I wore sweats to bed, maybe I wouldn't need the blanket.

I went into my room and stripped it off the bed. Went back out and handed it to him. "You can have any part of the couch you'd like." Thankfully, it was still intact. The intruder hadn't touched it.

"I've slept on worse."

How do you thank a man who changed your lock, remembered to buy pots for your plants, and spent his night sleeping on your couch to make sure you were safe?

You get out of the situation alive.

▸▸ CHAPTER 21 ◂◂

Detective Leo Baroni snored.

Not a lot. Just a little. But then, he'd slept on the couch all night. He woke up when I heated an oversize mug of water in the microwave and then poured it into my French press. I hoped that at some point in the future I wouldn't have a desperate need for coffee first thing in the morning, but that time had not yet arrived. I swallowed a few gulps and then went into the bathroom and got ready for work.

By the time I came out, Leo had poured himself a mug.

When he dropped me off at the Blue Dog, he called my name as I got out of his car. I bent so I could see through the passenger window. "Just do me a favor. Be vigilant."

As I walked into the shop, a woman was typing away on a laptop at a table in the middle of the floor. A guy was sitting in a booth. He was wearing sneakers and cargo shorts, along with a hoodie in spite of the day's sky-high heat index. I couldn't blame him though. The manager kept the shop cool. He had a skateboard on the bench beside him.

It made me smile.

My ex had only worn sneakers when he was slumming. That's what he said once when I was lacing up my own. He'd immediately whisked me to CityCenter and bought me a pair of suitable casual shoes. His phrase, not mine. He'd brushed away my words when I tried to protest. "That's why I'm here. To take care of you."

His taking care of me had been hit and miss. He paid for everything—for extravagant things—week after week, and then suddenly left me to pay the bill for the most expensive of the dinners or charity balls he'd told me to sign us up for. My credit card debt had ballooned when I was with him.

Eventually, the woman at the table abandoned her laptop for her phone, and the skateboarder in the hoodie left. It was midshift when I realized he was still hanging around, standing just outside the front door. I saw his elbow now and then when he shifted positions. I told the manager.

"For how long?"

"At least an hour. I saw him when I came in this morning."

"We need to get our customers to come back. We don't want them scared away by someone loitering in front of the building." She went out to investigate.

She came back about five minutes later. "Looked like a student." George Mason University had a campus a block down the street. Students kept us in business. "Said he was waiting for someone. I asked him to wait somewhere else."

"Did you see where he went?"

She shrugged.

⏵⏵⏵⏴⏴⏴

As I rotated off my shift, Leo came in through the door and walked right up to me. He introduced himself, but there wasn't any need.

I already knew him.

I recognized him by his hair. By his cologne. By the way his whole body seemed to be watching and listening all the time to what was going on around him.

"I'm trying to make myself useful. You already know we don't have any footage of the shooter. And none of the customers, none of the staff, noticed anything out of the ordinary. So who else can we ask? Who else might have seen something? Who's a regular around here?"

The police had already questioned all of the customers who were in the shop the afternoon of the shooting. But I didn't know how many other people they'd spoken to in the businesses along our street. I texted my student that I was going to be a few minutes late and then I took Leo to a hair salon several doors down. The owner spent the time between appointments standing in front of his shop smoking real, honest-to-goodness cigarettes. He might have seen the killer run by that day.

He had us come inside. Tried to interest Leo in a trim. Leo demurred.

I asked him if he'd seen anything unusual the day of the killing.

"When was it again?" he asked.

"Monday."

"Maybe. I took some breaks outside. But the wind was terrible."

Leo took over. "We're trying to identify the shooter."

"Can you tell me what he looked like?"

"That's what we're hoping you can do."

"When was it?"

"Just before two. He shot the victim and then he left the scene. He might have been walking away from the coffee shop in your direction."

"There was one man. It would have been about that time. Usually, Americans aren't walkers, they're strollers. But this one was. That's why I noticed him."

"What do you mean by a walker?"

He shrugged. "He had something to do. Someplace to go. Hard to explain. He was just different."

"If we were going to look for a walker, what would we look for?"

"Intensity." He shrugged again. "Someone determined to get where they're headed. Walking faster than other people. You know."

"I don't."

"If there are other people on a sidewalk, a walker will look at them as obstacles. He won't slow down; he'll figure out a way around. Walkers aren't patient. Strollers don't care."

"Can you remember what he was wearing?"

"A suit. Dark."

"Age?"

"Forty? More or less?"

We thanked him for the information and left.

Leo grumbled on the way out the door. "That was completely useless."

"Unless he sees the man again. At least he'd know to tell us." I glanced at my watch. I only had a few minutes left. "We could ask Ruth if she saw anything."

"Who's Ruth?"

"She sells newspapers by the metro. She's there every day. She might have noticed something." As we walked toward the intersection, I pointed her out.

As we approached, she seemed to look over her shoulder.

Once.

Twice.

Usually she greeted me with enthusiasm. Sometimes even with open arms and a hug. She was friendly, chatty, and helpful. She'd give directions to tourists and rap on the window of the coffee shop when the meter readers were out in force. But that day, she was much more subdued.

"Ruth?" I motioned for Leo to step closer. "I was hoping you could help us."

"I'll do what I can."

"We wanted to ask you about something that happened earlier this week."

She clasped her hands in front of her so tightly that her knuckles went white. "I can't help you. I don't know anything."

"Are you okay, Ruth?"

She turned her head to look over her shoulder again. Nodded.

I introduced Leo. "On Monday, around two o'clock, there was a killing. A shooting."

"Behind the coffee shop."

Leo nodded. "That's right."

"You know? I come out here to sell papers every day because I'm trying to stay out of trouble, do things right. And then this happens. Isn't anywhere safe anymore?"

"Did you see anything?" he asked her.

"No. Didn't hear anything, didn't see anything. That's what I told that man."

"Which man?"

"The one who's doing the investigating."

"When was that? Do you remember which day it was?"

"Day after. I remember because all those reporters were all over the place."

"Did he tell you his name?"

"Not that I remember."

"Are you sure it wasn't on Monday?"

"No. It wasn't. Couldn't have been. Because I remember thinking if they really wanted to catch who did it, then why didn't they ask me the day before, right after it happened?"

"Was he a reporter?"

"Police. That's what he said."

"Do you remember what he asked you?"

She shrugged. "I couldn't tell him anything. He just wanted to know what I'd seen. There'd been a shooting. Had I seen anyone suspicious, anyone acting funny? I told him I hadn't. Only person acting funny was him."

"How so?"

"He's asking me all these questions and he isn't taking any notes. Don't you people write things down?"

"We usually do." Leo thanked her for her time and we walked back to the coffee shop.

"It's too bad she didn't see anything."

"She did. I think she saw the killer."

"But she said she didn't."

"I've never talked to her before. Never met her. And I was the only one here asking questions on Tuesday. If it wasn't me, who else would it have been?"

▸▸ CHAPTER 22 ◂◂

I tried to shake off the chill that had crept up my spine. "Um . . ." I glanced at my watch. "I need to go. I'm already late."

Leo's phone rang. He held up a finger as he answered.

My own phone pinged as I waited. I took it out.

It was another law firm where I had hoped to interview. They were asking if I could come in next Friday. I emailed them back and confirmed the date and time.

Now there were two possibilities for employment. I crossed my fingers that one of them would work out. At this point, I was no longer picky.

No one had told me that the key to gainful employment and personal success wasn't just the school I attended. It was all the thousands of other little things I'd never had the chance to learn before I entered. It was all the inside jokes about cultural touchstones that I didn't know. It was wearing the right brand of shoes and buying the right kind of clothes. And not even the right labels, but the right styles in the right labels.

It wasn't until college that I realized just how different I was. How the American dream was only for a certain sort of person. Money isn't just something you earn; it's a perfume that leaves its scent on everything.

Leo hung up. "The team tells me there's a man just around the corner who's been hanging around for no apparent reason. It's suspicious.

He's Caucasian. Tall. Thin. Light brown hair. Wearing khakis and boat shoes. Ring a bell?"

"No. There was a skateboarder earlier, but he was wearing shorts and a hoodie."

"We're going to walk around the corner together. I'll let you know which one he is. I want you to tell me if you recognize anything about him."

We walked just far enough so we could peer down the street. "Over there. By that tree, near the intersection."

I looked. He was a type of preppy that I'd seen a thousand times, but nothing about him seemed familiar. I shook my head.

"Okay." He made a phone call. Spoke to someone for a few moments. Hung up. "It's taken care of. We'll follow him for a while, see if we can figure out what's going on. You done at the library at eight?"

I nodded.

"I'll take you there and I'll meet you there after. Don't leave without me."

▸▸▸◂◂◂

That afternoon I tried to bring all my concentration to bear on my students. But at the back of my mind was the thought that maybe the FBI had found a lead in the case.

While my first student was working through some reading-comprehension questions, I checked my phone. There was a news alert about campaign financing for the upcoming election. I clicked through.

Campaigns were seemingly awash in cash. Everybody seemed to be trying to buy the elections. A vote was the most powerful weapon an American could wield. After all the noise, all the ads, all the social media campaigns, it all came down to voting. What were those votes worth? Trillions, apparently.

It was another good application for cryptocurrency. If campaign donations were limited to cryptocurrencies and their blockchains made public, then all contributions could be traced. With the way the technology was developing, within the next ten years there wouldn't be any more dark money in politics.

"Ms. Garrison?" my student slid her answer sheet in my direction.

I went over the answers with her and gave her another set.

While I was waiting for my second student, I called the hospital to see if Mrs. Harper had checked out.

She was still under observation.

My second student kept playing with her water bottle, spinning it one way and then the next. Even I could read it as a sign of distress.

I put a hand to it and stopped it from spinning. "Katie? What's going on?"

"What if I don't do well? What if I fail it?"

"You can't fail it."

"You know what I mean. I got a 21 on the ACT the first time I took it."

"And what did you get last time?"

"A 26. But what if I do worse?"

"All you can do is practice. And keep working the strategies I've given you. If you've done that, then you get what you get."

"Can you tell that to my parents?"

"Remember the rules? This is between you and me and the test, okay?"

"Okay."

"You need to think of yourself. Who are you? What do you want?" That was asking a lot of a seventeen-year-old. I didn't know if I could answer those questions myself at twenty-eight. But I was part test coach, part life coach. "You're going to start applying to colleges this fall. So maybe take some time this week and think about the things you really like to do and the kinds of places that give you energy. What are your favorite things? Who are your favorite kinds of people?"

"But thinking about going away to school makes me feel sad. And lost. And lonely."

That was the thing about growing up. It sounded exciting and glamorous when you were in high school, but once you got into college, once you graduated, it was lonely. You did feel lost.

At least I had.

▸▸▸◂◂◂

What were my favorite things? Who were my favorite people?

I didn't know.

I'd told my student to think of herself, but that was advice I couldn't follow either.

Why not?

Because I couldn't. I didn't know who I was.

I knew things *about* myself, but I didn't *know* myself. I had this idea that other people carry in their minds some image of themselves. Some sort of picture of how they look.

Not me.

I had braces in middle school. My teeth are straight. I can feel them with my tongue. I know I have black hair. My driver's license says I have brown eyes. But are they edging toward amber? Or more toward green? I'd have to look in a mirror to say which, and I'd have to do it right then, while I'm standing there looking at myself.

In fact, I'd done that once during my undergrad years. I recorded audio of me looking at myself, reporting what I was seeing. It didn't help; I still couldn't turn all those disparate features into a composite face.

Sometimes I felt my face the way a blind person would, trying to translate what I felt into how I looked. But I couldn't do it because I can't map faces.

Who was Whitney Garrison?

I didn't know.

Did it bother me? I didn't know that either. The thing is, how would my life be different? What would change if I suddenly recognized a face? I supposed it was like asking a blind man what would happen if he could see.

After I broke up with my ex, I stopped trying to explain myself to people. One of the casualties of our relationship was trust. He taught me people can break it.

Another casualty? Confidence.

I'd been with him for a year and a half. Before that, I would have told anyone that I was a smart, independent woman. After I left him I just felt stupid. Stupid for not being able to see what he was doing to me. Stupid for putting up with him for so long.

Why hadn't I left sooner?

Was it the face blindness? Had the experience of never feeling normal left me with an insecurity he'd been able to exploit? Was that what he'd sensed in me? And if he had, then how? How had he seen it when I hadn't even told him about my face blindness at the beginning?

Normal people didn't go around explaining their weaknesses to everyone. They didn't say, "I never learned how to swim," or "I can't sing," or "I'm color-blind," did they? I suppose, if I was honest, I hadn't given many people the chance to know about that side of me.

But I figured I was a step ahead. Not everyone knows their own handicaps. And not everyone who knows them admits to them. I just did the things I could, and I tried to stay in my own lane. I learned not to put myself into situations that required the things I couldn't give.

What things?

Recognition. Reliance on friendship. It was like being tone-deaf. I couldn't give what I didn't have. No amount of trying would give me what I lacked. I was un-abled.

And it was fine.

I wasn't lonely in the way people think of loneliness. Work kept me busy. Coaching kept me busy. Being a junior associate at a law firm would keep me busy too.

I had a good life. A very good life. I had no complaints.

None at all.

▸▸ CHAPTER 23 ◂◂

My last student, Eli, had issues.

"How are you feeling about the test?"

He shrugged.

"We've done a lot of practice tests. You've improved three points from when you started."

"I know. But it's stupid. The whole test is stupid."

"I agree. The test is stupid. It's a snapshot of what you remember during a three-hour period of one day in your entire life."

"Then why do I have to take it?"

"Because it's the way people have decided this game is played."

"I have this friend who never even studied and took it the first time and almost got a perfect score."

"I did too."

"That's not fair."

"It's not. And we can sit here talking all day about how it's not fair, but starting in August, you'll still have to apply to colleges, and some of those on your list aren't test-optional. You're going to have to send them your scores. So it's up to you. You either play the game and do the best you can, or you don't. But either way, what they'll see is what you get."

As I was finishing up my advice on the reading section, an alarm started clanging.

We flinched. And then we straightened, looked around.

Lights were flashing.

Was it a fire alarm?

There always seems to be a delay in action when an alarm goes off, as if no one wants to be the first to decide it's the real thing. But the library didn't give us a chance. A voice came over the loudspeaker and library staff appeared as if by magic. They came up the stairs at a run.

"Fire alarm! Everyone out! Let's go!"

My student shoved his papers into his backpack and took off. I had more to take care of. My notes. His score sheet. My bar exam study guide and index cards. By the time I packed up, I was alone on the second floor.

The lights were still flashing, the alarm still clanging.

I threw my backpack over my shoulder and went toward the stairs.

A man with a messenger bag slung across his chest emerged from the bookshelves along the opposite side of the room and started toward me.

Something about the way he was moving so purposefully, not for the stairs but for me, sent a pulse of dread through my chest.

Out of the corner of my eye I saw—was that Harold? I couldn't tell because I couldn't see any glasses. But a man was sitting at a carrel over by the windows that looked out onto the tennis courts. His hands were clasped around the top of his head and he was rocking back and forth.

I abandoned the stairs and headed back through an alley of books, toward him.

The man with the messenger bag changed directions as well.

Leo's warnings echoed in my head. I was supposed to be vigilant and keep an eye out for the killer.

But what if the alarm was real? What if there truly was a fire? I couldn't let that man by the carrel remain at the back of the library, surrounded by books.

I threw a glance over my shoulder as I quickened my pace.

The man was gaining on me.

I should be heading toward the stairs, toward people, toward the exit, not deeper into seclusion.

I'd almost reached the carrel. "Sir? Sir! You can't stay here."

He didn't appear to hear me. Just kept rocking back and forth. Now I could hear him moaning.

I put a hand to his shoulder. He paused in his rocking, turned toward me.

"We have to go. Sir?" I moved my hand to his elbow. "I can help you."

He just kept rocking.

I moved around behind his chair so I could see the other man.

Three more steps and he would reach us.

"Sir?" I shook him by the shoulder. "Please!"

A hand closed around my arm and pulled me away from the carrel.

It was the man with the messenger bag.

I tried to pull away, but his grip only tightened.

My body resurrected the feelings of being trapped. The panic. The utter helplessness. But I fought against it. Twisting my arm, I tried to free myself.

It didn't work.

I put a hand to his chest and pushed, but it didn't have any effect.

He caught it with his own and levered me toward the bookshelves.

But I wasn't going to give up without a fight. I swung my backpack at him and kicked him at the same time.

He dropped my arm.

I used my weight as an anchor and pulled my hand from his.

At the end of the shelves, behind the man, a woman appeared. "Hey!" She strode down the aisle toward us. "I know you heard the alarm. You're going the wrong direction. Everyone is supposed to leave!"

The man pivoted from me, pushed her out of the way, and took off toward the stairs.

I squatted beside the man at the carrel who was still rocking back and forth.

And then the alarm stopped ringing. The flashing lights shut off. A deafening, tenuous silence settled over the library.

The man at the carrel slowly stopped rocking. His hands came down.

I noticed a pair of glasses on the floor. And a hat with a blue feather lay nearby. It was Harold.

I bent and picked them up.

He took them from me. "Sorry. Sorry. I'm sorry. Since the war, things haven't been the same." He could have been talking about Vietnam or Afghanistan for all I knew. He put the glasses on. "That's why I always come to the library. It's usually quiet here."

I squatted beside his chair. "You okay?"

"I'm fine. I'm fine. I'm good." He swiped at the perspiration beading up on his forehead.

The woman came over. A library lanyard hung around her neck. As she talked to Harold, I left them, moving toward the stairs. They were glass-sided, curving down in a long spiral to the ground floor.

I went down a few steps so I could get a better view. I'd told Leo I wouldn't leave the library without him, and I wanted to keep my promise. I didn't see him. But I did see the man who had been up on the second floor with me. I recognized him by his messenger bag.

He was heading toward the doors.

Had he seen me standing there at the top of the stairs?

"Whitney!"

I searched the crowd, trying to find who had called my name.

"Whitney!"

There! Leo was rooted in the middle of the lobby, holding his position as people flowed back into the library. I recognized his hair. I pointed in the direction of the door. Made a gun with my hand. Then pointed again, out behind him, to the doors.

Leo used his arms as leverage, as if trying to swim through the crowd. But by the time he fought his way through the door, the man had disappeared.

Leo quizzed me once he came back inside. "So, this man. Why are you so sure he was zeroing in on you?"

"He wasn't headed toward the stairs like everyone else. He changed directions when I did."

"Can you tell me anything about him? Anything at all?"

"I don't know. Lights were flashing. The alarm was ringing. And Harold was—"

"Who's Harold?"

"He's one of my friends. All the noise, all the lights. He couldn't handle it. So I went over to try to help him. That man followed me."

"He might have been trying to kill you. So no offense to Harold, but you need to tell me what you noticed."

"Sorry. I don't know." I closed my eyes. Tried to remember. He'd made me feel small. Vulnerable. Imperiled in a way I hadn't felt since I'd moved to Virginia. "He was tall."

"Black? White? Brown?"

"I don't know. I have a hard time with skin colors."

The side of Leo's jaw pulsed.

"He had a messenger bag over his chest. That's how I recognized him to point him out to you."

"What kind of bag? Canvas? Leather?"

"Leather. Brown."

"An attaché? Like something you'd normally carry in your hand?"

"I don't think so. I'm remembering it as a messenger bag."

"Can you remember what else he was wearing? Shorts? Jeans?"

"No. Twills. Or khakis."

"Any other impressions? Anything that would help us find him?"

"Hair was lighter colored."

"Blond?"

"I don't know. Maybe? I don't remember."

"Beard? Mustache?"

"I don't think so. I'm pretty sure he didn't have either. If he did, I would be able to remember them."

"If we're going to catch this guy, we need your help."

"And I can't give it to you. I'm sorry, but *I can't*! What do you want me to do?"

▸▸ CHAPTER 24 ◂◂

Leo's phone rang. He spoke for a moment and then hung up. "They have the suspect. The one from earlier by the Blue Dog."

The one I hadn't recognized? "He's here?" At the library?

"The FBI is questioning him outside. I know you can't recognize faces, and I know you said he wasn't familiar, but we're going to let you see him again. Tell me if there's anything you recognize about him at all." Leo took my backpack from me. "You ready for this?"

I took a deep breath. Nodded.

We walked out into the evening together. A fire truck was parked by the curb. Its lights were flashing, tinting everything with their fiery glow.

He nodded to a loose cluster of people standing over by the community garden area that lined the walkway. In the middle was a man who turned toward us as we approached. "That's *him*!" He was wearing a button-down and twill pants. A leather messenger bag was slung across his chest.

"Right. The one from earlier."

"No! That's the man I was telling you about. The one from upstairs who grabbed me while the alarm was ringing."

One of the agents pulled the wallet from his back pocket and flipped it open. Drew out a driver's license. "This says his name's Hartwell Anderson Thorpe IV."

I heard myself gasp. Hartwell Thorpe? I felt my face flush as a familiar, blanketing numbness spread from my face down my arms to my feet. I tried to fight it off. I forced myself to straighten my shoulders, to lift my chin.

Do not retreat.

A bully's biggest weapon is psychological. He wins by invading your head, changing the way you perceive the world. But I refused to be frightened anymore. So I walked up to him, reached out, and slapped him across the face as hard as I could.

He took it. He just stood there and took it. "I deserve that."

Those words only made me want to slap him harder. I was contemplating how much it would hurt my fist if I punched him, how much satisfaction it might give me if I kicked him in the shins, but Leo had already put a hand to his chest and stepped between us, facing me. "So you know him then?"

"He's my ex-boyfriend."

"The shooter is your ex-boyfriend?"

Hartwell's reaction was immediate. "Shooter? Wait. Wait a second."

My reaction wasn't far behind. "It was *you*?" I struggled with the concept, trying to reconcile what I knew of Hartwell with Cade's killer.

"Shooter?" Hartwell was shaking his head. "What are you talking about? What did she tell you? Did she tell you I'm a—I'm a shooter?" He leaned around Leo to speak to me. "Tell them, Whitney. I don't even own a gun."

"Whitney?" Leo hadn't moved. He was still protecting me from Hartwell. Or maybe he was protecting Hartwell from me. It was difficult to tell.

"I may have cheated on her, but I swear to you I didn't shoot anyone!" Desperation thinned his voice.

One of the agents took over the questioning. "Do you know Cade Burdell?"

Leo stepped away from Hartwell and stood beside me.

"Cade? Yeah. He worked in my dad's office. Good guy. Why?"

Disappointment had hollowed out my stomach. It would have been gratifying to see Hartwell forced to own up to something. And to have found Cade's killer. "I don't think he's the person we're looking for." I wished he were. It would have solved all my problems.

The agent ignored me. "Where were you on Monday afternoon?"

Leo nudged me with an elbow. "He's clearly been stalking you."

Hartwell heard him. "Stalking her?" He took a step toward me.

Leo slipped back between us.

"Wait." Hartwell held up a hand. "Just wait. Hold on. I haven't been stalking her. I'm not a stalker. She just didn't know I was following her; she can't recognize me. Did she tell you that?"

"So there's a reason you've been following her." Leo's tone was dangerously even.

Hartwell's Adam's apple bobbed. "No. Yes. I mean yes."

The FBI agent's head had tilted. "Care to tell us what it is?"

"I wanted to talk to her."

"You've been following her around this week to *talk* to her?" Suspicion laced Leo's words.

"If I'm being honest? Longer than that."

Wait. *What?* I stepped to the side so I could see around Leo. "For how long?"

"I came to the coffee shop. Ordered coffee from you."

"When?"

He shrugged.

"From *me*? *I* took your order?"

"Yeah."

"How long have you been coming to the Blue Dog?"

He shrugged. "Whenever I was on this side of the river, meeting with my client."

His client. His company's big cybersecurity contract was with the FDIC. I pointed a finger at him, but when I spoke it was to the agent. "His company is HARTAN."

A murmur went around the group. Everyone had heard of HARTAN. In an otherwise bleak market, its stock was soaring.

"He owns it. And it was awarded a huge contract with the FDIC last year."

An agent was pulling her handcuffs out.

"Don't do this, Whitney." For once, it was Hartwell doing the pleading. "HARTAN has nothing to do with you and me."

The agent tried to take hold of his wrist.

He wrenched it away. "I wasn't stalking you at the coffee shop. I knew you wouldn't recognize me. It wouldn't matter, so—"

"It matters."

"I know. I have no excuse. I'm sorry. I can see now that . . ." His voice trailed off. "The alarm went off and I was trying to get you out of the building. You were always so stubborn. I was stupid and I'm sorry. I want you to come back. That's what I wanted to say."

"The thing is, you didn't think you were stupid back when we were together."

Leo had given up trying to stay between us. He stepped away and I had a clear view of Hartwell.

"I think you thought you were clever. You thought you could cheat on me in plain sight. And that is inexcusable. It's cruel."

"I know. There's no excuse. I hurt you."

"And I have a restraining order. Which you've just told me you've violated multiple times."

The agent finally captured one of his wrists. "Did you ever wait for Ms. Garrison after her shift?"

He tried to shrug a shoulder. "Once or twice. When I didn't have to hurry to a client meeting."

"Where would you wait for her?"

"By the alley. She didn't always leave that way, but I figured if I could catch her when she did, then maybe we could talk in private."

"After she'd leave by the back, then what would she do?"

I was having trouble breathing. I thought I'd left Hartwell on the other side of the river. But he'd been here, right beside me, the whole time.

"She usually walks around toward the metro and jumps on a scooter."

Fear took root in my stomach. He'd been watching me—for days, for weeks—and I had never once noticed him.

"So where would you wait for her? By the door?"

"At the end of the alley. I didn't want to scare her. I just wanted to talk."

"Which end?"

"Fairfax Drive. I know how this makes me look, but it wasn't like that."

It was like that. It was exactly like that.

"Were you there Monday?"

"What day was that?"

"The eighth."

"Yeah. I think I was. I'd have to check my calendar to be sure."

"Then you must have seen it!" The words leaped out of my mouth before I could stop them.

The agent talked over me. "Tell us what you saw while you were waiting."

He shrugged. "Nothing. As I got to the alley, I got a text message from my client. Had to call him. By the time we were done, I assumed I'd missed her, so I left."

"Did anyone run by you?"

He didn't reply for a long moment. "Yeah. I think. Maybe? There was some guy. He was trying to make the light so he could cross the street."

"What street?"

"Fairfax."

"Which corner?"

"Monroe."

"Do you remember what he was wearing?"

He shook his head.

"Jeans. Birkenstocks. Running shorts. T-shirt."

"No. A suit. Look, Whitney, I really miss you. And I really meant what I said. If you'd just give me a second chance, I wouldn't screw it up."

I shook my head. "No." No more chances.

"Then I apologize. For everything. I'm not a bad guy."

"Actually, I agree with you, Hartwell. You're not a bad guy. You're the *worst*."

One of the agents snorted a laugh.

Leo put a hand on my arm. "Did you try to deliver a package to Whitney on the weekend?"

"A package? What kind of package? What are you talking about?"

I added a question to Leo's. "Were you the one who knocked over my planter?"

"Well . . . yeah."

The blood drained from my face. He not only knew where I worked. He'd found out where I lived.

"That's one of the times I came by."

One of the times?

"I knocked on the door and everything. I wanted to talk to you, Whitney. But you weren't there. I thought maybe you were and you just weren't answering. So I sat on the wall for a while to wait and then I got to thinking maybe it wasn't such a good idea. And when I jumped down, I knocked it over. I'm sorry."

"Did you ever talk to the owner of the house? Mrs. Harper?" Leo asked.

"Who?"

"The woman who owns the house. You didn't tell her you had a package for Ms. Garrison?"

"No. What package?"

I interrupted. "How did you even know where I live?"

"I got your address from your father. I called him."

"How did you know where I work?"

"I asked at your old job." The job he had always tried to get me to quit. Because "people like us order coffee, we don't make it." That's what he'd always said. But in that one thing, I'd resisted him. That job was my medical insurance. Before I moved I'd told my manager about the restraining order, but Hartwell was charming when he wanted to be.

"Did you ever enter Ms. Garrison's apartment? Did you ever ransack it?"

"Excuse me?"

"Did you break into Ms. Garrison's apartment?"

"What kind of person do you think I am?"

Leo answered. "The kind who violates restraining orders."

The agent continued. "Did you ever try to approach Ms. Garrison inside the library before today?"

"No."

"Did you pull the alarm today?"

"Why would I pull the alarm if I wanted to talk to her? I, uh— Are we done here? Can I go now? I need to meet my client."

"You realize the library has security cameras."

"I would hope so. Can I go?"

It seemed like the FBI was going to question him further, but I wanted more. I wanted him in jail. "I want to press charges."

Hartwell swept a hand across the top of his head. "Charges? I haven't done anything. What for?"

Leo answered before I could. "Continued violations of the restraining order."

"Those weren't violations. And she really didn't mean to file for one. She was just mad at me. I'm not the bad guy here."

He most certainly was. "I want to press charges." I wasn't just mad at him. I was scared. Terrified.

Hartwell took a step toward me.

Leo put a hand to his chest.

He backed off. "Don't do this, Whitney."

"You can work it out with the FBI."

▸▸ CHAPTER 25 ◂◂

As we were talking, a man approached. Leo reached out and shook his hand. They spoke for a moment. Then Leo gestured me over. "Whitney? This is Agent Beyer. He's in charge of the investigation now."

His hair was a fading brown. His height, his frame were both average. He was stylish without being trendy. Nothing about him was memorable, except for the manner in which he held himself. He was absolutely professional. If Leo couldn't be in charge, then I was glad that Agent Beyer had been chosen.

The agent extended his hand.

I shook it. Guessed he was probably about ten years older than I was.

He handed me my journal. I slipped it into my backpack. He wanted to know what happened in the library. I told him everything.

"You didn't know it was your ex?"

"He didn't say anything—he just grabbed me. I might have recognized his cologne, but I don't think he was wearing any." They still hadn't taken Hartwell away. He seemed to be arguing with the agents about something.

"Did he try to take you anywhere?"

"There wasn't time to tell. One of the staff members came up and he let me go."

"You say you have a restraining order?"

"Since April. Which he's clearly violated, more than once."

"I understand. I can help you report that if you want to."

I did want to. It was terrifying that he had been hanging out at work, and in my neighborhood, and I hadn't even known he was there.

Leo broke in. "She wants to press charges."

I hoped there would be jail time involved. I wanted him to think twice—three or four times even—before he violated that restraining order again.

I had a question for the agent. "So my ex was your suspicious person? *He* was the one loitering by the coffee shop?"

"That was him."

"And you knew I was in the library and you let him come in?"

"We didn't—"

"Even when you didn't know it was Hartwell, even though you didn't know I had a restraining order, he might have been the killer."

"You have a restraining order against him. Violent people tend to be violent. And he knew Cade Burdell too. He admitted that. Is he the jealous type?"

Most definitely.

"Maybe your ex *is* the killer."

"How is that— Is that possible?"

"In any case, we didn't know you were at the library. Not until Detective Baroni contacted us, after the alarm went off. We're just lucky he was here."

What if he hadn't been? Hartwell might still be following me all over Arlington. "A lot of strange things have been happening to me in the past few days."

"And Mr. Thorpe has just admitted to them."

"Not all of them."

"Which incidents are unaccounted for?"

Leo answered. "I detailed all of them in my notes. He didn't admit to the attempted package delivery over the weekend. He didn't admit to having broken into her apartment."

Agent Beyer didn't speak for a long moment. "Timeline says the package can't be attributed to our killer. Unless the killer is Mr. Thorpe." He signaled to an FBI agent and then turned aside to speak with her for a few moments.

"I've asked someone to watch Mr. Thorpe," Agent Beyer said when he returned to us. "But I do need to talk to you, Ms. Garrison, about your relationship to the victim, Mr. Burdell. That's how you can be most useful in our investigation."

Leo gestured toward Hartwell. "Can we do it somewhere out of sight of him?"

I sent Leo a silent message of thanks. Just seeing Hartwell had brought back everything. All of the things I'd been working so hard to forget. And the thought that he might be Cade's killer made me sick.

"Of course. Yes. By all means," Agent Beyer replied.

I had a suggestion. "There might be a room available in the library." It didn't close for another half hour.

Soon I found myself sitting across from Agent Beyer, beside Leo, as I answered questions about Cade.

"I listened to the voicemail he left you," the agent explained. "I'd been working with him on a matter related to his work at the FDIC. I really need to know what he was hoping to find out from you."

"That's just it. I don't know."

"It seemed to strike him as important. Important enough to reach out to you."

"I know. And I wish I could help you. But I just don't remember talking to him about anything like that."

"If you do remember, I need you to call me. Immediately." He passed me his card. "Cell phone. Anytime, day or night."

I pulled out my wallet and put it inside. "Can I ask you what you were working on with him? That might jog a memory."

"It was a hacking incident back in 2010."

"Of the FDIC?"

"That's right."

"It hasn't been solved?"

He shook his head. "We know who it was. It was China. There was a big investigation at the time. A commercial firm was brought in to unravel it all."

"But Cade hadn't been working at the FDIC that long."

"Only since last fall."

Something wasn't making sense. "Is there anything else you can tell me? I don't remember ever having a conversation with him about the FDIC." Did anyone ever have a conversation about the FDIC? It was one of those government agencies no one ever really thought of. "If you gave me some context, it might help."

"I really can't."

There wasn't much to say after that.

He did ask me a few questions about face blindness, though. How I handled the disorder. What kinds of things I might recognize about a person.

Leo drove me home. He drummed on the steering wheel as he waited for the light to change at Kirkwood.

"You could just turn on the radio."

"Hartwell Anderson Thorpe IV might be our guy. But if he isn't, we're back where we started. If it's not him, then who is it?"

I didn't know. That buoyant feeling I'd had earlier in the day, when I'd anticipated a break in the case, had been weighted down with dread.

"We need to rethink this. We need to rethink everything. When do you work tomorrow?"

"Seven."

"That's at the coffee shop?"

I nodded.

"Are you at the library too?"

"Yes. All afternoon."

"*Somebody* pulled that fire alarm. It might have been our killer, might not. Thorpe might be the killer, might not. But there are too many unattributable events happening wherever you go. Give me your work schedules for the rest of the week and I'll let the FBI know. I'll see if they can assign an agent to you."

That was a huge relief. I felt the knot in my stomach begin to unwind.

The light turned. He drove through the intersection. "So. Hartwell Thorpe. *The* Hartwell Thorpe. You want to talk about it?"

"Not really."

He held up a hand. "Okay. Thought I'd ask."

"I just feel like I should have been smarter. I should have known better. I should have realized what he was like sooner."

"The thing is, sometimes we don't recognize people for who they are. But it's not our fault; it's theirs. It's his."

I knew that. I really did. But I didn't feel it yet. I couldn't. I was having the hardest time forgiving myself for my own betrayal. "For a while with him, I thought it might be okay."

"What would be okay?"

"Everything." I had a social circle. I had a boyfriend. I had a life. "We were talking about moving in together. He'd made plans. I didn't renew my lease because we were looking for an apartment together. And then he cheated on me." That had been the last straw. I'd managed to excuse almost everything—the emotional abuse, the physical abuse, the controlling behavior—but cheating? It was one ask too many.

"If he did that, he's a jerk. If you have a restraining order on him, that means he's abusive. And he's a stalker. He knew you couldn't recognize him. He took pleasure in getting as close to you as he could without you knowing."

He had. It terrified me.

"He's dangerous."

"I wrote him a note when I left. Put it on his kitchen counter. And then I moved across the river. I thought I was really smart. The thing about renting a basement from someone is that your name isn't in anyone's property records. It's not on utility bills. And I changed my phone number. I'd never really done social media, so that wasn't a problem. I tried hard to cover my tracks."

"He's gone to a lot of trouble to find you."

"He's all about winning. All about appearances. When I dumped him? It must have been like a slap in the face. It wasn't part of his plan."

"Thorpe has been caught. And if he's the shooter, we'll nail him for that too."

"But does being caught normally stop domestic violence in your experience?" I knew the answer. I didn't need him to tell me. "He's a congressman's son. They're fabulously wealthy. The world operates according to different principles for him." And when I'd been with him, the world had operated that way for me too. I hadn't known how to pull all the levers available to people like them; Hartwell had pulled them for me. Was that why I'd stayed as long as I had? And did that make my staying better or worse?

"Principles or no, the most dangerous people are those who can't understand that they've done something wrong."

"I know. The world of finance is rife with them." Every scandal, from Enron to the housing meltdown in 2008, was conceived in the minds of people who didn't understand—or didn't care—that they were breaking the law.

"If the shooter turns out to be someone else, at least we get Hartwell for violating the restraining order. Let's hope for some jail time. Maybe that will scare him into compliance."

"I'm a realist. If I don't hope for anything, if I don't want anything, then I can't be disappointed."

Leo harrumphed. "Maybe not, but are you happy?"

"Happiness is a luxury. It's something I can't afford."

"Why not?"

"Because I'd have to pay for it."

"It doesn't cost anything to—"

"It costs everything." Only people who didn't have to worry about money said things like that. "And besides, I can't have what I can't have. It's axiomatic."

"But most people have aspirations. Most people have dreams. Goals."

"I do have goals. At this point in my life, I need them to be practical. I want to pay off my student loans."

"That's more of a necessity than a goal."

"Right now, it's all-consuming. When I have some breathing room, then maybe I can add some dreams to my list."

"Why can't you have both?"

"Because I made a Faustian bargain when I took out my student loans, and now I have to pay for it."

He said nothing. But I could tell he wanted to.

"What?"

"You told me your MO is to smile and try to get along with people."

"It is."

"You've hardly smiled at me since I've met you."

I gave him one just to show that I could.

"That's better."

When he parked along the curb in front of Mrs. Harper's house, he told me he was spending the night again. I didn't wait for him to get out of the car. I walked up the driveway in front of him, hoping to keep him from seeing I was crying. Was it anger? Regret? Exhaustion? I swiped at the tears before they could reach my cheeks.

My phone rang. My father.

"Dad. Hi."

"Whitney? You don't sound like yourself."

"I think I'm coming down with a cold."

"Doesn't sound like a cold. You okay?"

"I'm fine." He didn't know about Hartwell. Didn't know there ever had been a Hartwell. I was going to tell him after we'd moved in together.

"Well. Just wanted you to know that everything was finalized. It's all good."

"What's good?"

"The house. Everything's signed. Gave the keys up today."

I didn't know what to say. "I'm sorry."

He sighed. "No. Don't be. It's all for the good. It's time. A family's moving in. They'll enjoy it. It's a house for a family."

It was a house for *our* family.

"Just wanted you to know."

"Thanks. Dad?"

"Hmm?"

"I love you."

"Well. Love you too, sweetie. Take care of yourself. Proud of you." He hung up.

A hand touched my shoulder.

I jumped. Whirled around to face—Leo. It was only Leo.

"Just wanted you to know that I'm here. I didn't want to scare you."

I tried to calm my racing heart. "Sorry. With Hartwell and everything—"

"No need to explain."

I thought I'd escaped Hartwell. His sudden reappearance made it feel as if my life was rewinding, as if all the strides I'd made since I left him were for nothing. He was reeling me back in. Of all the bad choices I'd made in my life, he was the absolute worst.

What was it about him that had seduced me?

His confidence? The way he so conspicuously sought me out?

It was flattering. I could admit that to myself now. I had been flattered because he'd been part of the in-group. He was the king of the in-group. And for once, one of those people saw me.

Saw me.

Liked me.

Wanted me.

Everyone wants to be wanted; that's our collective kryptonite.

And then someone showed me the pictures on Instagram. Of Hartwell with another woman.

Why did I take their word for it if I couldn't recognize him?

I recognized the restaurant and I recognized the table he was sitting at with her. Because it was *our* table at *our* restaurant. And that's what hurt the most.

▸▸ CHAPTER 26 ◂◂

Leo was up before I was the next morning. He'd already made coffee. Already had a mug waiting for me at the bar.

"Do you have a ride-share app?"

I nodded.

"Do me a favor. Use it today, okay?"

"Sure."

"For everywhere. Even to the library. I don't know how long I'll be tied up, but you can reach me on my phone."

"Okay. And you can always check in with my phone. See where I am. Right?"

"I already do. On a regular basis. We changed your locks. Be smart about things. I'll probably see you tomorrow." He walked out the door, paused. "Lock the door behind me."

He didn't have to ask twice.

I got ready for work and was about to request a ride on my app when there was a knock on the door.

I levered off my shoes and tiptoed toward it. Bent so that anyone trying to look through the mini blinds wouldn't see my shadow. Then slowly, carefully, I lifted the corner of one of the slats. Took a peek.

It was a woman. A pair of sunglasses was nestled atop her sculpted blonde hair.

I let the slat drop and opened the door.

"Are you Whitney?" She took a step over the threshold. I had no choice but to retreat.

I nodded.

"I'm Jessica Harper."

Jessica. Jess. Mrs. Harper's daughter. The one who swam in high school. The one who'd graduated from Washington and Lee University and then gone on to become a periodontist.

I offered my hand. "It's so nice to meet you in person. How is your mom?"

She walked in. Put her purse on the bar and gave the room a glance. "Wow. This brings back a lot of memories. It's a time capsule. You were so good to lease it like this. I brought Mom home from the hospital late last night so I stayed. Took forever for the emergency room to examine the X-rays and then put the cast on."

"She's out? I'm so glad! Is she doing okay?"

"She'll be fine. But it's hard for her to get around. She's upstairs. I wanted to talk to you in private: I need you to leave."

I blinked. "Leave?"

"Move. I need you to move out."

"I'm sorry. Are you—" Had I heard her right? "Are you asking me to move out? Of here?"

"It's a question of lifestyle. I saw your boyfriend leave this morning. When you signed the lease, it was my understanding that—"

"He's not my boyfriend."

"Then you're subleasing? I'm really not comfortable with that."

"I'm not subleasing. He's a—" Did I really want to go into who Leo was and why he was in my life? It probably wouldn't be very reassuring. "He's just a friend."

"Mom told me about the break-in."

"That wasn't my fault."

"But the point is, Mom can't have a tenant with questionable behavior living in her basement. Especially now. I thought you knew that when you signed the lease. I need someone stable. Someone reliable."

"I don't have questionable behavior. And I've been very reliable."

"I can't be worrying about my mother's safety all the time."

"You don't have to. She's perfectly fine. Perfectly safe."

"Not with you living here. Apparently there was an incident at work too? That's what she said the police told her."

"The police didn't explain it right." Had they explained it at all? "She really has nothing to worry about."

"You're supposed to be watching out for her. That's why you're here. She's not supposed to have to watch out for you. *You* were supposed to keep *her* safe."

"I do. I try. And if you're going to evict me, I need some time to find another place to live. You can't just—"

"My mother's safety is my primary concern. I know she likes you. But this isn't going to work anymore. Not for her, not for me. She can't live by herself. That's the other reason you need to leave. Immediately. I'm going to take her back to my place and then try to sell this house. It's time."

Jessica lived about an hour away out in Loudoun County. "But this is her life. She has women's club and bridge club and garden club and—"

"I'm sure she'll be able to find plenty of other things to do. She had a heart attack back in March. If she had another one while she was living here by herself, it would kill me."

And if her daughter made her move out to Loudoun, away from all her friends, it just might kill her. "Have you talked about this with her?"

"I've told her I'm taking her back with me for a few weeks. We'll talk it over once she's there. I don't think it will be very difficult to convince her."

Mrs. Harper was not going to like that. But what could I do? I was just her tenant. I wanted to think I was her friend. But I wasn't her family. If her family was looking after her now, I needed to look after myself.

"If you're going to break the lease, then I need to be compensated. I'll need my deposit back as well as this month's rent."

"This is a question of safety."

"It's also a question of breaking a lease without any warning."

"Have you paid the rent for this month? I could—"

"I always pay a month in advance. Those were the terms of the contract."

"I'll refund it, but you'll have to wait until we sell the house."

"That won't work for me. I'll just stay here until then."

"You can't. I don't want you here if Mom's not here. Please, don't make this difficult."

"Then please don't violate the terms of the lease."

She held up a hand as she turned away from me toward the door. "Fine."

"And if I'm going to be made to leave, I'd like to talk to your mother before I go. She's become a friend. I won't leave without saying good-bye."

She stood in the doorway for a long moment. Then she sighed. Shrugged. "We can go upstairs together. But don't say anything that will upset her."

We walked up to the deck and in through the kitchen door. "Mom?"

Mrs. Harper's voice came floating out from the dining room. "Is that you, Jess?"

"It's me. And I brought Whitney."

We walked through the kitchen into the dining room.

"Whitney! Hello. I'm so sorry about you having to leave the apartment. I know this must be difficult for you."

I leaned down to give her a hug. "I'm just glad I was here when you fell."

As I straightened, Mrs. Harper took my hand and gave it a squeeze. "I hope you don't take any of this the wrong way. Jess just thinks I need to be smart about things. She's going to take me out to her place. I'll have this cast on for a while. And then I'll have to go to physical therapy. It's probably best. I hope you understand. You can see how it is." She released my hand. "A nice girl like you? I'm sure you'll be able to find something else."

For under five hundred dollars a month? Where?

▸▸ CHAPTER 27 ◂◂

I went back down to the apartment. Shut the door. Stood there trying to stop my thoughts from spinning. I had to vacate the apartment and I had to get to work. Simultaneously.

But how?

Where was I going to go? What was I going to do with my things?

I dragged my big duffel bag out from under the bed. Dug my reusable grocery bags out from under the bar.

At least I wouldn't have to move any large furniture.

Except my bed.

And my dresser.

All the rest was Mrs. Harper's.

I pulled my few remaining dishes from the cupboard and stacked them on the counter. Bundled up the dish towels I called my own and crammed them into a dented metal mixing bowl.

Dish soap? Laundry detergent? Toilet bowl cleaner? I'd bought them. I would take them. I set them next to the bowl. Added a stack of bath towels and sheets. And what would I do with my plants? It was too soon to tell if they were going to take root. Maybe I could leave them underneath the deck. Just until I found another place to live.

If nothing else, the ransacking of my apartment meant I had less to move.

Niggling at the back of my mind was the question of where on earth I was going to move to. But first things first.

I needed to leave.

And I needed to get to work.

I texted my manager, warning her I was going to be late. I told her it was police business. And it was. Sort of.

I pulled my clothes from the closet and crammed what I could into my dresser drawers. The rest I shoved into the duffel and garbage bags. The textbooks I hadn't wanted to part with, my journals, and the books I needed for the bar exam went into the grocery bags.

And then I couldn't put off moving any longer.

I texted someone I knew from law school, asking if I could spend a couple days at her place. On the couch or the floor or any other surface that might work.

Several minutes later she texted back that she'd moved. She was living in Austin now and hey, if I ever came to Texas, she'd buy me a beer.

I texted another friend from my old circle.

No response.

And that was the extent of my social network. All the other people I'd known had been friends of Hartwell. And the point of moving out of DC was to leave him behind.

I searched on my phone for storage units. There was one in the south part of the county that was running a special. I could use it for a month for twenty-five dollars. For the second month, the full rental rate would be applied. Surely by then I could find another place to live. If I could hire an extra-large ride-share, pay for the time to load and unload? Maybe I could take care of everything for less than a hundred dollars.

It was the best I could hope for.

How many nights could I afford at one of the old-time drive-up motels in Arlington? Three? Four? Not more than four. I didn't know what the deposit might be at my new place.

I refused to think ahead to what—or where—that new place might be.

▸▸▸◂◂◂

Arlington was the fourth-smallest county in the country. It was also among the top ten wealthiest counties in the nation. But if you lived in certain sections south of Arlington Boulevard, you'd never know it. It was in one of those areas that I found the storage company.

After assuring my driver that I would absolutely pay him for the time it took to rent the storage unit and then unload his SUV, he agreed to transport me. We also had to wait for the manager to unlock the gate so we could get to the unit. To access it we drove into an alley lined on both sides with units.

It wasn't ideal—the doors to the units were roll-up/roll-down and accessed from outside—but it was cheap.

I found my unit number and then motioned the SUV forward. I unlocked the door and rolled it up, rocking onto my toes to give it a final push. The floor of the unit had been swept, but it still had a sort of indefinable scent, as if the ghosts of things stored there in the past weren't yet at peace. Although the driver parked right in front of the door, unloading still took more time than I wanted.

I tugged my mattress from the SUV, pulling it toward me. Then I got underneath it, supporting it on my back. With a big heave, I tossed it toward the unit. The box spring was different. I tipped it out of the SUV and then progressed, inch by inch, toward the unit, trying not to scuff it. Once it hit the metal floor, I slid it in. Next came the dresser. I took the drawers out and moved them separately. Then I tackled the dresser itself. It wasn't that heavy, but it was chest-high and awkward to manage. It scraped on the pavement as I duck-walked it into the unit. The boxes and bags and duffel were easy. I didn't worry about organizing anything, but unloading still took about twenty minutes. And after that, I had to get back to the central part of the county for work.

▸▸▸◂◂◂

When the rush at the coffee shop died down, I took a look at the community bulletin board by the entrance. You weren't supposed to post housing or babysitting or other service offers. The store manager didn't want to have any liability if things went wrong. Sometimes, however, they'd get posted when we weren't looking.

But not that morning.

I called my university's housing office. Asked if they knew of any available rooms or apartments. They gave me a few leads, but when I called about them on my break, they'd already been snapped up by the multitude of college interns who descended upon the city every summer.

I looked on Craigslist, but my requirements were specific. I needed a place within a scooter's commute of work, and it had to be less than five hundred a month.

I was looking for a unicorn.

▸▸▸◂◂◂

A woman came in about forty-five minutes before my shift was over. She stood just inside the doorway for a long moment as if trying to decide whether to enter. She was glittery in a way I recognized from my time in Hartwell's circle. Her fingernails sparkled. A rectangular purse with a gold-chained shoulder strap was looped over her shoulder. And her hair was perfect. It was the kind that faded from blonde to brown so imperceptibly and looked so natural that I assumed it was. Until I reminded myself hair didn't do that.

She half turned to the booths and the windows before changing her mind and starting in my direction, toward the counter.

"May I help you?"

She ordered an iced latte. Unlike most customers, she didn't walk to the pickup area as she waited for me to prepare it. She shadowed me as I moved, talking over the hiss of the machine and the gurgle of the frother. "Can I ask you a question?"

I smiled. "Sure."

"Were you there? The day the man was killed?"

My smile wilted.

"He was my boyfriend."

Grief pierced my soul. I didn't even know Cade had been seeing anyone. "I'm so sorry. I knew him. We worked together on the Hill."

"I just want to see. I want to know where it happened." She was playing with the stack of coffee sleeves, running her nail over their corrugated edges.

"I was here that day. I was the one who found him."

Her hand stilled. "Can you show me?"

I hadn't been through that door since the shooting, but I told her I would take her. I explained the situation to Corrine and then joined the woman in the hall, reminding myself that today was today. It wasn't Monday. There was no killer lurking outside. I took a deep breath and pushed the door open, went out, and held it for her.

She paused on the threshold. Squared her shoulders as she took a deep breath. Then she joined me. Took a look around. "This is where he died? Out here?"

I pointed to the pavement in front of us. It seemed to me that I could still make out that puddle of blood.

"They really didn't explain it to me very well."

"They think he was shot from the roof."

"The roof?" She tilted her head to look up. "You did say you were here. You found him."

I nodded.

"Did you see the shooter?"

"Not really. Mostly just his shadow."

"I just— I can't believe it." She collapsed, curling into me, sobbing.

I let her cry for a while and then I angled us toward the keypad. "Maybe we should go back inside?" Thinking about the murder, imagining the killer up there on the roof, made me uneasy.

She straightened, shaking her head. "I'm sorry. I'm so sorry." She dug into the purse that dangled from her shoulder and fished a Kleenex from it.

"Did he say anything to you about what he was working on at the FDIC?"

She shook her head. "We hadn't been dating very long. Just a couple months. But I could tell he was a keeper."

"He was a good guy. The best."

"Yeah." She sniffled. Crooked a finger to catch a tear. "There was one thing he said. He told me he didn't really like his job."

I was surprised. "It seems like it would have been a good fit for him. With his interest in economics and everything."

"I know. I mean, he liked the job part of it. He called it a dream job. But if that were true, then he should have been happy, right? But he was so stressed. And then he didn't want to go out anymore." She paused. "I mean, he still— We were still dating. He just didn't want to go out on actual dates. He said it wasn't me. Swore it wasn't me. He just said he felt like he couldn't trust anyone anymore."

▸▸ CHAPTER 28 ◂◂

Leo called to check in while I was in a ride-share headed toward the library.

I told him I was fine. "Mrs. Harper got released. She has a broken leg. Her daughter's going to take care of her, out in Loudoun, until she's out of the cast." I didn't want to tell him about being evicted. It wasn't his responsibility. But he did seem to think *I* was his responsibility. "They've decided to sell her house, so they asked me to leave."

"Leave the apartment?"

"Yes."

"When?"

"This morning."

"They asked you to leave? As in pack up and move? Right now?"

"Yes. But it's fine. I don't want you to worry about it, but I did want to let you know."

"What are you going to do?"

"It's already taken care of." I'd do what I'd always done: I'd figure something out. "Oh—Cade's girlfriend came to the store today."

"Yeah? We talked to her a couple days ago. That must have been tough."

"She wanted to see where he died."

He grunted. There was a shout in the background. It sounded like he put a hand over his phone and shouted back. "Got to go. That all she said?"

"She said—well, she *thought* he said that he didn't like his job, but in light of the shooting—"

"What did she say?"

"She said he couldn't trust anyone."

"He turned out to be right."

"I know, but the thing is, you'd only say something like that if a person you had actually trusted turned out not to be trustworthy."

"True."

"Hindsight might be causing me to read into it, but it might be interesting to know who he worked with. To try to figure out why they weren't so trustworthy."

"We're already on it. Got to go." He hung up.

▸▸▸◂◂◂

I glanced around as I walked into the library. Leo had said there was an agent assigned to me. Was it the man browsing the new releases? Or the woman walking up the stairs to the second floor?

I could drive myself crazy trying to figure out who it was. I told myself the important thing was that someone was watching me. In actual fact, *two* people might be watching me. An agent and a killer. I didn't have to know who the former was, but I really wanted to know the identity of the latter.

My first student came to me in a panic. "The test is next Saturday!"

"I know."

"I don't think I've studied enough."

She was one of my few students who actually had.

"I took the test you gave me on Saturday morning. And then I took another one in the afternoon. And one on Sunday. I kept getting new things wrong. So I started another one yesterday, but—"

I held up a hand to stop her. "New strategy. You're not going to study yourself completely crazy anymore."

"O-kay. So what am I going to do?"

"You're going to follow the schedule and then, when you're done for the day, when you've covered the topics you said you would, you're going to put the books away and you're going to remind yourself of a few things. Write these down."

She opened her notebook and sat there, pen poised above the paper.

"I'm really smart."

She wasn't doing anything.

"Kayla!" I tapped the sheet of paper. "Write it. 'I'm really smart.'"

She started writing.

"I'm a really hard worker." I paused for a moment. "Got that?"

"Yeah."

"This is just a test." I let her write that too.

"This test will be scored, but it doesn't get to grade me. It doesn't get to tell me who I am or what I'm allowed to do. This test doesn't apply to real life."

"Could you repeat that?"

I hated college admission tests. With a passion.

And yet we weren't ready yet to push beyond them. We wanted something that would tell us who we were and what we deserved and what kind of success we could expect. We wanted a yardstick to measure everything by. But we hadn't found a way yet to measure kindness or intuition or the capacity to dig in and work and work and work at something until it got done.

Tests were useless at measuring the things that mattered most.

And they were the only thing I was good at.

The irony that I was not following my own advice was not lost on me. But in my favor, the bar exam actually would get to tell me who I was going to be and what I was allowed to do. In order to be a lawyer, I had to pass it.

▸▸▸◂◂◂

I stayed at the library long after my last coaching session; I stayed until they closed. It was stupid to go anywhere by myself, so I prolonged the inevitable as long as possible. I booked one of the public computers and did some research on the FDIC hack that Agent Beyer had mentioned.

It had been a huge scandal. The FDIC had tried to keep it hidden, but an unidentified witness reported it to Congress. It had taken a congressional investigation for them to give up their information about it. The FDIC hacks had been pinned on China. And more recently, I discovered, so had the hack of the verification system of a recent stablecoin launch.

Stablecoins bridged the gap between traditional currencies and digital currencies. They were a cryptocurrency backed by a more stable asset. This one had been backed by the US dollar. In exchange for one dollar, verified account holders of FDIC-insured banks were given one stablecoin, which could then be used to trade on the cryptocurrency exchanges.

Why had China hacked into the system that verified all users had FDIC-backed accounts? What had they hoped to gain? For reasons unknown, China was stealing vast amounts of data. What were they doing with it?

No one knew.

It was possible they were using it for internal political purposes, to identify and keep track of exiled dissidents. Or maybe to identify Americans who might be willing to spy for them. But those cases might comprise just a tenth of a percent of people whose personal information they now had.

What *could* they do with the information they'd stolen?

That was the intriguing part. Who knew what future algorithms they might develop that would help them mine the data for nefarious purposes? They had social security numbers, government security clearance files. The FDIC hack had given them bank records of hundreds of thousands of Americans. They had information on spending habits, mortgage payments, and personal identifiers. If companies like Amazon and Google could target ads based on social media activity, what might China be able to do?

Just about anything.

But that 2010 hack had already been investigated. China was the culprit. All of that happened a decade ago; it was public information. So why was the FBI still investigating? And what did Cade have to do with it all?

I still didn't remember having any conversations about the FDIC with him. I hadn't even known he was interested in working there. But China? That seemed relevant.

When Cade and I were on the Hill, China had just made a major announcement about its interest in blockchain technologies. At the time, everyone had discounted China's interest in cryptocurrency. What the Chinese said, and what we'd all assumed, was that they wanted to develop the blockchain architecture that supported digital currencies. They were going to test it on a cryptocurrency they had created. Cryptocurrency was only one of its myriad applications. But knowing they had hacked the stablecoin verification system made me want to reexamine that assumption.

So, yes. I was sure Cade and I had spoken about China. But we'd done it in a tertiary way. I wished I knew why he'd gotten involved with the FBI.

Eventually, the library announced they were closing. I couldn't stay there, and I couldn't bring myself to tell Leo I was homeless. I just couldn't. So I did the next best thing. I took a ride-share over to the Blue Dog and had the car wait in the alley while I punched my code into the keypad. Then I waved the car off and pulled the door shut behind me.

The shop had been closed for over an hour by then. The last employee of the day had gone home.

I made my way down the hall and then out onto the floor.

The manager had security cameras all over the place, but what were the odds that she actually ever checked them?

It was a risk I'd have to take.

The shop was different at night. The seating area was bathed in the soft white glow of streetlights. During the daylight hours, the shop pushed itself out into the world through its large floor-to-ceiling windows. At night, the darkness pressed back in.

The scent of espresso lingered, but the only noise came from the hum of the appliances.

Out on the sidewalk, a man walked past the windows. He paused. Turned for a moment and seemed to look into the shop.

Had he seen me?

I retreated back to the hall and punched in my code to access the back room. After clearing off the desk, I sat down. I pulled my books out of my backpack and then unzipped an outside pocket and reached for a pen. The key to Mrs. Harper's apartment was there too. I'd have to figure out how to get it back to her.

I zipped the pocket shut and spread everything out.

At home, I could make all the coffee I wanted. Here? Unless I wanted to gin up the huge coffee makers and clean up after myself, I'd have to make do with tea. But at least in the shop I was secure.

I was safe.

I worked on the topic of evidence for a while.

An hour later, when my neck began to crick, I called my dad.

"Whitney, hi. How are—" His voice slipped away and I heard a thud on his end.

"Dad? Are you okay?"

I didn't hear anything.

"Dad!"

He came back on. "I'm fine. I'm fine. It's just—I had the phone on my shoulder. You used to be able to do that with the old phones. You could set it right on top of your shoulder and it would never slip off. Of course, you couldn't walk around with the phone either. It wasn't portable."

"You're okay though?"

"I'm fine. Fine. I just—" He broke off in a sigh. "I wish you were here to help me."

"With moving in?"

"No." He chuckled. "No. I'm fine with that. Frankie came over to help. No. I'm trying to get my finances straightened out. You have a head for numbers."

I liked numbers. I always had. They never changed clothes or hairstyles. They were easy to tell apart. "I'm happy to look at anything you want."

"That's the trouble. I don't know what I want." He sighed again. "Once I figure this all out, maybe we can talk again."

"Anytime."

"You can give your old man advice for a change."

We talked for a few more minutes, and then he hung up before he thought to ask about my day. That was good though. As much as I'd made a habit out of lying to him, I still didn't enjoy doing it.

I put a hand to my back and stretched. Did some head rolls.

It was stuffy in that shut-up, airless room.

I stood and walked its length a couple times. Did some jumping jacks and some knee lifts. There weren't any good sleeping options in the shop, so I was determined to use the night to my advantage.

I sat back down. Returned to the study guide. My answers for the section were:

1. A
2. D
3. A

And the correct answers were?

I flipped to the back to find them.

1. B
2. A
3. C

How was that possible?

I double-checked my answers against the key.

Somehow I'd completely misread all the scenarios.

I went back to the cases. Skimmed them. Reviewed the questions. But how on earth could B, A, and C be right? I still couldn't see it.

I read the cases in earnest, looking for the things I'd missed.

How could it be that I'd studied for months and was doing *worse* on the reviews than I had in the beginning? I was starting to sound like one of my students.

I turned to the back once more. *Review Section II Answers*—Wait. Review Section II?

I flipped back to the cases and questions. I wasn't on Review Section II. I was on Review Section III. And the answers to those questions were, in fact, what I had chosen. A, D, and A.

I wasn't stupid. I was just tired.

And really hungry.

I closed the book, put my head down on top of it, and cried, even though I knew crying wasn't productive and I couldn't afford it. I convinced myself that maybe what I needed wasn't food. Maybe it was just a break. I stood up, took a few more turns around the back room. Then I headed out into the hall and to the front of the shop for a change of scenery.

The glow of streetlights diffused the dark. It reflected off the sidewalk and in through the windows. The chance of anyone noticing me in the darkened shop was slim, so I walked the length of the front counter—back and forth, back and forth—swinging my arms, doing head rolls, until I shook off my drowsiness.

It was peaceful there.

The refrigerators and freezers produced a steady hum. Now and then, a car passed, headlights sweeping the sidewalk. As much as Arlington wanted to promote itself as an in-burb of DC, during the weekdays there wasn't much nightlife. Or any life at all on the streets late at night. I slid into a booth, stretched my arms out across the table toward the opposite side, lay my head on my arm, and stared out into the night for just a few minutes.

▸▸ CHAPTER 29 ◂◂

I had almost drifted into sleep when I heard something at the back of the shop.

My eyes sprang open. I sat up. Listened.

Above the hum of the refrigerator, beyond the bathroom at the back of the hall, something was bumping up against the back door.

I stood.

There it was again.

The front door was locked; it opened only with a key. A key I didn't have. My only way out was the way I'd come in: through the back.

I had no idea who was out there. But with the shop closed, it couldn't be anyone with good intentions.

I could slide over the counter and curl up behind it, in the work area. But if someone actually came into the store, it would only be a matter of time until I was found.

Ditto if I took refuge underneath a booth.

The back room?

There were wire racks and shelves, but at the moment they were filled with boxes. If I could have moved them, I might have made a place for myself to hide and put boxes in front of me, but they were heavy. Immovable. And I might not have time to punch in the code to get in there.

Was that the outside keypad beeping?

I fled to the only place I could think of.

The bathroom.

Is a smaller *place to hide—a place with no outlet—really a good idea?*

It was the best I could think of right then. I ran into the last stall of the three, hopped on top of the toilet, curled into a ball, and sank my head into the circle of my arms. I let my forehead come to rest on my kneecaps.

I heard the back door open.

Heard the bathroom sink drip.

Drip. Drip.

The flowery scent of the hand soap was suddenly nauseating.

The door shut with a thud.

There was silence for a moment and then footsteps went past the bathroom door, down the hall.

Maybe I could sneak out when the intruder wasn't looking.

But in order to know he wasn't looking, I would have to take a look. And possibly expose myself to his view in the process.

The footsteps came back up the hall.

Maybe he wouldn't notice the bathroom.

The footsteps paused.

The bathroom door squeaked open.

A foot scuffed against the tile of the floor.

I heard the first stall door open. It banged against the metal frame. The impact vibrated up through the toilet, through the seat, and into my feet.

The second stall door was pushed open.

I leaned a shoulder into the solid wall beside me and squeezed my elbows in toward my head.

My stall door pushed open.

I held my breath.

When nothing happened, I opened a crack between my arms. Took a peek.

A man was standing there, mop in hand, head cocked. "I'm used to mold growing on toilets, not girls."

I blinked, trying to reconcile his benign form with the sinister vision I'd created in my head.

He extended a hand toward me. "I'm not going to hurt you, but you got to come down off of there."

I'd forgotten that the manager had a cleaning crew come in at night after the shop closed.

I stepped down off the toilet. "Sorry."

"Shop's closed. You're going to have to leave."

"I work here. Really. I can show you. I just forgot about—" I gestured toward his mop.

After a few minutes of trying to explain myself and then giving up, I punched in the code for the back room and got my ID out of my pocket. I also found the magnetic name tag I used for my apron and showed them to him, finally convincing him that I was legit.

His name was Rick. "Usually there's no one here when I come. Got the place to myself. Kind of nice."

"I don't have anywhere else to go."

"You run away from home?"

"My home ran away from me."

He snorted a laugh. Put a pair of headphones to his ears. "Don't mind me. Just going to clean this place up."

▶▶▶◀◀◀

I went back to my studies. I didn't have any trouble staying awake. My senses were on high alert.

Rick left around two o'clock. I didn't dare to fall asleep—I was afraid I wouldn't wake up before the first employee came in at four. My plan was to make it look as if *I'd* come in to open the shop. I could claim I'd mixed up my dates. The person scheduled to open wouldn't know I hadn't clocked in.

Around three forty-five, I put all my books away, stowed my backpack in a locker, and drew an apron on over my head. I pulled out my hair tie, ran my fingers through my hair, and then put it back into a ponytail.

This time when I heard the keypad, I didn't panic. When Ty came into the back room, I greeted him.

"Hey. Are—?" He cocked his head. "Are *you* supposed to open?"

"I thought so. Sunday, right?"

"Uh, no. Maybe. I mean, today's Saturday, but maybe—"

I feigned surprise. "Seriously?"

"Yeah. Tomorrow's Sunday."

"Really? Sorry. I've been a day off since Monday. With all that happened." I shrugged. Figured it didn't hurt to make a play for sympathy. "Since I'm here? I might as well help you."

There was a knock at the back door.

Ty started toward the hall. "I'll take the deliveries if you can get the brews going."

I worked behind the front counter brewing regular and decaf while Ty checked in the deliveries and then put them away.

We finished our prep with some time to spare.

Ty picked up a couple mugs and poured us both a cup of coffee. "You okay? Back from the time warp?"

What? Oh. "Yes. Definitely firmly planted in Saturday now." I took a sip.

"Hey. They ever catch that guy? The shooter?"

"Still looking for him."

"They can write me a parking ticket two minutes after my meter expires, but they can't catch a killer. Welcome to America."

I made sure to clock in when my actual shift started. During my break, I called Mrs. Harper.

"Whitney Garrison!" Her voice was clear, though she sounded tired. "It's so good to hear from you!"

"Are you doing okay?"

She told me that her family had convinced her to sell the house. No surprise to me. "I suppose they're right. It *is* awfully big for just one person. And I *was* getting lonely. They say it needs to be painted and the carpet taken up. And maybe even a new roof. I guess it does, but it seems like an awful lot of work to go to if I'm just going to put it up for sale. Anyway, I'm sorry you had to find somewhere else to go with such little warning."

"I'll be fine." I wish I could have said that I was going home, that I planned to move back in with my dad. She would have liked that; it seemed to bother her that I lived so far from him. I would have felt safe there. And maybe memories of my ex and images of Cade wouldn't be able to catch up with me if I left them here on the East Coast.

But I wasn't a child. Going home wasn't an option.

Besides, my father had sold the house. I didn't have a home anymore.

▸▸ CHAPTER 30 ◂◂

Leo came in after I went back out on the floor. He wanted to talk to all of us. "I need you to tell me again about your regulars."

Ty was the first to answer. "The guy who got killed was a regular. Joe. Came in every day around one thirty."

"Aside from him. Have you noticed any others?"

Corrine piped up. "There's Whitney's boyfriends."

I couldn't keep from rolling my eyes. "He doesn't want to hear about them." And I didn't want him to think I liked to string men along.

But Leo disagreed with me. "I'd love to hear about Whitney's boyfriends. Tell me everything."

Corrine bumped Ty out of the way and took his place. "There's been a couple. We keep telling her she ought to ask one of them out."

"Would you be able to identify them if they come in?"

"Sure. Whitney pretends like they don't exist. That's her strategy. It drives them crazy."

Mostly, it was face blindness. I just shook my head, playing along.

"Tell me what they look like."

"Sure. Well, there's one, he's been coming for a couple weeks now. He sits right over there"—she pointed to a table by the door—"and gives Whitney sad puppy-dog eyes. Comes in around eleven. Stays for, what—an hour?"

I shrugged.

"How would I recognize him?" Leo asked.

"Besides the puppy-dog eyes? I don't know. His name's Austin. Typical prep boy."

"When you say typical, what do you mean?"

"Something about the hair. And the clothes. What's wrong with him, Whitney?"

"Not my type." Not after Hartwell.

"Well, if you don't want him, can I have him?"

Leo ignored Corrine's question to me. "Have you seen him lately?"

"He was here yesterday. He usually comes in around the same time as the other one."

"Which other one?"

"He's like . . . hipster, variation three. You know?"

"Can you be a little more specific?"

"It's the nice pants. And the nice shirts. You know the kind. And the mustache. Mostly the mustache. He's Mustache Man."

"What kind of mustache?"

"You know. The—" She drew a couple curlicues in the air in front of her.

"I'm not following."

"The one that turns up at the ends."

"A handlebar?"

"That's it. A handlebar mustache."

"I saw him. In the security footage. He was here the day of the shooting. When's the last time you saw him?"

"I don't know. Tuesday? Wednesday?"

"Can you tell me anything else about him? Besides how he looked?"

Try as she might, no matter how many different ways Leo asked the question, she couldn't remember another thing about him. Nobody knew his name or where he was from.

"Is there *anything* else you can tell me?"

"I mean, what else is there?" Corrine asked.

"Anything. Where he works. Where he lives. Is he a commuter?"

She thought for a moment. "Here's something. He always orders tea. Iced."

"Tea." Leo sounded dubious.

"Green tea. Not that there's anything wrong with that, you know? You do you. That's what I say. But doggone. Now I'm sad. Because that's what I like: a man who thinks for himself."

"And you said he was one of Whitney's boyfriends?"

"He wasn't my—"

Leo held up a hand.

I clamped my mouth shut.

"I was kind of angling for him at first. He had that vibe," Corrine said.

"What vibe?"

"That thing going on."

"What made you stop?" Leo asked.

"He wasn't interested."

"What made you think that?"

"He was always glancing out the window when I was trying to talk to him."

"Where was that? Where did you talk to him?"

"Right here. He sat where you are. Only he'd never face the counter. Not unless Whitney was around. Then he was all"—she made a gesture with her hands—"locked on. You know?"

"Anyone else try to flirt with him?"

"I mean, I think we all did, didn't we?"

"Didn't we what?" Maddie asked.

"Mustache Man. We all gave him a try, right?"

I spoke up. "I didn't."

"True. Everyone except for Whit." Corrine pointed a finger at me. "I'm gonna take a page out of *your* playbook next time."

"So it was Whitney from the start?"

"Was it?" She turned to ask me.

I shrugged. Trying to play it off like I normally had. But underneath my nonchalance, a chill was working its way up my spine. "I don't think so."

"When did it start?"

"I don't know. Last week? Yeah. But he actually asked about you a couple days ago."

"Me?"

"Yeah. He wanted to know when you'd be in next. And I said to myself, chalk another one up for Whitney."

"When was that?" Leo asked. "Do you remember what day it was?"

She turned around and grabbed Maddie by the elbow. "Hey. Do you remember what day we ran out of lids?"

"Tuesday. Because I wasn't here and I heard about it my next shift."

"Tuesday. It was Tuesday."

Tuesday. The day after the murder.

▸▸ CHAPTER 31 ◂◂

When it got busy, Leo left the counter so we could get back to work. But I asked him if I could talk to him before he left.

"What do you think? About the man with the mustache?"

"It wasn't Hartwell. We have the video. It wasn't him. Whoever he is, he seems like a man with a job to do. He sat right there and watched every day while Cade picked up his coffee. He watched him come in, watched him go out. Learned his habits." He pointed to my chest. "Saw your name tag and everyone else's. And dang—a handlebar mustache. Have to hand it to the guy. Cheesy, but effective. Pull off the mustache, throw it away, and you're a totally different man. Don't even have to dye your hair or shave a beard. Bottom line? We don't know anything more about him than we did before we started asking questions."

One thing was clear to me. Corrine, annoying though she was, could be a valuable ally. Granted, she wasn't very discreet, but she did notice everything.

If I told her about my face blindness, maybe she could watch my back.

I wasn't thrilled about voluntarily telling someone that I had a giant blind spot in my life. The last time I'd done that was when I'd told Hartwell.

And the thing was, I didn't tell him right away. I didn't want to.

He was so . . . everything. Everything I'd ever dreamed about and thought I couldn't have. He was cute. How could I tell, if I couldn't remember faces? I couldn't. But I watch people. And I noticed he had a certain effect on women. So he was cute.

Or gorgeous.

Or something.

He was very confident. The kind of confidence, I suppose, that comes from being the son of a congressman and being raised with money. And then heading a start-up that made millions.

He was such a gentleman. He opened doors for me. He waited to take a seat until I sat down. All those things that proper people are supposed to do? He did them without thinking. They were instinctual.

And he was never late. For anything.

Wherever we were supposed to meet, he was always there first. I could count on it. That meant that he was always looking for me. I'd never had that in my life before. *I* had always been the one doing the searching. I had always been frantically looking around trying to find a way—clothes, hair, shoes, voice, gestures, gait, *something*—to figure out who people were. To finally have someone know me? Have someone name me and look for me? I didn't have to worry about causing anyone any trouble. Once I got used to all of that, I told him about my face blindness. And he was okay with it.

He asked so many questions.

How had I recognized my parents? By their clothes? By their hair? But what if they changed something? What if they had to wear glasses? Or gained weight? Or lost it?

I told him there were so many other ways to tell people apart. Their voices. Their scent. The way they walked or the way they gestured when they talked.

I never dreamed that one day he would use it all against me.

Everything was perfect.

Until he started undermining me. Started making me question

myself. That's when I began to defer to him. And then he began to bend me to his will. That's when I surrendered, trading away my autonomy for his approval. And then he started hitting me.

But I talked myself into staying with him because I thought we were worth it. I didn't want to be the kind of person who gave up when things got difficult. Every couple had disagreements. If I really loved him, wouldn't the truest measure of my loyalty be my commitment to working things out?

He talked about moving in together. And that's about when he started cheating too. It took someone who knew us both to tell me. The humiliating part? It had been right there, the whole time, on social media.

I just couldn't see it.

And I didn't know how to recognize the signs.

I didn't know that being careful not to provoke his temper would lead to giving up my opinions so I could safely tiptoe around even the most noncontroversial things. And I didn't know that tiptoeing would turn into having to walk oh-so-carefully across eggshells all the time.

Now I did.

That slight detachment he always had wasn't preoccupation; it was boredom. That perpetual looking around wasn't networking. It was being on the lookout for something else. Someone else. Someone better. Someone new.

When I confronted him, he didn't deny it.

He never even tried to deny it.

That's what hurt the most.

He blamed it on me instead. If I'd been a better girlfriend, he wouldn't have had to look around. That's what he said.

I'd been so naïve.

That's why I hadn't told anyone at work about my face blindness. I didn't want anyone else to use it against me. But now? Their not knowing had the possibility of making things a lot worse for me.

And I didn't need to tell everyone.

Corrine noticed everything. And everybody. If I let her know, she could help keep me safe.

I pulled her aside as she was leaving the counter to clean up a spill in the back room. There was no one in line and only a few customers at the tables. I asked if I could talk to her about something.

"You want to know who that yummy guy is, right? The one over there in the blue shirt?"

"I really don't."

She told me all about him anyway. "And you know what his drink is? Guess."

"I have no idea."

"A flat white. With a dash of nutmeg. Is that not just perfect?"

"Corrine? I need your help with something."

"I'm keeping him to myself. No hard feelings?"

"No hard feelings. It's about the murder investigation."

She'd already ducked through the swinging door into the back room. I followed her.

She reached for a mop. Handed it to me. "Would you mind carrying that?" She picked up a jug of cleaner. Nudged a pail out of the corner with her toe and put a squirt into it. Pointed to a puddle in front of the refrigerator. "Orange juice. I dropped a bottle. Don't step in it."

I tore some paper towels off a roll and blotted the spill.

"So what was that about the investigation?" She headed to the door.

I rose, threw away the paper towel, and followed her out into the hall. I kept the door open so we wouldn't have to punch in the code again. "The detective's interested in the regulars."

"Yeah. That's what he said. Because they might have noticed the killer." She put the pail in the big service sink and turned the water on.

"There's something I need to tell you. I have this condition."

When the pail was full, she turned the water off and then hefted it out and walked past me through the door.

I let it close behind us.

"It's called prosopagnosia. Face blindness."

She swished the mop around the bucket. "I've never heard of that."

"I can't recognize faces."

"What do you mean?"

"My brain literally can't map faces. It's like trying to buy something and the barcode won't scan. The computer has no idea what it is because it won't connect with the database."

"Hate it when that happens!" She took the mop out and got to work. "But—you mean . . . you know who *I* am, right?"

"You're Corrine."

"So you know *my* face."

I put a finger to her name tag. "I know you. I know your beautiful curly hair. I know your voice. But mostly I can read. And this says Corrine."

"So you *don't* know me?"

"As long as we're in this store, I hear your voice, I see you're scheduled for my shift, I know you. But if I saw you at the grocery store and you weren't wearing your name tag, or you were wearing a sweatshirt with the hood up—or even if you weren't—I would walk right by you."

"Seriously? But what if I was like, 'Hey, Whit!'?"

"I hope I'd recognize your voice. But if not, then I would just say, 'Hey, how's it going?' and I would desperately pray that you would say something that would help me put you into context."

"Wow. So you don't know me. After all this time? And all the shifts we've worked together?"

"I *do* know you. I just can't *recognize* your face."

"Can you recognize yourself? Like if you look in a mirror do you know it's you?"

"I know that I have to be seeing myself because who else would it be? But sometimes, if there's a mirror in a restaurant or a reflection in a window, if I'm not expecting to see myself? No. I have no idea."

"So you really *don't* know me! That makes me feel bad."

"It makes me feel worse. Especially when there's a killer out there who knows who I am."

She gasped. "And you have no idea who he is!"

Exactly. "That's where my favor comes in."

"What do you need me to do?" She stuck the mop back into the pail and pumped it up and down.

"I just need you to help me see people. The victim was my friend. He'd asked me to meet him out there in the alley. He thought I had some information that he needed. If the killer shot him because of what he knew, then what might he do to me?"

Corrine gasped again. "So he's after you too?"

"Maybe. So I need you to tell me if you see anyone suspicious. Anyone you keep seeing when you might not expect it. Is there anyone hanging around outside? Anyone who looks like they don't belong? I need your eyes and your brain. Because mine don't connect."

"Of course. Sure. Yes. So how will I know if it's him? Besides the handlebar mustache. That's the guy, right? But the important thing is not to worry. I've got your back. If you think it's someone else, just tell me what he looks like and I've got you."

Maybe I shouldn't have told her. Because clearly, she didn't get it.

▸▸ CHAPTER 32 ◂◂

Leo texted me to say he'd be back at the shop in time to take me to the library. On Saturdays I worked a short shift so I could spend more time with my students.

But at 9:50, I still didn't see his SUV.

I thumbed open my car app and scheduled a ride. There was a driver just a few blocks away. As a car pulled up to the curb several minutes later, I looked at my app. Gray Toyota Camry. License plate TEJ 492.

I walked to it, bent to look in the passenger's window.

The driver rolled it down.

"Who are you here for?" I asked him.

A car pulled up behind him. Honked.

"Here for Whitney?"

Relief untied the knot in my stomach. I opened the back door and got in. The driver circled the block and then headed toward the library.

As we waited for a light to change, the car behind us honked.

My driver raised a hand.

The car honked again.

The driver turned to speak to me over his shoulder. "I think this guy behind us wants you."

"What?"

"This guy behind us. In the car."

I looked out the back window. Behind us was the same car that had honked at the curb. But I didn't know anyone who drove a white Nissan. "I don't know that man."

"Maybe he knows you."

As we neared the library, I undid my seat belt and slipped my backpack over my shoulders so I could hit the pavement at a run.

But my driver pulled into the parking lot at a leisurely pace and did a slow-motion stop in the drop-off area. By the time I could actually get out, that car was right behind us again.

There wasn't anyone walking through the parking lot or on the walkway to the building. When I stepped out of the car, it would just be me out there. Alone.

I leaped out, slamming the door behind me, ready to make a run for it.

As the car drove off, I heard a popping sound behind me.

I'd taken two running steps toward the library before someone caught my arm.

It was a man wearing jogging shorts and a T-shirt. His dark hair was slicked back from his face.

I wrestled free. Started to run again.

But he grabbed me, throwing me to the ground behind a row of bushes.

Panicked, I kicked out. Thrashed my arms.

"Bullet," he said.

What?

"*That was a bullet.*" He jammed his hand in his pocket, even as he kept me covered with his body.

"Let me go!"

"Whitney! It's me. *Leo.*"

He wasn't wearing his usual suit jacket and pants. His hair wasn't even right. It wasn't falling onto his forehead.

"I was in the car right behind you. I was trying to save you from calling a ride."

He didn't look like Leo. He didn't smell like Leo. "Let me go!"

"I would, but I don't know that it's safe." Keeping one hand on my arm, he moved off my back and positioned himself on the ground beside me. "I'm sorry I was late. I was trying to get your attention back at the Blue Dog so you wouldn't have to pay for a ride."

"You weren't driving your SUV."

"I know. It's a loaner. I had to take mine into the shop. That's what I did after I left."

"And you're not wearing a suit jacket."

"I thought I could squeeze in a run before picking you up."

Now I could see that it was Leo. His bangs were drenched in sweat. He'd slicked them back from his forehead.

He'd been moving his head, trying to see through the bushes. Now he shifted sideways and rose just a little before dropping back down beside me. "We're going to wait until Beyer's team shows up."

I was past being scared. I was just plain mad. And I was shaking. "I thought you were the killer."

"I didn't even think. I'm sorry. I didn't mean to scare you."

I shook my head because I couldn't form any words.

"I don't—I just—I wanted to tell you, as soon as I could, that there's been a development."

"You couldn't text?"

"If I hadn't come in person, you might be dead right now. And I was just down the block at the gym. My timing was off, otherwise I would have met you outside the shop."

"What's the development? Have you identified the killer?"

"No. But we've identified the person who trashed your place."

"Which is the killer, right?" What wasn't I understanding?

"Maybe. The person who trashed your place was Hartwell. Fingerprint match."

Hartwell.

My white-hot anger was replaced by a cold, dark rage.

It made perfect sense that Hartwell would invade my space and take revenge on me by destroying my things. But knowing it was him didn't make it any better. It just made the shadow that he'd cast over my life even longer. Made my future seem even darker.

"That's what I wanted you to know."

Agent Beyer's team came to investigate. One of them interviewed Leo and me while the others roped off the crime scene and began their investigation.

I had a group session first that afternoon and I was able to start them on a set of practice questions before I answered the FBI's questions. But there really wasn't much I could tell them. I hadn't seen the shooter. I'd heard the bullet, but I couldn't tell them which direction it had come from.

"Detective Baroni said my ex, Hartwell Thorpe, was the one who trashed my place?"

The agent nodded.

"Doesn't that strengthen the case that he's the killer?"

"Cade Burdell was part of an ongoing investigation at the FDIC. That's the angle we're pursuing right now."

"HARTAN is a contractor for the FDIC. And HARTAN is Hartwell's company."

"I can't really go into the details, but the investigation doesn't involve Mr. Thorpe or his company."

"Maybe it should."

The agent wouldn't say anything else about it.

We knew nothing about the shooter. He knew way too much about me.

My hands were shaking again. I tried to ignore them.

Didn't help.

I tried to actively stop them from trembling.

It only made the tremors worse.

When the agent left, I rose to follow. I had to get back to my students.

But Agent Beyer came into the room.

He sat down beside me. "I know you're frustrated with this investigation. We are too. But we're going to catch this guy. We are. I can't tell you everything about our investigation in the FDIC, but you already know that it has to do with that hack back in 2010. The Chinese had a contact in the FDIC back then. Cade discovered that person, whoever it is, is still there."

"What?"

"That's what he was working on with me. We're trying to identify the mole. That's what the coffee orders were all about. Cade suspected someone was watching him, so we set up the robo mobile coffee order. Every day at 1:20 we could communicate. That's why he didn't have any identification on him. And that's why he was so hesitant to link himself to you."

"So it was the *Chinese* who killed him? I thought Hartwell was a suspect."

"We have to consider everyone until we can rule them out. Mr. Thorpe is one, although he's only been interacting with the FDIC for a couple years. Detective Baroni's Mustache Man is another. But frankly, that's what it looks like to me. The Chinese or someone working with them."

Then the whole thing was much bigger than I'd thought.

And much more terrifying.

▸▸ CHAPTER 33 ◂◂

Agent Beyer left us. Before I rejoined my students, I asked Leo a question.

"Doesn't the FBI do safe houses?"

"I was going to ask you if you wanted me to make the case for one. It might be tricky because you can't actually identify the suspect."

"Cade thought I had important information."

"But you don't know what it is."

My face must have shown him what I thought about that.

"I get it. I can suggest it to the FBI."

"If they could work it out though, I'd have to stay there, at the safe house, right? I wouldn't be able to leave, for my jobs?"

"That's my understanding."

"Well then, never mind. I can't."

"We'll catch him. Soon." He told me to take a car home and to be careful.

Did I tell him I didn't have anywhere to stay?

No.

If he was working to identify the killer, I wanted him to be focused on that, not on me. I'd be safe at the Blue Dog. Safer, apparently, than I had been when I was living at Mrs. Harper's.

Since the library closed early on Saturdays, I only had one private student session. As she reached across the table to take a set of practice problems from me, her sleeve lifted, revealing a nasty bruise.

"You okay, Allie?"

"What?"

"Your arm."

She grabbed the hem of her sleeve and tugged it down to her wrist. "Fine." But as she extended her arm to pull her homework from her backpack, I could see several other similar marks on the inside of her wrist.

"What's going on?"

"Nothing."

"Because if I kept getting bruises in the same place all the time, then I'd stop doing the thing that was causing them."

She had everything going for her. She was bright, poised. She was active in sports and had a full list of extracurricular activities and volunteer hours. Most of my students didn't have a prayer at getting into the Ivy League. She just might. And she was aiming for Harvard.

"I work hard. I set goals. I don't really have time to sit here every Saturday afternoon. I have a chance of going to nationals this year in my sport. I have to keep training. And cross-training. So that's how it started. It was an incentive to stay focused. I made a goal. I'm wearing this rubber band 24–7." She pulled her sleeve up to show me. "If I don't get a hundred on this practice test, then I have to snap myself."

I bit my tongue to keep from saying something I'd regret. Something that might stop her from talking.

"Is that what the welts are from?" I tried to keep my voice steady. Tried to remain calm.

"It really stings at first, when you do it. But the welts go away after a while. Then they turn into bruises. Every time I look at them, I think, 'See? That's what happens when you fail.'" She was speaking so evenly, so matter-of-factly, as if snapping herself with a rubber band was just another goal-setting tool. "And I don't fail that often. It works."

She was only seventeen years old.

"What would happen if you didn't get into Harvard?"

"I'm getting in. That's what I've told everybody. That's why I have to ace this test."

"But once you take this test, once you submit your application, it's not up to you anymore. Your part in the process stops. The school's admissions officers take over." It was the same way in the real world. That's what interviewing was all about. You presented your best argument for why a company should hire you, but after that it was up to them.

"I have the grades. I have the athletics. I have the extracurriculars and the volunteer hours. All I need is this test."

"But this test isn't a guarantee. There's nothing you can do to make them take you."

"I'm giving them everything they want."

"But even if you get a perfect score, it won't make them take you. You know that, right? All it gives you is a chance."

"You got into an Ivy. That's what it says online."

"I did." But that was in a different era. "If I had to do it again, I would go to a school in-state. Do community college for the first two years."

"What if someone told you that you wouldn't have gotten into your Ivy though? That it wasn't up to you? That it was someone else's decision? Would that have made you try less?"

"I'm only saying that—"

"Because when someone tells me I can't do something, I do it anyway. I do it faster, stronger, better. You only fail if you don't try hard enough."

That's what I used to think too. But sometimes, no amount of trying could make something happen. Nothing could cure my mother. Nothing could make me recognize a face. "As far as your part of the process goes, that's true. I'm just telling you that there's a whole other part that you don't have control of. That's all."

She didn't see it. Couldn't see it. Or maybe she didn't want to see it. But I'd done what I could.

She was the opposite of me. She was doing everything she could to get in; I had done nothing but had gotten in anyway. But I hadn't seen clearly either. I'd thought an Ivy was the key to my future. I didn't understand that it would shackle me to debt for the rest of my life. And I hadn't had the agency back then to advocate for myself, to pursue scholarships. I thought people would think less of me if they knew I needed money. I didn't want to stand out by standing up to ask. I didn't want anyone to know what I didn't have. That sense of shame, the fear of not fitting in, kept me from getting the financial help I'd needed.

As Allie worked on her practice problems, I continued my search for a new apartment. A new room. Anything, really. But the cheapest studio I could find was a thousand dollars. The cheapest room I could find was eight hundred.

The kind of situation I'd had at Mrs. Harper's was the kind that never gets advertised. People knew that Aunt Suzy needed someone to live with her. Or Grandma Sally had a spare bedroom and the need for a little extra money. But those situations went to people who could be trusted, not to strangers. I'd been so grateful Cade found it for me.

I might have been able to pick up a nanny suite if I'd wanted to work as one, but I didn't have time to watch kids even if I could have. And I couldn't. Face blindness. How could I be counted on to recognize them?

I thought of posting an ad at some of the local community centers and churches.

Quiet law student

Looking for room or studio

Willing to trade rent for odd jobs and light housekeeping

But the killer seemed to be following me. He might see those notices too. And then he'd have my phone number.

As Allie continued to work through her review questions, I did some more research on China. I'd done a project on the strength of the dollar relative to other currencies when I was interning on the Hill.

Congressman Thorpe had used it to help support his position on a financial oversight bill.

When Cade and I talked back then, a lot of our conversations had been in the context of the fallout from the trade wars a few years before. Cade especially had lamented how some of the markets that had been available to the nation were now lost.

The countries we'd been trading with hadn't been able to sit out the trade wars until things stabilized. They still needed things like food and cars, so they'd found other countries to supply them. When we stopped buying goods from China, in effect, we'd also stopped buying things from places like Malaysia and Sri Lanka and Japan, which had supplied parts for all of those goods assembled in China. We'd sacrificed our relationships with them for some angry rhetoric and short-term political gains. If they'd found more stable trading partners in the meantime, then why come back to us?

Though Cade and I had our friendly policy differences, we both agreed on one thing: it would be helpful to everyone if people who understood economics were the ones tasked to make economic policies.

Ours were the kind of conversations that happened all over the Hill when people were out of range of listening ears.

Most Americans assumed that nations act in their own interest. My project showed how the Chinese, in temporarily hurting their own citizens and allowing themselves to lose some face in the trade wars, had diminished US influence abroad, blocking us in some markets almost entirely, as they established strong trading partnerships with our competitors.

One of the things I was most proud of during my internship was that the congressman had used my data to support his claims that our banking laws needed to be strengthened, not weakened. He'd been so passionate about that bill. I still couldn't believe he'd voted against it.

Besides the fact that Cade had discovered China's ghost at the FDIC, I couldn't figure out how to connect our conversations about China or my research on currencies to his death.

As my student finished up, I put together some thoughts for my upcoming second interview. On one side of the page I wrote down questions I needed to have answered: expected junior associate workload, practice groups, current projects, billable-hour thresholds, and career progression. On the other side, I noted aspects about the firm I wanted to research: firm history, partner bios, and recent cases if I could find them.

Then I started thinking about the interview itself. Firm handshake. Look the interviewer in the middle of the face. Try to remember something, some distinctive trait about her. Or him. Or *them*, if it was a panel.

Please, let it not be a panel!

I'd need to review the notes I'd made about the first interview.

I'd wear my other good suit, which I would have to retrieve from the storage unit. And I'd carry my notebook in that attaché my parents had bought me after I earned my undergraduate degree.

Attaché!

In my rush to vacate the apartment, I'd left it at Mrs. Harper's house on the shelf in my closet.

I thought of calling Jessica to see if she would set it aside, but I discarded the idea. She didn't owe me any favors, and I was pretty sure that I was not her favorite person. I might have called Mrs. Harper, but I didn't want her to have to think about the loss of her house any more than she probably already was.

I still had my key. It was only five o'clock. I could just stop by and get it without bothering anyone. I'd be in and out before anyone even noticed.

▸▸ CHAPTER 34 ◂◂

I had a car pick me up from the library.

I gave the driver Mrs. Harper's address and asked if he could wait for me when we got there while I went inside.

"I'll have to charge you for the time. Got to warn you."

"I know. Thank you."

When we arrived, I asked him to pull up to the top.

As he pulled in, I took my phone from my backpack. If I was going it alone, at least I could be ready to make an emergency call if I needed to. "I won't be long."

I jogged around to the back, let myself in and then locked the door behind me. I walked over to the staircase that led up to the main floor and locked it too. Just in case. I didn't want to be surprised by any more intruders.

I went to my closet and got my attaché.

My dad called as I was leaving. I paused by the bar.

"Dad. Hey. Can I call you later when I—"

"I think I've finally figured it out."

"Wait. I'm sorry. What did you figure out?"

"I figured out how to make everything work."

"In terms of what?"

"With my finances."

"Can I call you later?" I almost said, *once I get home?* "I'm out right now."

"Oh. Sure. Yeah. I've decided to do something a little different. Figure, why not? What's the worst that can happen?"

With finances? Quite a bit. "Don't do anything until after we talk, okay?"

"Sure. I just figure, I don't have much left to lose, so why not bet big?"

Definitely we needed to talk!

"Just because you declared bankruptcy, just because you sold the house, doesn't mean you have nothing, Dad." Did it? "You have something, don't you?"

"Yeah. But it's not much. I didn't have any choice but to file. I really didn't."

"That's why there are bankruptcy laws. Sometimes it's the only option."

"It was like a slug in the gut though. Never been so ashamed." There was a slight slur to his words.

Had he been drinking? "It's not your fault Mom got sick. You have nothing to be ashamed of."

"It just felt like I was always standing around, holding my hat out, asking for money."

There it was. The ultimate sin. It wasn't the actual asking for money; it was *having* to ask for money, regardless of whether you actually did or not.

People who grew up with money couldn't understand how the world worked when you didn't have it. They made it seem as if not having it was the consequence of some sort of choice a person made. Having money made you one of the good guys. Not having money meant that in some way you must be a bad person.

Take the loans! You deserve a good education.

Can't pay back your loans? You worthless person!

Which was it?

Everyone was good at explaining how things worked. Anyone could tell you the mechanics of success, what the requirements were.

Graduate from high school.

Graduate from college.

Get a job.

Get a better job.

Thing is, no one took the time to tell you about the rules that weren't written down. And if you didn't know about them? You didn't know how to follow them.

I told my dad I'd call him later and hung up. Then I left the apartment, locking the door behind me. I promised my plants I'd come back for them as I jogged up the stairs. When I came around the house, I saw a police car sitting at the base of the driveway, lights flashing. My driver was leaning against his car, arms crossed, talking to a policeman. An older man, frail and bent, hovered nearby. As I appeared, the old man gestured toward me. "Like I said, she went around to the back of the house."

The policeman turned his head in my direction. "Is this her? Is she the one you saw?"

The older man answered. "That's her."

I approached them. "Is there a problem?"

The police officer stepped toward me, arm extended, palm up. "What do you have there?"

I held up the attaché. "I used to live here. I just moved out. I left it behind by mistake."

The old man scoffed. "Likely story. Marjorie told me to keep an eye on the place while she was out in Loudoun. She broke her leg. Went to live with her daughter for a while. She had me come over to get a key before she left so I could check on things for her."

"I used to live here. I just moved out. I only came back to get my attaché."

The policeman stepped toward me. "I'm going to need you to come in for questioning."

"But I wasn't trespassing. I was only trying to get my things." I couldn't be charged with trespassing. I couldn't be arrested. I might not get sworn in as a lawyer, even if I passed the bar, if a conviction came up on my record. It would ruin everything. "I promise I used to live in that house, in the basement. I forgot the attaché when I moved out. I was only trying to retrieve it."

"Be that as it may, I have to take you to the station. We can sort it all out there."

▸▸ CHAPTER 35 ◂◂

I spent an hour trying to convince the Arlington police that the whole thing had been a misunderstanding. I asked them to call Jessica. They did, but they had to leave a message. While I wasn't quite able to get them to believe me, they did finally agree to call Leo.

They left me alone in a room while they went out to make the call. A while later, the door opened. I didn't bother to turn around.

"So what do you have to say for yourself?"

Again? "I was telling the other officers that I wasn't trespassing. I was only trying to get my things."

"It's me. Leo."

I turned around. It *was* him! I felt like my head was going to float away as my worries lifted from my shoulders. "You have to make them understand."

"They think you were trespassing."

"I wasn't—!" I closed my eyes. Took a deep breath. Opened them. "I already told you: Friday after you left for work, I was asked to leave the apartment by Mrs. Harper's daughter."

"Right. You were asked to move out."

"Mrs. Harper's daughter didn't want me around. Too many bad things were happening. I wasn't a safe person. She thought if I stayed, something bad might happen to her mom."

"So you went back to the house this evening to do what?"

"I went back because I have an interview on Monday and I needed my attaché that my parents got me for graduation because—"

"Wait. Back up." He slid into a chair across from me. "You got kicked out, that I already know. But where are you staying?"

I refused to cry. I absolutely, positively refused to cry. But my chin rebelled. It started to tremble. I blinked once. Hard. Twice. But the tears came anyway.

I turned my head. Pulled my sleeve down over my hand and used it to swipe at them. "There are not a lot of places to live in Arlington at the low, low rate of five hundred dollars a month. I haven't gotten a job offer yet as a lawyer, so all I have are the Blue Dog and my students. I can't not work, so I have to live close enough to get to the coffee shop at four in the morning if I have to open. But the metro doesn't start running until five. And the bus doesn't start running until five. And that's out in Fairfax County. It would take me at least half an hour to get all the way here. So if I don't find something close enough to scooter, then—"

"But where did you stay last night?"

I shook my head.

"You had to stay somewhere."

"I stayed at the Blue Dog."

"Don't you have any friends you can stay with?"

"Not anymore. Because of Hartwell."

"So you don't have any place to go."

I shook my head again. And I was really, truly afraid that I wouldn't be able to find one.

"First things first. Let's get you out of here."

▸▸▸◂◂◂

The police complex was in an area of Arlington I didn't know very well. Leo turned down one street after another as we drove. I couldn't tell whether we were headed toward Virginia Square or away from it.

Finally, I felt I had to say the obvious. "I appreciate this, Leo. Appreciate you showing up and getting me out. But the coffee shop won't be closed for another hour and I can't go back there until everyone is gone. I don't think spending the night there is manager-approved."

"We're not going there."

"Then where are you taking me?"

"I'm taking you home."

"Home where?"

"Home. To my home. My house."

▸▸▸◂◂◂

Leo lived on a quiet street just a block from one of Arlington's major arterials, across from a county park. He had one of the brick colonials that sprouted a chimney from one side. It looked like a child's drawing: front door in the middle with a black shutter–framed window on each side and three windows across the top. The front door was painted dark red.

Flower beds stretched across the foundation, away from the front steps toward the corners of the house. At some point, someone had added a sun porch onto the right side. It was shaded by a magnolia and a holly tree.

He parked the loaner Nissan in his driveway and then came around to my side of the car as I grabbed my backpack and the troublesome attaché. He opened my door. Cupped my elbow as I got out.

I followed him across the lawn, up the front steps, and in through the door.

It opened into a living room that had black leather and chrome furniture and a big TV that hung on the wall above the fireplace.

He took the attaché from me and set it on a table underneath a window that looked out into the front yard. He put my backpack on the floor beneath it.

Beyond the table, on either side of the chimney, were doors that opened into the porch. Sun filtered past the border of trees and in through the windows. Dappled shadows danced on the checkerboard-patterned floor.

And all of a sudden, I longed for home.

I longed for the days when the worst thing that could happen to me was having too much homework. I longed for the evenings when I could sit on the couch next to my mother and tell her about my day while my father sat in the armchair across from us, interjecting comments, trying to make me laugh.

"You hungry?"

I shrugged. "I could eat something." I was ravenous. Starving.

"Let's see what I can find."

I followed him past the front door, out of the living room into a dining room, and then turned into one of the tiniest kitchens I'd ever seen. At the far end was a door to the backyard.

Even the bar area in my basement apartment at Mrs. Harper's had been bigger. I had to stand out in the dining room while Leo rummaged through the cabinets simply because there was nowhere else for me to stand.

He opened the fridge, took out a serving bowl of pasta. Opened the cupboard and handed me a plate. "Help yourself."

I could have eaten it all, but he clearly intended to have the leftovers for himself. Otherwise, why would he have made so much? I portioned out a tidy quarter of it and transferred it to my plate.

"You have to have more than that."

I shaved off a sliver more. He sat with me at the table as I ate. I told him about my project for Congressman Thorpe. "It seems like it should be connected with Cade's death. The project was about China. Cade was giving information to Agent Beyer about a Chinese hack. But I can't figure out how to make the connection."

He propped his chin on his fist. "Right. His work with the FBI and your work on the Hill have the same key word. I'll mention it to Agent Beyer. Do you have a copy of that report anywhere?"

"No. But the congressman's office might."

When I was done, he took my plate from me and walked it into the kitchen. When he reappeared, he had a key in hand. He put it on the table and slid it to me. "This way you can come and go when you want to. But I'd still prefer it if you don't go anywhere by yourself. Ideally, it would be me bringing you back here in the evening. Need anything else?"

I shook my head.

"Okay. Then I'm off the clock." He went into the living room, picked up a remote, and turned on the TV. As he stood there beside the couch, he invited me to join him. He gestured to the TV. "This? This, right here, is drama." He was watching baseball.

"I don't even know which team is which."

"The Mets are in gray. Playing the Red Sox. They're in white."

"Whose side are you on?"

"Not the Mets."

"Whose side should I be on?"

"I don't know. Where are you from?"

"The Northwest."

"The Mariners. When they're playing."

"What do I do when they're not? What's your team?"

"Yankees; I'm from Jersey. But they're not playing. So I root for anyone who can beat their rivals. Tonight? I'm going for the Red Sox even though I normally wouldn't because there's a chance that if they can beat the Mets then they knock them out of the playoffs."

"Sounds a little Machiavellian. The enemy of my enemy . . ."

". . . is my friend. Right."

I smiled. Walked over to my backpack so I could get my books.

"Wait," he called. "What's your favorite color?"

"Red."

"So go for the Red Sox. They wear red too."

"And what do I do the next time I see a game and they're not playing?"

He shrugged. "What color do you hate?"

"Orange."

"So go for anyone not wearing it."

"So easy."

"It's as simple as you want to make it."

I perched on the edge of the couch and stayed for a few minutes to watch, rooting with Leo against the Mets. It was something I hadn't done before. Hartwell hadn't watched much television, and when we went to the stadium in DC it was mostly to hang out and network in his firm's suite. It wasn't to watch the games.

We high-fived when the Red Sox got a run. When I finally left Leo, to study at the dining room table, he was laser-focused on the game.

▸▸▸◂◂◂

Several hours after that, I slowly became aware that Leo was standing at the end of the table. Had he said something?

"Pardon me?"

He put his palms to the table, leaned toward me. "I said, 'You win.'"

"Win? Win what?"

"The Who Can Stay Up Latest contest."

I glanced at my watch. It was past midnight. My few hours of studying had turned into four of them. "Sorry. There's so much material to cover. Sometimes I forget to come up for air."

"You can keep studying. I just wanted you to know that I'm going to bed."

I shut my book. Set it on top of my study guide. "Me too."

I followed Leo up the stairs. The hallway at the top was small and square. He gestured to the room on the left. "That's yours. I call it the Baby Bear Room."

The Baby Bear Room only had enough space for a twin bed and a child-size dresser. But that was all the room I needed.

"Still starting your shift at six?"

I shook my head. "I don't work at the Blue Dog on Sundays. But I do have to go to the library. I have students tomorrow."

"I'll drive you. I'll pick you up. We still don't know why your friend was killed. You're the only link we have to his murder. I need to keep eyes on you until we get this guy."

Left unsaid was the thought that both of us must have been thinking. He needed eyes that could recognize what they were seeing.

He needed eyes that worked.

▸▸ CHAPTER 36 ◂◂

One benefit of sleeping at the Blue Dog? I didn't regret my lack of pajamas. And I didn't have to get dressed in the morning. In Leo's guest bedroom, though I took my jeans off, I wore my shirt to bed.

I crept into the bathroom when my alarm went off and took a quick shower, and then I got dressed and went downstairs as quietly as I could. The one thing I could do to repay Leo for his kindness was make an excellent pot of coffee before he woke up. I rummaged through his cabinets and found the filters for his coffee maker. I made myself a peanut butter sandwich and slipped it into my backpack. That way I wouldn't have to worry about dinner.

I heard Leo pad down the stairs and soon he was leaning into the kitchen from the dining room. "You sleep okay?" He was wearing a T-shirt over a pair of running shorts. His black hair was sticking out all over the place.

I shrugged. I never slept okay. It was a hazard of always worrying whether the next day was going to be the one when the fragile world I'd built fell apart.

"Was it the bed?"

I shook my head. "It was my head."

"Yeah. Sometimes I have trouble sleeping too. I think about all the ways these things can go wrong."

These things? Things about the investigation? "What things?" I poured him a cup of coffee.

He took it from me. "Things. Everything. Every single thing."

"Like what?"

He shrugged. "It wouldn't be fair to share. I don't want to scare you."

"Or you could look at it this way: if I know what you're up against, then maybe I can find a way to help you."

"Okay. So here's the highlight reel. The big one: What if he gets you before we get him?"

That was mostly what I worried about too.

"And what is China doing at the FDIC?"

"They're not only in the FDIC." I told him about the stablecoin verification hack.

"Maybe that's what it is." He took a sip. "Maybe it's not the old hack everyone's worried about. Maybe it's this new one."

"But the verification system isn't the FDIC's. It's the stablecoin company's. They verify that account holders have actual accounts at FDIC-insured banks. The system isn't linking to the FDIC." At least, that was my understanding.

"So now I'm back to not knowing anything. I could tell you I understand all this crypto stuff, but when I actually sit down to think about it?" He shook his head. "It all slips away from me. It feels like people make it up out of nothing. They used to print money; now they get computer programs to create it."

"Money is money. The value is in people wanting it. It's worth what we all say it's worth whether it exists on paper or in digital form. We know the strength of America is the strength of her markets, and the strength of her markets is the stability of the dollar, right?"

Leo shrugged. "Don't look at me. I'm the guy who just works hard and saves hard and doesn't ask questions."

"That's what the FDIC is supposed to do: ensure the stability of the dollar by insuring deposits and supervising the nation's financial institutions. So maybe we assume that's exactly what China *doesn't* want.

They *don't* want our currency to be stable. Why else would they put someone at the FDIC to keep their hands in all that data?"

He took another sip. "Okay. I'll play. We assume malicious intent. But what can they do? And more than that, what can they do now that they couldn't do ten years ago? Third question: Why wait so long to do it?"

"I don't know. But whatever Cade found made someone jump."

"What kind of guy was Cade? Have you ever pictured him asking you his question in person? Tried to figure out what conversation he was talking about?"

"I have. And I still don't know."

Leo ran a hand through his hair, raking his bangs back from his forehead. "Seems to me, if we're assuming malicious intent, and we know China has stolen information from the FDIC and embedded itself in that verification system, then we have to assume they have the ability to mess with our economy. The question is how much of a mess would they be able to make."

"There was over two billion dollars tied up in that stablecoin. And tens of thousands of accounts at FDIC-insured banks at up to $250,000 per account."

"Then that's a big mess."

It was the kind of mess that Hartwell used to propose when he talked about cryptocurrencies. He always argued that I was much too naïve. That people would find a way to corrupt the technology before a framework could be put in place to protect it. Hartwell could always stay two steps ahead in any argument. That was his superpower. It was thinking that far ahead that made him a visionary. "It might be worth talking to Congressman Thorpe."

"Why?"

"Because he was sitting on the Science, Space, and Technology Committee back in 2010. He might know something about the original hack that would help us. And there was a bill that was just voted down in the House. It had to do with strengthening that banking system. It's one he worked really hard to get through the committee when I was there. But when it came to the floor just recently, he voted against it."

"Be nice to know why, wouldn't it?"

I raised my mug in his direction. "And I know he sat through the hearings on cryptocurrency. I was there. At the very least, considering he knew Cade too, maybe he could look at the information about Cade from a different perspective. Sometimes that's all it takes."

"I can suggest it."

I reached behind me for the coffeepot. "More?" I held it up.

"Yes, please. Lots." He held out his mug while I poured. "Hey—want some toast? I have this great recipe."

"Maybe."

"It involves a toaster. I'll do some up for you."

We traded places. He made some toast and buttered it. Put it on a plate and handed it to me. I took it into the dining room.

He joined me several minutes later with a plate of his own. His had eggs on it. He paused as he passed my chair, tilted his plate, and shoveled half of them onto mine. Handed me a fork. "So this bar exam. When is it again?"

"Just over two weeks."

"So once you pass it—"

"Don't jinx me."

"*If* you pass it."

"Stop talking, Leo."

"Okay, so how about this: What if you don't pass it? What's your backup?"

"I don't have a backup plan."

"No plan B?"

"No contingencies. That's why I'm studying so hard."

"But what if life doesn't go your direction?"

"Life has never gone my direction. I'll give you the summary. I was born with face blindness."

"Yeah. That one, I know."

"I got through high school, graduated with a 4.0, aced the SAT. Accepted scholarships to the school of my dreams."

"Sounds real tough."

"I thought the patchwork of scholarships they'd pieced together was good for all four years. My parents were wonderful, but they didn't go to college. They trusted me to sort through the application process."

"So it *wasn't* a full ride?"

"It was. But the scholarships were renewable annually. I didn't understand the fine print, so I didn't renew them. I had to take out loans for the other three years."

"Okay."

"After my undergraduate degree, I was going to go back home, but I got talked into applying to graduate school."

"How do you get talked into something like that?"

"The usual way. 'Everyone is doing it.' And it kind of made sense. My undergraduate is in finance. Fascinating, but not a lot of opportunities at the lower levels. Not in what I wanted to do. So I went back to school. I worked part-time during my master's degree because—"

"In? What's your master's in?"

"International economic policy. The clock on repaying my undergrad loans started once I graduated. I could have deferred, but recall that I did study finance. With compounding interest, that loan would have gotten a lot worse. I had to take out more loans for my master's. And more for my law degree. My father doesn't know any of this. And I definitely haven't told him about the shooting."

"So the plan is?"

"Pass the bar. And then do what every law student does: get a job with a big firm. Do the associate thing for enough years to substantially pay down my loans, and then I can intersect with the path my father thinks I'm already on."

"You don't seem like the corporate type to me."

"A lot of law students are the corporate type at first. It's like being a med student. You have to slog through the rotations before you can actually be given the chance to work in your specialty."

"Well, what do I know? It's a plan. But I'm a little ambivalent on the whole lying-to-your-dad thing because parents always seem to figure that kind of stuff out. Other than that, sounds good."

"So glad it meets your approval." I took my plate and Leo's into the kitchen. Turned on the light. Scraped the crust of his toast into the sink, turned on the water, and flipped the switch for the garbage disposal.

The switch emitted a sharp buzz just before the lights went off.

I froze. "Leo? Leo!"

"Here." I heard his chair scrape and his footsteps cross the dining room floor.

My hand was shaking. Stupid hand. "What did I do?"

He slipped past me and opened the door to the basement. "It's an old house. I have to get it rewired. But for now, you can't turn on the light and the garbage disposal at the same time."

"Sorry."

"Now you know. Circuit breaker's in the basement. I'll go down and flip it back on."

When the lights came on, it was as if everything had changed. I tried to tell myself that it was due to nerves. If things looked distorted, somewhat larger and brighter than before, then it was because my heart was racing, my eyes darting. The house wasn't any less safe, any less welcoming or secure. But it took a while for my hands to stop trembling. And it took a few minutes before my heart stopped feeling like it was trying to escape through my throat.

▸▸ CHAPTER 37 ◂◂

As I was slinging my backpack over my shoulder getting ready to leave, Leo's phone pinged. He picked it up. Read something. Then he told me he wouldn't be able to drive me to the library. "My boss is on the way over to pick me up."

I told him I'd catch a car.

As he put the dishes in the dishwasher, someone rang the doorbell.

"Can you get that? It's just my boss. Can you tell her I'm almost ready?"

I walked to the door and turned a screw to look out the old-fashioned peephole.

The woman outside started knocking. "Leo? I know you're there! We don't have time to screw around."

Leo passed me at a jog on his way to the stairs. "Go ahead. Open it."

He'd drilled paranoia into me. It was a little disorienting to have him suddenly ask me to open the door. "You're sure you know who it is?" I gave him a last look as he disappeared up the stairs and then I opened the door. "Leo said to tell you he'll be right here." I stood aside so the woman could enter.

But she stayed outside, on the stoop. "You're the one, aren't you?"

"Sorry?"

"The blind girl."

"Woman. I'm the *woman* with *face blindness*."

"Are you staying here? With him?"

"Um—" What was the appropriate response? Kind of, but not really? "Just for a few nights. It's not, um—"

She tilted her head.

"It doesn't have anything to do with—"

She tilted it the other way.

"He was kind enough to—"

Leo joined me, pulling on a sports coat. "Hey." He smelled like toothpaste.

The woman placed a hand on the doorframe. "What's she doing here?"

He was wrestling with a tie. "When that thing with the prowler happened, she lost her lease. She didn't have any place to go, so—"

"You're not doing this, Leo."

Leo was shaking his head. "It's not what you—"

"Save it. We'll deal with it later." She pointed a thumb toward her car. "Let's go."

▸▸▸◂◂◂

Leo's voice echoed in my head as I got into the ride-share I took to work.

Keep your phone with you at all times. Don't be stupid. Stay out in the open, among other people. Don't go anywhere by yourself.

By the time I got to the library, I didn't want to get out of the car. I wanted nothing more than to hide out somewhere until the killer was caught. But I had to show up for my students; otherwise, their parents wouldn't keep paying me.

My second student canceled on me; I spent that time doing some work of my own, thinking about that hack back in 2010 and why it might still be important to the FBI.

What if China did want to destabilize our economy? How would they do it?

The answer was simple: by making the markets crash.

How could they do that?

It wouldn't be very difficult. Aside from being a trading partner, they held quite a bit of our economy in the palm of their hand. I'd learned that during my research project. They were the largest foreign holder of US government debt. They were the largest foreign owner of both commercial and residential real estate. They sent over three hundred thousand students to our universities. If they made concerted moves on all of those fronts . . . If they suddenly sold all the debt they owned, it could send a shock through the debt market. If they dumped all the real estate they owned, it might tip the housing market. If they stopped sending us their students, all those full-tuition payments would pull the rug out from dozens of universities that relied on that funding.

The harder thing would be to send us into recession, to make the markets lose so much confidence that they wouldn't bounce back in two or three weeks. In order to do that, they'd have to really shake the faith of the average consumer.

How could they do that?

I puzzled over that question for a long time.

Toward the end of the hour, I got up to take a break. I said hi to Harold. Poked around the fiction section to see if any of my favorite authors had books I hadn't read. As I reached the end of the aisle, a man in a red baseball cap passed by at the other end.

I found one of my favorite authors. Fantasizing about life after I took the bar exam, I pulled out one of her books. Opened it to the first chapter to figure out if I'd read it before.

I had.

I went on to the next aisle. As I stopped in front of another shelf, in my peripheral vision, the man with the baseball cap drifted by again.

Was he following me?

I decided to do an experiment. I went back to the aisle I'd just been in.

Several seconds later, he drifted by again. In the opposite direction.

He *was* following me.

Immediately, I went back to my table in the center of the room. I texted Leo.

At library

Man following me

He replied almost immediately.

Texting agent now

A moment later, a woman who had been looking up something on the library's digital catalog took a seat at the table beside mine.

It made me feel slightly better. At least I knew someone else was on my side. And maybe now, someone who could remember faces would get a look at his.

I spent a jumpy fifteen minutes looking over my shoulder until I saw the man disappear down the stairs, a stack of books in hand.

Leo came into the library to get me several minutes before I was done with my last student. He sat down at the table behind us, sideways in the chair, arm draped over the back. I could tell it was him by the way he sat there. And by his hair. My fingers itched to push it back into place.

As my student walked away, he slid into the vacated seat. "He's not still here, is he?"

"Who?"

"The man who was following you."

I felt my cheeks get hot. "No. Turned out he was just looking for books. He left with a stack of them."

▸▸▸◂◂◂

Leo drove us back to his place. We stopped to pick up my plants underneath Mrs. Harper's deck on the way. Once we got back, I dove right into studying.

As I sat down to open my books, I grabbed an index card. But China was still on my mind. I'd already decided they could tank the markets if they really wanted to.

As I'd told Congressman Thorpe when I'd presented my report, our economy had vulnerabilities. That should have been apparent to anyone who was watching. Especially in terms of China. None of its investments in our economy was new information. None of them had been made in secret.

China could provoke a national financial storm if they wanted to, but on an international scale, our economy would still be viewed as relatively stable. The proof of that? No other currency was seriously considered as an alternate reserve currency to the dollar.

But FDIC hacks had given China granular access to our financial system in an entirely different way. What could they do if they were inside the system? Pretend to be US citizens. Open bank accounts.

Markets were an experiment in mass psychology. In a volatile market, enough reactions by fake account holders could show up on consumer confidence polls. Enough polls with down-trending numbers could convince actual US citizens that something was seriously wrong with the economy.

What else could US citizens do with bank accounts?

Receive social security payments. Transfer money in and out. Engage in automatic payment of bills. But all of that eventually involved spending money, which would be helpful to our economy. That would seem at odds with a goal to ruin it.

What else, beyond buying things, could US citizens do with money?

Invest in the markets. Support a charity. Donate to a cause. Only US citizens, for example, could contribute to a political campaign.

There were a lot of ways in which China could use personal information and fake bank accounts, but I still couldn't make anything fit together. None of it lent any clarity to the investigation.

Leo came inside, bringing the scent of gasoline and freshly cut grass with him. He disappeared into the kitchen. While he banged things around, I sank back into my books. Soon the scents of garlic and basil began to make my mouth water.

Eventually the garlic and the basil turned into a pizza. He brought it out to the table in the pan and split it right down the middle. Half for me, half for him. He slid mine onto a plate and set it in front of me.

"You made this?"

"I did."

"From scratch?"

"Mostly. It's your classic tomato pie courtesy of The Italian Store."

The Italian Store. It was a place I aspired to, a bastion of Italian goodness in two locations in Arlington. It wasn't a splurge for most people, but it was for me.

"I use their dough."

I took a bite.

"And their sauce. And a few other things. But I put them all together on the pan."

"That's good enough me."

He ate his half from the pan. I ate mine on a plate that also served as a paperweight to my study guide.

It was nice to be with someone who wasn't trying to control me, who wasn't trying to change what I wore or how I presented myself. With Leo I found myself wearing my jeans and a baggy T-shirt again with no guilt. No second thoughts.

"Are you guys any closer on Cade? Or the killer?"

"Getting there."

"Because something's been bothering me."

"There's a *lot* that's been bothering me." He muttered the words.

"The FDIC insures individual accounts."

"Right."

"But only up to $250,000."

"Yep."

"The Chinese have invested billions in our country."

"True."

"But it's not in $250,000 bank accounts."

"No."

"It's in research and buildings and government debt. So where's the FDIC connection? I can't see one."

"Neither can I."

But I couldn't stop trying to make the pieces fit.

The conversation with my father had also been bothering me, so after dinner I called him.

"You want to hear about my plan?"

"Tell me everything."

"It's this new money. Crypto."

"Crypto*currency*?"

"That's right. I met a guy, says you can make a fortune off it if you time it right."

I had a passion for cryptocurrency but not as a core part of an investment plan. Especially not for someone near retirement. "Some people have made money off it. But that was when it first got started. And it's people generally who've been holding it for a long time."

"Well, this guy's mining it. You know what that is? You get a computer, get a program, put it to work solving puzzles, and it's like finding Easter eggs."

My unease was growing by the moment. "Where did you meet this person?"

"Through Frankie. Kind of a friend of a friend from bowling."

Warning bells clanged in my head. "You haven't given him any money, have you?"

"Frankie and I are going to talk to him tomorrow night. He's in town for a few days."

"Promise you won't give him any money before you talk to me."

"Sweetie, don't worry. I've been around the block a time or two.

The bankruptcy took almost everything, so it'd just really be nice to goose the retirement fund. Otherwise, it's going to be you."

"What's going to be me?"

"My retirement plan. If I can't take care of myself—" He broke off. "But don't worry. That's plan B. Plan A is I figure out how to make a bunch of money fast."

"That never works, Dad."

"It does for some people. Why can't some people be me for a change?"

Because it didn't work like that in real life for people like us. Although to some extent, my dad was right. People who had money weren't necessarily better or smarter than the rest of us. They were just lucky. Lucky to be born into the right circumstances and lucky that bad circumstances had never touched them the way they had the rest of us. "Dad, you can't build a plan around luck. Please. Promise me you won't invest any money until after you've told me what their pitch is."

"I know what I'm doing."

"Please, Dad!"

He told me he loved me, tried again to reassure me, and then he hung up.

Cryptocurrency might be new, but human nature hadn't changed. Money in any form was still money and there would always be people willing to scam others to get more than their fair share.

▸▸ CHAPTER 38 ◂◂

Monday morning, I took my attaché instead of my backpack to work. I also took my interview shoes. Leo promised me a ride to the storage unit to pick up my other interview suit and then a ride into DC for my interview.

I'd arranged for Maddie to come in early to cover part of my shift.

Corrine and I worked together—briefly. It always took me a while to hit my full stride in the morning, but Corrine was one of those people who always took life straight up. And she could multitask too. Somehow she was able to take orders, pull shots, and keep up a running conversation. That morning was no exception.

"If I had a dollar for all the men who come in here just to look at you? I wouldn't be here anymore. I'd be on a beach somewhere in Tahiti."

Everyone always talked about beaches in Tahiti, but had anyone actually ever been to one? Was there anything to them, were they truly beautiful, or was it all just hype? "Let's review. Of the most recent, one was an ex-boyfriend. And one might be a cold-blooded killer. I wouldn't wish to be me if I were you. Come to think of it? *I* don't wish to be me."

"Forget about those guys. There's a new one."

"New one what?"

"New *guy*. He was asking about you Saturday."

"When?"

"After you left."

"How long after?"

She shrugged. "I don't know. Before three, right? Because that's when my shift ended."

"The problem with my life right now is that there are too many men. And they're all causing trouble. I don't need another one."

"You might like this one though. I like this one."

She liked everyone.

"I'm just trying to help you out, that's all. After what you told me about the face thing."

"I'm not interested."

"But he's interested."

"That doesn't mean I have to be."

"I told him all about you."

Shaking my head, I turned back to the espresso machine. It wasn't until I'd pulled a couple shots that the implications of her words sank in. "Corrine?" I raised my voice so she could hear me over the hiss of the machine. "What exactly did you tell him?"

"Him who?"

"The guy who asked about me Saturday."

"Oh! That you're super smart and super nice. And you aren't dating anyone."

Who needed a dating app when she was around? "That's it? You didn't tell him anything else?"

"Like what?"

"Anything about the murder?"

"You know? You don't have to let it all hang out up front. Just a suggestion, take it or leave it, but I'd say, give it a couple dates and then work it in. Like, 'Oh, by the way, I found a dead body.' Because people who'd date you because of that, you wouldn't want to date anyway. *That* would be creepy."

I went back to pulling shots.

She slid past me on her way to the mobile pickup counter. "And I might have *maybe* sort of mentioned your face thing. Because I didn't want him to feel bad if he came in sometime and you didn't recognize him."

"But I told you that in confidence!"

"It was for a good cause."

"Considering that it's my information to give out, could you not give it out in the future?"

"Okay, yeah. Sorry. It was just me trying to do you a favor."

I let it go. It was all that I could do.

▸▸▸◂◂◂

On my break, I discovered that Mrs. Harper had left me a voice message.

I called her back. "Mrs. Harper? Is everything okay?"

"No. But it's my own fault, isn't it? Once I get this cast off, I should be fine. Jess has a check for you. We wanted to put it in the mail, but we don't know where to send it."

I gave her Leo's address.

She repeated it back to me.

"That's right."

"Wonderful. I'll just— Hold on for a second. Jess is headed out. I'll ask her to take it with her."

I heard some talking off-line. In a few moments, Mrs. Harper came back on. "That's fine then. It's all taken care of." She spent the next few minutes telling me about what life was like with a cast and how she'd watched her grandchildren swim at a meet over the weekend. "Oh— and you'll never guess what happened. I found that package!"

"What package?"

"The one that nice young man delivered. I was packing for the trip Doris and Helen and Irene are taking without me when he came by. Wouldn't you know? I must have set it down in my suitcase and then put a sweater right on top of it. I just found it this morning. So we're mailing that to you too."

Leo and I had already decided that there never had been a package. That it had just been a ruse to gain entry to the house.

"Are you sure it's my package?"

"It has your name right on it."

"Is there any way you can tell me who it's from?"

"Let me check with—" She paused for a moment. I heard her call her daughter's name. She soon came back on the line. "Jess is already gone. She took it with her when she left so she could mail it. I'm sorry. But how long can it take to get from Loudoun to Arlington?"

It couldn't come quickly enough!

Leo came by early. I told him about the package after he ordered his coffee.

"You mean there really was one? Huh. And she didn't know who it was from?"

"No idea."

"We should find out in the next couple days."

He ordered a coffee and then took it over to a table. He sat there pretending to read the paper as he waited for me. I don't know if anyone else realized he was pretending, but his posture was too rigid, too stiff to believe he was absorbed in the articles.

As we left for the storage unit, I saw the guy with the sling again. He crossed the sidewalk in front of us and stumbled. I put a hand to his arm.

"Sorry." He righted himself.

"You okay?"

"Fine. I'm fine. Sorry."

At least he wasn't carrying an armful of papers this time.

Leo had his SUV back. He helped me into it.

"You haven't noticed anyone different?" he asked as we drove to the storage unit. "Anyone new around?"

"How would I know?"

"Good point. Anything unusual, then?"

"The guy with the sling." I said it before I put any thought into it.

"The what?"

"That guy with the sling."

"The one who almost tripped over us?"

"Yeah. He ran into me last week. He was carrying a notebook full of papers and dropped them all over the sidewalk."

"You'd never seen him before last week?"

"I might have. But I probably wouldn't have noticed. I only recognized him by the sling."

Leo let a few moments go by before he responded. "When was this?"

"It was Wednesday? Maybe. I think."

"Time of day?"

"As I was leaving work."

"Same place?"

"Last week he was in front of the Blue Dog heading toward the metro."

"Are you sure?"

I thought back to when I'd first met him. "I don't know. That's the direction he was going. He asked if I could do him a favor, but my car pulled up right then. I had to go."

Leo grunted.

"Why?"

"Anyone you've noticed around that coffee shop in the past couple weeks has got to be considered a suspect."

My face went numb. My vision blurred around the edges. "The guy was wearing a sling. He might as well have been helpless."

"You can wear a sling even if you don't need one. Makes a good disguise. And you can never be too paranoid."

"He seemed like a nice guy."

"Never said he wasn't. You remember what I told you, right? Never go anywhere—"

"Without someone else. I know."

"Not until we figure out who the killer is." He sighed. "I wish we knew what that favor would have been."

▸▸ CHAPTER 39 ◂◂

While we were driving to the storage unit, my dad called.

"Hey, sweetie. I'm sorry about yesterday. I just really need this to work, that's all."

"But your friend who introduced you to—"

"Frankie."

"Your friend Frankie. How well do you know this friend?"

"Well. Very well." There seemed to be a sort of warning in his voice.

"Okay."

"You know things were rough for me after your mother died."

"I know."

"I don't think you do. And that's okay. You weren't here, so you couldn't see it. And I'm glad you didn't. But I can't live in that space. Do you understand what I'm trying to say? I loved your mother. I still do. But I can't love her any more or any less now. She's gone."

It's true that I'd never lived in the house after Mom had died. He must have been haunted by all the memories. I should have thought of that before now. I should have said something. Should have suggested that he sell the house. If he'd done it sooner, maybe he could have paid off some of those bills. I swallowed the lump in my throat. "I know, Dad."

"So I'm making some choices."

"Okay. I understand. I just want you to be safe."

"I know you do. You're a good girl."

"I'm glad you sold the house." Or I would be, once I had the time to process it. "It was time. And I understand the need to invest. It's just that no one knows what's going to happen with cryptocurrency." I had my hopes. I knew what I wanted to have happen, but there weren't very many rules in place to govern it yet.

"No one knew what would happen with desktop computers or cell phones either. New things are always risky. But I'm willing to take a chance. What do I have to lose?"

When I was growing up, my father had always known everything. And he'd always been right. I didn't know how to let him be wrong. "Can I just ask you—can you limit your exposure? They say if you gamble you should only bet as much as you can afford to lose."

"That's good advice. Thing is? At my age? I have to gamble. I don't have enough years left to do things the right way. Listen, whatever happens, I won't hold you responsible, okay? I asked for your advice. I choose not to take it. That's all I wanted to say."

I told him good-bye and tried to push him out of my thoughts so that I could shift my focus toward the interview. Second interviews were good. Third interviews were better, of course. I told myself the only thing I had to do that afternoon was get invited back for the next round.

Leo drove right up to the gate guarding the storage units. He asked for my access code and got out to punch it in.

The gate opened.

We drove up to the unit. Leo stood beside me as I unlocked it, and then he rolled up the door for me.

"I just kind of threw everything in there. I can't remember where my things are exactly. It might take a few minutes to go through every—"

The door had risen far enough for me to see inside. Nothing was there.

He gave the door a shove that rolled it up to the top. "Are you sure this is your unit?"

It had to be, didn't it? I double-checked the number. "This is it. This is where I left everything."

Leo had taken me by the arm. He was pulling me away. "Leave it."

"But—"

"We'll have to dust everything for prints. I don't think there will be any, but—" He walked around the car with me and opened the door, then went around and got in on the driver's side. "Time to talk to management."

▸▸▸◂◂◂

I didn't waste any time telling the manager what had happened. He nodded along until I got to the everything-is-gone part.

"Whoa, whoa, whoa." He pressed his palms to the counter. "He said you sent him down."

"He? He who? You told me I was the only one who would have access to my unit. That's what I put in the paperwork. I didn't give permission for anyone else to access it."

"He said you were busy, asked him to come by and take care of it."

"But I didn't! I don't even know who you're talking about. Who was it that came?"

"Just calm down. He knows you, said you were short. Dark hair, brown eyes, all kinds of pretty."

Leo put a hand to my shoulder. "This man? Can you describe him for me?"

"Sure. He was, uh, 'bout this tall." He held up a hand roughly even with his ear. "White guy. Had a hat. Pork pie. Hadn't seen one in years. My grandfather used to have one."

"Hair color? Eye color?"

The man shrugged.

"Anything else you can tell me about him?"

"Uh-uh. Wait. Yeah. Wore a necklace."

"Necklace? Gold? Silver?"

"No. It was a leather thong. One of those."

"Facial hair?"

"No."

I'd finally found my words. "But I don't understand. He just came in here and said, 'Give me a key to the unit, and you gave it to him?"

"No. I mean, he didn't know the unit number, but that's okay. I remembered you. And then I pulled up the information and it was all good."

"But he took everything. He stole it all!"

"No, he didn't."

"There's nothing left."

"That's because he put it in a bigger one."

"A what?" Leo and I spoke in unison.

"He said you all had decided you needed something bigger."

"I don't—" I shook my head. "I don't understand. You're saying he came here and said *I* told him to move everything. To a *different unit*?"

"That's right." He put a key on the counter between us. "I put you in number 143."

"Did he pay for the new one?" Leo asked.

"Sure did."

"Credit card?"

The manager shook his head. "Cash."

Leo verified there were security cameras and arranged access to the footage. Then he pulled his phone from his pocket and dialed a number. As he started talking, he stepped outside.

I slipped the key into my pocket. "So that's it? You gave him the key to the old unit and assigned him a new one?"

"That's it. Nice man."

I went to join Leo. He had me wait in the SUV with him. About ten minutes later, several squad cars swung into the parking lot, lights flashing. And then a van drove up and joined them.

Several people got out of the van. They rolled back the side doors and dove in. When they came out, their arms were full of equipment.

One of them came up to talk to Leo while the other pulled on an olive-colored protective suit and helmet.

"Which one is it?" one of them asked Leo.

"Number 143." He gestured beyond the gate to the storage units.

The manager came out to join me. "What's all this?"

Leo stepped back to speak to him. "Can you open the gate for us?"

"If you can tell me what's happening!"

"We think the man who switched the units is a suspect in a murder case."

"A— I'm sorry. What?"

"He killed someone. And he may have left something inside the unit. We're taking the necessary precautions. You might do better to stay in the office. Maybe behind your counter?"

The man was already retreating toward the office door. "Hey—no hard feelings. I thought I was doing the lady a favor. I was just trying to be nice!"

Leo put a hand to my back. "Why don't you go with him?" He applied gentle pressure, propelling me toward the door.

I joined the man inside. But we didn't take shelter behind the counter. We stood at the window and watched.

In the alley, two other people in protective suits were consulting with each other.

A third person appeared on the roof. It looked like he was planning to—

"What is that? Is that a saw? A drill?" The man shook his head. "Oh no. No, no, *no*. They are *not* going to put a hole in my roof!"

In fact, cutting a hole in his roof looked very much like what they were doing. The man on top handed the drill back down.

They gave him some sort of cable. He bent down over the hole as the people on the ground fed it up to him.

"What's he doing that for?"

"I think they're trying to figure out if there's a bomb in there." That was the only thing that made sense to me.

"A bomb! If he blows himself up, it's not my fault. And if he blows people's stuff up? It's not me going to pay for it!"

The man lay down on the roof as people yelled things up to him. After a while, he pulled the cable out and handed it to the people on the ground.

Leo came down through the gate and got me. "Didn't figure you'd hide behind the counter." He took me outside with him.

"Everything I have is in that unit."

"They didn't see any signs of a bomb."

"Are you sure it's safe?"

"They're sure it's safe."

"And we trust them because . . . ?"

"Because they're experts."

Everything I had assumed to be true these past few weeks, the past few months, had turned out to be false. I wasn't sure if I could trust anyone anymore. "Can we wait here? Until we know for certain?"

"Sure. Yeah." He yelled up to the people by the unit, told them to proceed.

In the end, one person was designated to open the unit. Everyone else took cover.

It was so quiet, we were listening so intently, that we heard the key turn in the lock. As we waited to hear something—*anything*—a bird twittered.

Right here! *Right* here! *Rrrright* here!

A car drove up to the gate. The driver started to get out, but someone broke from the group and went over. He must have asked the driver to remain inside because he got back in his car.

Up at the storage unit, the man unlocked the door. Inched it up.

I held my breath, hoping that nothing would happen, no bomb would explode.

When the door reached the top, the man let the handle go. He stood there, hand on a hip, surveying the unit.

"What's the matter?" I whispered the words to Leo.

"Don't know."

"If my things aren't there—" If they weren't there, I didn't know what I'd do. I'd gone from the depths of despair to the heights of hope in less than half an hour. I didn't know if I could make that journey again.

The man in front of the unit gestured for us to come join him.

Leo took me by the hand and we walked up together.

The man in the suit stepped aside. "You missing anything?"

It was all there. At least it looked to be. When I'd moved my things into the previous unit, I'd just dropped the boxes and bags on the floor and shoved the mattress against the wall. The killer had put my box spring and mattress together and then made it up with my sheets and comforter. The boxes were piled beside it in a way that could only be described as tidy.

It was bone-chillingly creepy. "Wh-why would he do that?"

"Because he could. Because he wants you to know that he's one step ahead of you. He wants to freak you out."

"It's working."

▸▸ CHAPTER 40 ◂◂

Agent Beyer arrived. I walked with him away from the storage units. Away from Leo. "We have to think about the possibility that this was your ex-boyfriend."

I couldn't decide whether that would make things better or worse. "I thought he was in jail for violating the restraining order."

"He was fined, not jailed. He paid the fine on Friday evening. He's been out since then."

"He violated my restraining order, we caught him in the act." I couldn't keep my voice from rising. "He confessed to breaking and entering, and now he's back on the street?"

Leo came over and joined us. "Everything okay?"

Agent Beyer ignored him. "I don't make the rules. We've sent an agent to his office to question him."

"You're the one who told me violent people do violent things! How is it that they never even notified me?"

"Metropolitan Police DC is a different agency. I have no jurisdiction there. I don't know how they do things, but I do want to catch our shooter. The problem is, right now, I can't distinguish between your ex and the killer. Can you give me some background on your relationship?"

"What do you want to know?"

"Anything. Idiosyncrasies, habits. Basically, I'm trying to identify his footprint so I can distinguish it from our shooter's. I need to know what to take seriously."

"You need to take Hartwell seriously. Extremely seriously."

"I understand that. But I also need to find a killer. And that's in our national interest. Will you help me?"

I wanted to protest that Hartwell was just as cunning, just as dangerous as the shooter was, and that discounting him from anything would be a mistake, but I understood. Hartwell was my problem. Cade's killer was theirs. So I started at the beginning.

"I met him at a law-school mixer. He got me an internship with his father, on the Hill." That ought to have been the first warning sign. A man who wouldn't respect boundaries and took advantage of nepotism wouldn't respect me either. "His father chairs the House Financial Services Committee. And he sits on the House of Representatives Committee on Science, Space, and Technology. Which is another coincidence in a long string of them."

"How so?"

"They investigated the original Chinese hacks at the FDIC back in 2010."

"Okay."

"And the other coincidence is that the Financial Services Committee had been working on a bill to strengthen some important financial oversight measures and banking laws. They would have affected China."

"That's coincidental how?"

"It was being worked on while Cade and I were there."

"Ah. Any insights yet on what he was hoping to talk to you about?"

"No. I keep trying to remember our conversations. But if they didn't involve which interest group lobbying Congress was offering free food for lunch, they were mostly about issues the congressman was interested in. Or staffer gossip. Or China. We did talk a lot about China."

"That seems relevant."

"I did a project for the congressman on currency and the global markets. Cade was our tech guy, but he had a thing for macroeconomics. He was interested in global trade."

"And what was your particular interest?"

"I did a report for the congressman on the relative strength of the dollar. We became the world's reserve currency after World War II. The general assumption is that that won't change anytime soon. But the way China's invested in our economy has given them a lot of power. And during the trade wars, they put themselves in a better long-term position than we did."

"Is this what you and Cade talked about?"

"We talked about some of it. And I've been doing a lot of thinking lately, since he died. Our place in the global economy is more tenuous than we realize."

"Does that have anything to do with the hack at the FDIC?"

"No." And I really wished I didn't have to admit it. I wanted there to be a connection. It seemed like there should be.

"Let me know if you remember anything."

I told him I would.

"Let's keep going with your ex. You had a restraining order. Can you tell me why?"

I didn't want to. Especially not with Leo listening. I didn't want to tell the agent—didn't want to tell anyone—that I was in a relationship, had *stayed* in a relationship, where my boyfriend had hit me.

"He was abusive."

"I understand that. Emotionally? Verbally? Physically?"

"Yes. All of those."

"Did he hit you? Punch you? Kick you?"

Leo broke in. "Is this sort of detail really necessary?"

"Patterns of domestic violence are well-established. They occur on both a cyclical and an escalating basis. I need to know what that cycle was for Ms. Garrison so I can accurately predict Mr. Thorpe's behavior. He's entangled himself in this investigation. I need to be able to mitigate his impact."

I knew all about the long downward spiral of domestic violence. I knew that eventually, if I had stayed in that relationship long enough, I would have ended up as a statistic. I would have ended up dead.

I made one last plea. "I detailed this when I filed for the restraining order. Can't you get what you need through that?"

"We could. We will. It's just quicker hearing it from you."

I gave in. "The last night I was with him, he punched me in the face. He said it was because I didn't trust him. Then he shoved me into a wall. When I stumbled and fell to the floor, he kicked me."

"Where?"

"In the side."

I suspected that he'd broken one of my ribs. I didn't have the money to meet my deductible, so I wrapped a long-sleeve T-shirt around my middle and cinched it up as tight as I could.

"Can you tell me anything else about him?"

"If you aren't his girlfriend, then he's charming. He has a way of getting whatever he wants."

"The charmers are the worst. Makes you feel like a fool in hindsight, when you find out you've been taken advantage of."

I nodded.

He cleared his throat. "When did you leave him?"

"At the end of April."

"Are there any vacation homes, second residences he might go to?"

"The family has a vacation home on the Chesapeake. One in Jackson Hole. An apartment in Paris."

"How often do they visit?"

"Jackson Hole is for Christmas. The house on the bay is used in the summer, especially when Congress is in recess. Paris is just for fun—long weekends, mostly."

"How do they travel to the vacation homes? By car? Boat?"

"Plane for Jackson Hole. Both my ex and his father are pilots."

"Any places he frequents when he's in DC?"

"He eats out most nights."

"Where?"

"Wherever is trending. Or Adams Morgan. The family has season tickets at the Kennedy Center. They're members at one of the country clubs in Maryland. Hartwell entertains in his firm's suite at the Nationals baseball games."

"Is there anything else you can tell me? Any other habits? Quirks?"

I shook my head. "Not that I can think of."

He let us go. I followed Leo back to his car, making sure I stayed behind him. I didn't want him to look at me.

By that time, my interview was long past. But I called the firm anyway, using the phone number I'd been given. "May I leave a message with Ms. Buckingham?"

"This is Ms. Buckingham."

My stomach clenched. "I'm Whitney Garrison. I was your three o'clock interview this afternoon." Should I tell her what had happened? Would she even believe me? And if she did, would she decide I was too much drama for her firm? "I'm sorry I wasn't able to meet with you."

"The courtesy of a call would have been appreciated."

"I apologize. I've been working with the FBI on a case and there was a development. Is it possible to reschedule the interview?"

"While I'm sure working with the FBI is very interesting, I'm looking for a lawyer who prioritizes her obligations. I hope you understand."

"I do. I understand. I'm sorry I can't be that person right now."

▸▸ CHAPTER 41 ◂◂

Leo loaded all my things into his SUV. He said he didn't mind storing them in his basement.

I wasn't scared. I wasn't inconsolable. I wasn't despairing.

I wasn't anything.

"Hey." Leo reached out across the console and touched my hand.

I flinched.

"That was brave. To talk about your ex."

I said nothing.

"Some people think domestic violence only happens to poor people too stupid to recognize what's going on." He paused. When I didn't say anything, he continued. "I've worked a lot of domestic incidents. One thing that has surprised me is how many batterers are successful. And gregarious. They're the people everyone wants to be. We're called to cases all over the county, south *and* north. It's not a class problem. It's not an intelligence problem. It's a human problem."

He was trying to make me feel better.

"I just want you to know that the things he did to you have everything to say about him and nothing to say about you."

"They have everything to say about me. I should have known better."

"Now you do."

"What was it about me, what did I lack that I thought would be provided by him? Why didn't I break up with him after the first time?" Or the second or the seventh or sixteenth?

"You were probably hypnotized by the lifestyle. It would seduce anyone. Fancy cars, fancy friends, all that money."

Leo's words made it all worse. "So yes, at first it was like that, but I come from—" I paused as all the words I wanted to say got hung up in my throat. I tried again. "I won't say I come from nothing because that's not true. I come from a family who loved me very much. I come from a family with modest means. I never lacked for anything. Growing up? I had everything I needed and even some of the things I wanted. But that doesn't prepare you for what to say when the guy who lacks for nothing tells you that you're everything. It doesn't prepare you for how to resist things you want, so badly, to believe."

Neither of us said anything for a long while. Eventually, he broke the silence.

"At least he didn't steal anything from the unit. He could have."

"True."

"Could be we'll be able to lift some fingerprints."

"Great."

"Listen, I'm sorry about the interview. Can you call them back again? Ask them to reschedule?"

"You don't ask the assistant director of the practice group to reschedule. At least, not after you missed the interview without warning her."

"Sorry."

"It's fine." It wasn't fine. That firm had been my chance at doing things right. I'd done things the wrong way for so long. At some point in the very near future I needed to jump on the right career track and buy a ticket on the fast train to success. But I was starting to think I'd used up all my chances. Why not be honest with myself? "Real life, normal life? I don't think it's for me."

"Why not?"

"I wrote it off—marriage, having a family—a long time ago."

"Why?"

"How could I trust myself with a family? With kids? I would never be able to recognize my own child. What kind of life would that child have, knowing their own mother didn't know who they were? I'll stick to law, where everything is written down. And finance, where I can recognize the numbers."

"It might not be my place to say it, but I think you should concentrate on all the things you *can* do instead of the things you *can't*."

"I am. I'm good at school. I was an excellent student of international economic law. I'll be good at being a lawyer."

"The way you framed it made it seem like you think of it as second best. That if you *had* a choice, you'd choose family."

A piercing wind howled through my hollow soul. "Of course I would. Wouldn't you?" To know and be known? To belong to someone? To be part of something? Yes. I wanted it with all that I had. But I shrugged. "Sometimes, choices get made for you." And then you just had to deal with it.

▸▸▸◂◂◂

Leo had dinner delivered. I wasn't hungry. He insisted that I eat something.

We ate in silence until I pointed out the obvious. "This is the second time my things have been tampered with."

He nodded. "But I've got several different locks on the door in my basement. You don't have to worry about them." He paused. "Hey." The word came out softly.

"What?"

"You don't have to worry about him. About Thorpe. You're safe here."

It was a nice thought, but I wasn't ready to trust it.

I went to work right after we ate. As I studied, he disappeared into the basement and started doing something that involved sawing and hammering. I pulled the folder of information from the Financial Services Committee out of my attaché. I'd really been hoping that internship on the Hill would be worth something. I was hoping I could turn it into a job.

I opened the folder, reliving a moment where I had felt as if I was really making a contribution. I flipped through the notes I'd made in preparation for my interview until I reached the page at the bottom. It was a table that noted China's investments in the US over the past thirty years. In the most recent year, their direct investments in our economy totaled just over five billion dollars; they'd bought over a trillion dollars in US national debt and over twenty billion dollars of real estate, driving up prices in major cities around the nation.

It didn't mean anything necessarily, but then again, it might.

I went down into the basement where Leo and I had put my things. The tang of sawdust scented the air. I bent over my bags, looking for the journal from my internship. I wanted to look at it again.

Leo took hold of his safety glasses and slid them up onto his head. "You good?"

"Just trying to find something."

He went back to work as I kept looking. I looked in every bag, thinking maybe I'd jumbled up my things in my haste to get away from the storage unit, but I couldn't find it. It wasn't there.

It had been.

I'd paged through it when I prepared for my interview.

I finally admitted defeat and decided to focus on my studies. I was well into a review of tort law when my eyelids started to flutter. Then my head started to droop. I glanced at my watch.

It was only eight o'clock.

Leo had come up from the basement. He was behind me, on the couch in the living room, watching something on TV.

Pushing my chair back, I stood. Leaned over my chair to flip through the books.

Only ten more pages total. I could do ten pages.

But several pages in, my head started to nod again.

I put one of my reference books on the chair. That way I wouldn't be tempted to sit down. My eyes were dry. I blinked, hard, several times in hopes of moistening them.

Didn't work.

I went into the kitchen, turned on the cold water, and cupped my hands underneath so I could splash my face. Then I closed my eyes and did a few head rolls. Took a deep breath.

Only six more pages. That's all I had to do.

I went back to stand in front of the table, bending over my notes as I paged through the books. The air conditioner kicked on and I began to shiver. That was okay though. I wouldn't fall asleep if I was shivering. The challenge was to focus. I lifted a foot off the floor, giving my subconscious something to work on as I kept on with my review.

But my foot got so heavy.

I gave in and decided to kneel.

I don't know when I fell asleep, but I know when I woke up. A warm hand rested atop my head for a moment before it slipped down to my shoulder.

"Mmm." I opened my eyes. My head was cradled in the crook of my arm. I'd fallen asleep on top of a notebook.

Leo took me by an elbow and helped me to my feet.

My knees tingled with pain. Maybe kneeling hadn't been the smartest thing to do. I closed my books and stacked the notebooks on top of them. Then I attempted to move away from the table. Stiffness joined the pain in hobbling me.

"You okay?"

"Fine." I put a hand to my hair and swept it away from my face. "I'm fine."

"Should I say something about burning the candle at both ends or just keep my mouth shut?"

"You can't say anything I haven't told myself. After the bar I can take a break." I couldn't, actually. I'd be working the same number of hours—I'd just be doing it for some fancy law firm in DC. But I had an agreement with myself: I could lie to myself as much as I wanted just as long as it got me through the exam. I'd set up a hazy fantasy of a glass of red wine, an all-you-can-eat buffet of gourmet food, and a chalet in Switzerland as the reward for finishing.

For passing. For surviving.

The real reward?

A chance to work even harder to pay off more loans.

That's where the idea of Switzerland came in handy. I kept it so close that it was difficult to see around, particularly if I didn't want to.

"If you fall asleep as you hit the bed, you might be able to squeeze out six hours."

"I can't fall asleep yet. I still have work to do."

"Then maybe what you need is a break. *Raiders of the Lost Ark* is on. Come watch with me."

"I don't have time to watch a movie." I hardly had time to breathe. Besides, movies were confusing. I could never tell who was who.

"Just watch the opening. It's classic. It'll only take ten minutes."

"If I watch it will you promise to leave me alone?" Maybe I could jump-start my brain if I forced it to try to distinguish between characters.

"Promise."

It was about time for me to stretch anyway. Research showed that efficiency was highest when working for about an hour and then taking a fifteen- or twenty-minute break. Or half an hour with a five-minute break. Either way, three hours of solid work was pushing it.

I went over to the couch with him, took the pillow from the corner, and sat down.

At first I thought I wasn't going to be able to follow it. Everyone was wearing some sort of hat and clothes that were the same shade of brown. But then I noticed only one of them was wearing a leather jacket.

There was a scene with a whip and then there was a dark cave.

Somehow, the pillow found its way into my arms, my feet onto the cushions, my knees to my chest. There were big, hairy spiders. And a skeleton and poisoned darts.

But for once, I seemed to be able to keep the characters separate. At least the important one. At that point, the hero was the only one wearing a hat. And he was extremely clever.

There were death-defying leaps.

Betrayal.

Treachery.

And a chase through a rain forest.

Suddenly, I was pressed up against Leo's side and my face was hidden in the pillow.

He put an arm around me. "It's okay. He's the hero of the movie. Movies. All four of them. He's not going to die."

I put a hand out to draw the pillow down.

"Really."

Leo was right. He made it through the chase and then through an incident with a snake. But then, all of a sudden, the movie left the jungle. The next scene was in a university classroom. I sat up. Put the pillow down.

"Where'd he go? What happened?"

"Indy? He's right there. He's a professor when he's not out looking for artifacts. That's his class."

Oh.

"And all the girls are in love with him. But he doesn't care. And that man who just came into the classroom? He's a friend."

I stayed a little while longer. And then a few minutes after that.

As he came out of one of the scenes without a scratch, I realized I'd grabbed Leo's hand and anchored his arm around my shoulder.

I examined it in the flickering light of the TV screen. It was strong. And large. The hairs on the back of his hand caught the light.

He squeezed my hand and I turned to him.

He tightened his arm, drawing me even closer.

I let him.

He bent and kissed me on the lips. Just one brief, perfect kiss.

My breath caught.

He drew back for a moment. Kissed me on the forehead. And then he turned his attention to the movie. Several minutes later he went back to describing who was who for me. And several minutes after that, I'd given up trying to figure out what was going on between us.

I ended up staying there, with Leo, on the couch. He talked me through the entire movie. Let me clutch his arm when the scary parts came and cheer with him when the bad guys got caught. It was a luxury to worry about someone else for a while, even if it was a fictional character who would go on to star in three more movies. A luxury to feel like a normal person. It was a luxury I hadn't had.

Ever.

▸▸ CHAPTER 42 ◂◂

It was warm there, against Leo's side. And safe. There weren't any killers. There weren't any study guides. There was just him.

I must have fallen asleep because I woke with a start.

I was confused for a moment. The living room was dark. The movie was over; the credits were rolling. It took me a few seconds to remember where I was.

Leo's living room.

It took me a few seconds more to remember what had happened.

A movie. And a kiss.

I sat up. Scooted away from him. Put the pillow back in its corner. "You let me sleep."

"You were tired. I did everything I could to wake you up. You wouldn't budge."

I was standing by that time. The light in the dining room was still on, illuminating everything I should have been doing.

The past few days really must have gotten to me. That was the only explanation I had for abandoning my books.

Tears dissolved the words I wanted to say and then collected them in my throat. I had to swallow in order to dislodge them. "I can't do it." I couldn't do any of it. And worse than that? I didn't want to anymore.

Leo stood, extended a hand as if coaxing me back to him.

I took a step back, away from him. "Don't be nice to me. Don't be kind. I won't know how to—" I gestured toward the table. "I have to be able to—" I had to be able to focus, to concentrate, to not think too hard about the future. Because if I didn't, then the sheer impossibility of obtaining my dreams, of ever having a life other than paying down my debt, threatened to undo me. "I don't have anything to give you."

"I'm not asking you for anything."

Then he was the only person, the only thing in my life, that wasn't.

He kissed me on the cheek and then went upstairs.

I spent a few minutes gathering up my notes and books and then a few minutes more asking myself what I thought I was doing. I'd already determined boyfriends were a luxury I couldn't afford. And Leo needed to stay Mr. Leo Baroni, police detective.

No boyfriends.

No distractions.

No complications.

▸▸▸◂◂◂

We sort of circled around each other the next morning.

Concentric circles.

No touching.

"Whitney? Can we talk about—"

"Did you know there are over a thousand different cryptocurrencies?" I didn't want to talk about him. I didn't want to talk about me. I didn't want to talk about us. There wasn't an us to talk about.

He sighed. "Fine." He held up a hand. "We'll go the no-talking route. I had no idea."

"Neither do most people. But even so, it's not the currency that's the most valuable technological innovation; it's the technology behind it."

"I'm just going to say that I enjoyed spending time with you last night. That's it. When you want to talk about, we'll talk about it. If that's after we catch the killer, after you take the bar, then I'll wait."

Gratitude bloomed in my chest. "Thank you."

"Just let me drop you off this morning."

▸▸▸◂◂◂

A couple hours later, as I was bussing a few of the tables, I saw the man with the sling again.

He walked past the window.

I stopped picking up cups to watch him. I watched as he waited at the intersection for the light to change. I watched as he crossed the street. I watched as he walked into one of the apartment buildings that lined the opposite side of the block.

And then I breathed a sigh of relief.

When I could, I went into the back room, took my phone from my backpack, and called Leo.

"I think it's okay. About the guy with the sling. I'm pretty sure he lives in the area."

"How do you know?"

"Because I saw him walk into one of the apartment buildings."

"Which one? Which building? Can you give me the address?"

I tried to explain which building it was. Spatial directions were difficult for me. But I think I succeeded. Leo said he'd ask the FBI to have someone look into it. I slid my phone into my back pocket in case he needed to get ahold of me.

As I went back to the register, a guy wearing a preppy mixed-plaid button-down strode up to the register.

"Hey. So what's good here? Besides you?"

Once in a while, a particularly clever pickup line made me smile. Or even laugh. But his wasn't one of them. "The coffee's pretty good."

"Huh." He pulled out his wallet. "Then give me a large iced mocha." He handed me his credit card.

Ruth came into the shop while I was marking his cup. She was dripping with sweat. Having to wear that yellow vest probably made the heat worse. "Can I have some ice water?"

I smiled. "Of course." I pushed the man's cup toward Corrine, who was at the espresso machine, then slid a cup off the stack for Ruth.

"Hey." The man repositioned himself and blocked Ruth from the counter. "I'm kind of in a hurry here. And I paid for my drink."

Ignoring him, I went to fill Ruth's cup and met her down at the mobile counter to pass it to her. When I came back to the register, the man was still waiting for me. So I decided to say something to him.

"You know what I'm really looking for in a relationship?"

He put an elbow to the counter and leaned in. "What?"

"Someone who's kind." I signaled to Corrine and we traded places.

▸▸▸◂◂◂

An hour later, Corrine was grabbing a cookie from the pastry case for a mom who was busy trying to contain a very active toddler. She nudged me with her elbow as she passed. "I forgot to ask you—you have to tell me—what did you think?"

"Think? About what?"

I had to wait until she came back behind the counter for her answer.

"*The guy.*"

"Which guy?"

"The one."

"Why do I feel like this is some kind of code?"

"You know: *the guy*. The one who was asking about you. The one I told you about. I told him you were super smart, super nice. That guy."

That guy. "The one you told about my face blindness?"

"That one."

"You're saying I met him?"

"Yeah."

"When?"

"Out there." She pointed toward the window.

"Outside? How do you know?"

"Because I saw you. So cute."

"I talked to him?"

"You were with Mr. Detective. He kind of tripped while he was passing you."

"*That* was the guy?"

"Yeah."

"That's the same guy who was asking about me?"

"Yeah."

A ripple of apprehension raised the hairs on my arms. "When's the last time you saw him?"

"Just this morning."

"He was here?"

"Yeah. But you were busy."

I hadn't noticed him. "Did he ever tell you his name?"

"I can't remember."

"Haven't you taken his order?"

"Yeah. But it's always an iced coffee with coconut milk. So I've never needed his name."

"This is important, Corrine. He's never introduced himself to you?"

"I don't know. Maybe? Why don't you just ask him next time you see him?"

Something was wrong. If he was that interested in me, why hadn't he tried to flirt with me like other men did? Why hadn't he introduced himself? Why had he just let me go on my way that first day I met him without trying harder to keep me there?

Because he knew where I worked?

But if that was the case and if he really did live in that apartment building across the street, then why hadn't he sought me out to talk to me again?

There were too many men in my life. Everyone was a suspect. But

I couldn't live in a world where I trusted no one. It was too small. Too unforgiving.

"Hey, girl, I'm sorry."

"For what?"

"My bad. I forgot."

"Forgot about what?"

"Your face thing. I'll point him out to you next time he comes in."

"You don't have to. I can remember him."

"But you told me before that you couldn't remember faces, so—"

"He's got that sling."

"What sling?"

"On his arm."

"No, he doesn't."

"The sling—" I mimicked wrapping something around my arm.

"I know what a sling is. He doesn't have one."

"Are we talking about the same person?"

She put a hand to her hip. "The man you helped keep from tripping yesterday."

"He had a sling. He was wearing one. Every time I've seen him, he's wearing a sling."

"Every time I've seen him, he's not."

I called Leo again.

▸▸ CHAPTER 43 ◂◂

Agent Beyer came into the shop. He worked with the manager to access the guy's account and contact information. He said there were agents outside at various places. I tried to keep calm, taking orders, then switching with Ty to pull shots and make drinks.

Eventually the agent came over to the counter. "We think we have him. I want you and you"—he pointed to Corrine and me—"to come out with me. Just to see what his reaction is."

We took our aprons off and left them in the back room before joining him.

As we approached, one of the agents leaned away from the group. He gestured to the man in the center. The one who was wearing a sling.

"Is this the guy?" Agent Beyer asked. "The one who's been stalking you?"

Corrine nodded. "It's him."

The man reacted with outrage. "I am not a stalker!"

"We're thinking it's classic Ted Bundy," one of the other agents said. "You know: wear a fake cast to make girls feel sorry for you. Put them off guard and then use their sympathy to take advantage of them."

"This is not a fake sling!"

"But you don't wear it all the time, do you?" Agent Beyer responded. "Ever wear a fake mustache?"

"What?"

The agent repeated his question.

"Fake mustache?"

"You've been seen in this area quite a bit this past week."

"Because I live right over there." He pointed to the apartment building. "And I come in for iced coffee sometimes because— Is that a crime?" He seemed to look at me. "All I wanted was to ask you out on a date."

A date? "Why didn't you?" Every other man with an interest in me seemed to.

"Because I—" He shrugged. "Because— I was going to. I was trying to figure out what dating app to use. That's why I've been hanging out. I figured out when your shift was. I'd try to be here when you got off work. When you left the Blue Dog, I was hoping I'd be able to see you on the geo-locators, you know? Then I could contact you through the app. I was trying *not* to be a stalker."

▸▸▸◂◂◂

As I returned to work with Corrine, Leo caught up with me. I smelled his cologne on the wind before I turned around and saw him. But before I could say anything, Agent Beyer called him over. They huddled for a few moments by the curb before the agent got into his car. Leo joined me as he pulled away from the curb.

"They're going to check out the guy with the sling. Make sure he was telling us the truth."

"Have they found out anything more about Hartwell? If it was him at the storage unit yesterday?"

"The manager couldn't identify him by photo. We can't identify the man in the security camera's footage. Hartwell swears that he was with a client when the manager says the incident took place."

"And you're going to take him at his word?"

"No. We've asked him for his alibi."

"And?"

"He says he'll get us proof."

"So the *potential* of proof is being taken as a real, concrete answer?" The law only worked if it applied to everyone equally. "Do you know what he's probably doing right now?"

Leo didn't answer.

"He's probably convincing someone to lie for him to make it seem like he had an alibi."

"A lie only goes so far. Eventually the truth comes out."

"What if it comes out too late?"

"I know it's not what you want to hear, but I need you to trust the process."

Trust the process?

He'd been glancing up and down the street. Now he gestured toward the Blue Dog. "Let's get back inside where we're not so exposed." He opened the door and then held it so I could walk through.

We claimed a table at the far end of the room.

"It might seem like he can play by different rules, but he can't. They won't let him. You've got to trust that they won't."

"I wish I had some guarantee, because so far he's gotten away with just about everything."

"I only—" He ran a hand through his hair. "I didn't ask you to come back inside to make you feel bad. I didn't come back to argue with you. I wanted to tell you I'm off the case."

That wasn't what I'd expected him to say. "Off the case? Off what case?"

"Your case."

I sat back as I tried to make sense of what he was saying. "What?" He couldn't be off my case. He was the only person I really knew among those who were attached to the investigation.

"I'm off your case. They've reassigned it."

"Who has? The FBI?"

"Arlington County."

"I don't want it reassigned." As much as my feelings for him—and about him—were confused, I had no problem trusting his professional judgment.

"You don't have any choice."

"They can't just—"

"Conflict of interest."

"Whose interest?"

"Yours."

"I would think that a detective's interest would be required on a case."

"Not your case. *You*. In particular."

"Because of Sunday morning? When your boss came by?"

"Right."

"So is it against the law that you've taken me in?"

"Federal law? State law? No."

"Is it against police department rules?"

"It's not smart. Let's put it that way."

"Then why did you do it?"

"Because you had nowhere else to go and I'm a nice guy. I'm the good guy here, Whitney. You can't choose who you're attracted to. Or what cases you get. Me being me and you being you created a conflict of interest."

"But—"

"And I can't say I disagree."

"But—"

"Can you?"

"No. But—"

"Although I wouldn't say I agree either."

"Did you just—" I was trying to sort out what he'd just said. Or what he hadn't. "So you do think there's a conflict of interest."

"I'd rather say that I think there's an interest. Don't you agree?"

"Whose interest? On the part of what? I need to be super clear what you're talking about."

"I'm interested in you. So I agree with my boss. But I'm also interested in your case. I think I'm the best person to work it since I was there from the beginning. So I *dis*agree with her."

I didn't want to go from being called Whitney to being called Ms. Garrison or "that girl" by someone I didn't know. By someone who didn't really know me. I just didn't. "If I request you personally, then maybe—"

"Then definitely it will just confirm her suspicions that there's a conflict of interest."

"If I tell her it's because you're the only one I trust to—"

"Conflict of interest."

"But if I let her know that—"

"Interest."

"—the only reason I can finally sleep at night is because I know you? And I know that you're there? In the room next door?" Desperation quickened my voice as I tried, uncharacteristically, to outrun the reach of reason.

He reached forward across the table, cupped a gentle hand around my neck, pulled me close, and kissed me. "Then I'm glad." He released me. "And I'm wondering why you couldn't before."

A tear was making its way down my cheek. I ignored it. To swipe at it would only call attention to it.

He brushed it away with his thumb. "We're going to identify this killer. And then we're going to lock him up."

"It's not that."

"You sure?"

"It's not *just* that."

"Then what is it?"

"It's everything." Finding and locating a killer was the easiest thing going on in my life. Everything else, I had to figure out a way to live with. Killers were temporary. Everything else was permanent.

▸▸ CHAPTER 44 ◂◂

"Do you want to know what I think?" Leo asked.

"Do I?"

"You should go into hiding."

"Where? Under a bed?"

"Or down in my basement or the kitchen or wherever. I think you should stay inside until this is over."

"Leo, I've already told you. I have to work. It's not an option. Remember? And I have students today."

"The way I see it, if you get killed, you can't work. And it feels like we're close. Just give us—give the team—a couple more days."

"And then what? What if they need a couple more? Do you see how this goes? A couple more and a couple more and then I'm out of a job. Both of them. And I still don't have anything lined up for after the bar."

"I think your manager would understand."

She might. But the parents of my students wouldn't. "I can't drop off the face of the earth."

"Just hear me out."

I sighed. "I'm listening."

"Why can't you FaceTime or Skype with your students? Don't half of the test prep companies do that anyway?"

"Because I'm not with a test prep company. I offer personal, personalized service."

"But you could do that over the internet or over the phone, couldn't you? For just a couple days?"

"The parents wouldn't like it."

"But isn't the test just around the corner?"

"It's on Saturday. But the SAT is in August. I coach students for both."

"They're not going to drop you now. Not at the last minute."

"But they might let it be known that I did a bait and switch."

"So offer them a discount."

"Leo, I'm trying to make money, not give it away!"

"You wouldn't have to make it free. Just drop your fee by twenty or thirty dollars."

"And what am I going to tell them?"

"Tell them you have a family emergency, but you still want to honor your commitment to their student. What parent wouldn't want to hear that?"

Maybe. It might work. "But what am I going to tell my manager?"

"Tell her that you can just about guarantee sirens and police officers if you come to work, but that if she'll let you have a couple days off, maybe you can help put an end to all of it."

"How many days do you think this will be?"

"Let's start with two."

"So tomorrow, if you think, 'Maybe she should have made it three,' you'll tell me, right? So I can call the next set of parents?"

"Yes. I'll stay in touch with the detective who replaced me on the team."

I looked over at the work area. At Ty, who was busy making shots, and Corrine, who was at the register. I glanced away, looked out toward the window. There were a lot of big windows at the Blue Dog. I was actually quite exposed when I worked here. And so were my coworkers. Maybe Leo was right. The killer obviously knew my schedule. He'd observed me as I went about my day. Maybe the smartest thing to do was to stay hidden inside for a couple days.

"Okay. I'll do it."

"Thank you."

"You know, I've been thinking a lot about the timeline. Some of the things that have been happening have to be Hartwell. There's no other person they could be."

"We know he's been stalking you. He already admitted to the planter. We know he's the one who tore up your apartment. He may have been the one at the storage unit too."

"But who took a shot at me? It doesn't seem like something he would do. And the package is still a mystery. It couldn't have been the killer, could it? It was a whole day before the shooting even happened. It had to be Hartwell, right?"

"I want him to have pulled that alarm at the library too. But he swore it wasn't him."

"Do we have to believe him? Do we really need to give him the benefit of doubt?" Something was still bothering me. "Those first things—the package delivery, the handprint, the planter, the break-in. All of those things seem to fit together."

"What was the fire alarm at the library, then?"

"An attempt to get me to come back to him? That was his pattern. Take me for granted. I push back; he explodes. He apologizes and starts courting me again."

"I'm not quite sure I buy that." But he was nodding. I'm sure he'd heard all of that a hundred times in his years at the police department.

"So it sort of fits. But the storage unit and the attempted shooting don't. At the most basic level, Hartwell is a bully. He's not a psychopath; he's reactionary. His modus operandi was always to make his point and then punish me and yank on the leash. It was scary in its own way, but it wasn't terrifying. The storage unit? That was creepy.

And the attempted shooting isn't his style. All the planning that was put into Cade's killing seems more like the storage-unit switch and the library shooting than planter smashing and apartment ransacking. Does that make sense?"

Leo shrugged.

"Some of those events were meant to make me do something—make me go back to Hartwell or make me sorry that I left him. Some of the others—Cade's killing and the library shooting—weren't. They were to stop Cade and me from doing something."

"Good point. Still leaves me unconvinced on the storage unit. We're back where we started. With an unknown killer."

"One who's been following me. One who *had* to follow me to the storage unit and also follow me—follow us—to the library. Or at least know my work schedule well enough to know when to wait for me."

"Any thoughts yet on what Cade wanted to discuss with you?"

None. "I'd like to assume that it was something about China."

"Agreed."

"I wanted to go back and look through my journal again, but I couldn't find it."

"You just had it. Didn't Beyer give it back to you?"

I nodded. "But when I looked for it in your basement, I couldn't find it."

"You had it before you put everything into the storage unit."

"Yeah. And now it's missing."

"That seems significant. You should tell Beyer."

"And there've been things in the news lately. Nothing that seems to connect them to anything, not even to each other, except for the fact that they all have to do with China. Or they *might* have something to do with China."

"So, I wonder, does our killer know what you know, whatever it is Cade wanted to talk to you about? Or is he just afraid of what it might be?"

"Does it matter?" It really didn't. For all intents and purposes, the result was the same. For some reason, he needed me dead. "Is there anything else the FBI has learned? Any theories you can tell me now that you're off the case?"

It took a while before he answered. "There's quite a bit they know about the shooter, actually." He didn't say anything else.

"Since I'm the person he seems to want to kill, do you think you could share some of that information with me?"

"This shooter is taking you personally."

"I'm ahead of you there."

"In terms of *how* he tried to kill you. And what he did to the storage unit. If it really was him there."

"I guess I'd take it personally too if someone kept standing in the way of me achieving my goals."

"But we don't think he's a professional."

"On what basis?"

"It's more a question of default. If he were a professional, chances are he'd have taken you out by now."

"So you're thinking it's a good thing then?"

Leo shrugged. "I mean—yeah. It's a good thing."

"And how do they plan to catch him?"

"By watching him watch you and—"

"That's not really a plan."

"—and a little bit of luck."

▸▸ CHAPTER 45 ◂◂

My manager wasn't working, so I called her. She wasn't happy about Leo's plan. But she was even less happy at the prospect of more police cars and flashing lights. "I just want things to get back to normal."

"So do I."

"If I did agree, I won't be able to pay you for the time you don't work."

"I understand."

"We'll have to treat it as leave without pay."

"That's what I was going to propose."

"And to keep your insurance, you'll have to figure out how to add in extra shifts this pay period."

Of course I would.

"But I would rather you stay safe than get killed. Just keep me in the loop. Let me know when you can come back."

I thanked her and hung up.

I parked myself at the dining room table, texted all my afternoon students and told them I'd decided to Skype with them instead of meet in person. And then I started on my harder task. I called the parents of the students I would be tutoring tomorrow.

"The test is only a week away!"

"I know it is. But your son tested three points better on the last practice test he took." He'd actually tested four points better, but my policy was to underpromise and overdeliver. "He's been working really hard. And I'll still be able to tutor him. Just not in person."

"I really don't like this."

"I wish I didn't have to propose this solution."

"He doesn't have to meet you at the library. He could come to your place."

"I'm just afraid that what's going around over here might be catchy." And the people close to me might be targeted. Cade was. "I don't want to do anything that would jeopardize him right before test day."

"No. No. You're right."

When I finished the last of my parent calls, I called my dad.

A woman answered. "Hello?"

"Hi. Um." I held my phone out to make sure I'd dialed the right number. I had. "Is John there?"

"Johnny? Sure. Just a second." I heard her call my dad's name. Heard a male baritone answer.

"Whitney?"

"Hey, Dad."

"Um. Sorry. I was just in the kitchen. Frankie was closest to the phone."

Frankie. *The* Frankie? "That was *Frankie*?"

"Yeah."

"The Frankie from bowling?"

"Yeah."

"The one who knows the guy who knows—"

"Right. Yeah."

"Dad?"

"What?"

"I thought Frankie was a guy."

"Oh. Oh! No. Nope. She's a girl."

Neither of us said anything for a long moment. He broke the silence.

"So Frankie helped me move in."

"That's nice." I had a vision of an older woman arranging his kitchen cabinets and bringing him casseroles.

"We're together."

"Together how?"

"We're dating."

"Oh! Okay." The image of the casserole evaporated. "As in boyfriend-girlfriend?"

"Yeah. Uh-huh."

I heard Frankie's voice in the background. Heard my father's muffled reply. Then he came back on the line. "The thing is—this is serious."

"With Frankie?"

"Yeah. We've been friends for a long time, but we've been serious now since Christmas. That's why I'm doing the crypto thing. If we're going to have a future, then we need to build back that nest egg. You know what I mean?"

"Yes. Of course. Of course you do."

I heard Frankie's voice again.

"Just a second, sweetie." He must have put his hand over the phone. I heard him speak, but it was garbled. He came back on. "Frankie needs me to help her with something."

"Can I just ask you—once when I texted you, it didn't sound like you. There were emojis . . . ?"

He laughed. "That was Frankie. Sometimes she's closest to the phone. Reads me the texts. Texts back. She knows how to do all those phone things. Anyway. Gotta go. Talk to you soon?" He hung up.

Leo came over. Stood by my chair. "You okay?"

"No." I reached out and put an arm around his waist.

He bent and in one fluid motion, he had me sitting on his lap.

"It's my dad."

He kissed my forehead.

"I just— Right now? I need you not to kiss me."

"Okay. Can I still sit here?"

"Yes." I felt petty and ridiculous telling him what he could do in his own house while I was sitting on his lap. "I think my father has a girlfriend."

"Is that good or bad?"

"I don't know."

"Does he sound happy?"

"He sounds—" How did he sound? "He sounds like he has a life." One that I didn't have a part in.

"And how are you?"

"I'm not sure."

It's not that I begrudged him a relationship. It's that I didn't know how to picture him in one. He was living in a new place. He had a new person.

"Do you know her?"

"Who?"

"The girlfriend."

"No. It's a woman he knows from bowling. I'm trying to be a grown-up about this."

"Are you succeeding?"

"What I really want? I really want my mom back. But she's dead."

He said nothing.

"I know that's not possible and I know it's not fair to my father, but that's what I want. I know it's unreasonable. Because how can I go up to her and say, 'How dare you not be my mother!'?"

"Maybe you should go out to see him. You could meet her."

"When? After the killer stops chasing me? After my ex stops stalking me? After I pass the bar?" I paused. Then I said what was really bothering me. "They're talking about building a nest egg together."

"It's better than the alternative. At least they're thinking about the future."

"I used to be in that nest."

"You were in the other nest. The old nest."

"I want my nest back. Not to sit in it. Just to know it's there."

"It is there. Anytime you want to visit. In here." He tapped his chest.

We stayed there for a few minutes and then he got up, gently helping me to stand. He took my hand and tugged me toward the living room. "Let's watch a little baseball. Just for a few minutes."

I sat at one end of the couch. He sat at the other end.

We watched the game in silence for several innings.

"Leo?"

"Hmm?"

"If I lean up against you, I don't want it to mean anything."

"Got it. Proximity means nothing."

We watched the next inning that way.

Then he put a hand to my lap, palm up. "Want to hold my hand? No strings attached. I promise."

I put my hand in his.

He wrapped his warm fingers around my own. Squeezed. "It's going to be okay. And until then, you just hold on as long as you want to."

▶▶▶◀◀◀

The next day, Leo introduced me to Detective Melissa Sims before he left for whatever new case he'd been assigned to. She'd been given my case in his place. She told me the FBI had several agents in the area. Leo's house was located next to a county park, so it wouldn't have surprised me if some of the people out walking or kicking a soccer ball or batting a tennis ball around were actually agents. It made me feel better.

If I hadn't been hiding out, I would have called the morning a luxury. I studied until noon. Took a break for lunch.

My father called.

"Sorry about that misunderstanding. About Frankie. I should have told you about her sooner. I mean, I thought I did. But, you know."

"I know. I didn't get it. That's okay. It's just a lot. I've learned a lot I didn't know about you in the last few days."

"I really am sorry. But I'm your father. I felt like I needed to protect you from some of it. Why should you have to worry about all those medical bills? Or feel bad about my being forced to sell the house? Or file for bankruptcy? There's nothing you could have done."

"I know."

"So. I've been doing all the talking. What about you?"

What about me? What was there that I could even tell him? I'd kept so much from him that it was hardly fair to dump Hartwell and the shooting on him now. "I'm fine. Busy. Just studying for the bar."

Around two, Detective Sims texted me. She said the mail had been delivered and asked if I could come to the door for it.

She handed me a couple letters and a large bubble mailer.

It was from the Harpers.

I ripped it open.

There was a check inside with a refund of my rent and my deposit. And there was also another, smaller bubble package.

My name was on the front. There was no return address. I pulled on the tab to open it. Shook the contents onto the dining room table.

There was a folded piece of notepaper and some sort of computer part.

I opened the note.

It took me a moment to decipher the signature at the bottom. I heard myself gasp.

It was from Cade.

I read the letter with trembling hands. It changed everything.

▸▸ CHAPTER 46 ◂◂

I called Agent Beyer and I read the note to him over the phone.

Whitney—

Really don't want to involve you but I need to give this to someone I trust. Hold on to it for me. I'm working tech at the FDIC and I found something in that new secure system they installed. Turns out H's system has some foreign components. Something's going on. All signs point to China. I'll give you a call tomorrow once I figure some things out. I need some info about H.

"I'll come get it from you. You said it's a computer component?"

"That's what it looks like. It's made up of a couple parts. It's not very big, but it must be significant."

"I'll come over right now."

About half an hour later, he texted me that he'd arrived.

When he knocked, I let him in.

"Can I see it?"

I gestured to the table.

He read the note. Then he put on some gloves and examined the parts that Cade had included.

"I have no idea what this is, but if he thought it was important, then it must be." He put it into a bag and sealed it. "Any idea who H is?"

"I'm assuming it's Hartwell." Whenever we'd talked about him, that's how we referred to him. Since we were both working for his father, it seemed best. "He pitched his company's cybersecurity system as a secure, American-sourced alternative to those of his competitors. After the revelation of the CIA's ownership of an international encryption device company and with the fear of China's influence over Huawei's 5G network, everyone's wary of governmental and foreign interference. That's why HARTAN was awarded the contract at the FDIC."

Agent Beyer was nodding.

"But Cade had been planning to talk to me the day he died. I wonder why he didn't just bring that with him." I looked at the part Agent Beyer held in his hand. "He'd been in daily contact with you, hadn't he?"

"Yeah. He first contacted us after some recent hacks. We suspected there was a mole in the FDIC. That's why we set up the Joe account at the coffee shop. In case he was being followed. We communicated through mobile orders. Soy mocha, I didn't have any information to pass him. Brewed decaf, I did."

"And how would you pass that information?"

"We had a dead drop."

"Did he ever have information to pass to you?"

"Of course."

"How did he do it? How did you know there was something waiting for you?"

"If he grabbed a napkin on his way out, that was the signal."

"So you were there? At the Blue Dog?"

He nodded. "Yes. Every day."

"Then . . ." I was trying to reorder my thoughts. "Then you must have been one of our regulars."

"I was."

"Which one?" I had to have seen him. "Does Detective Baroni know this?"

He shrugged. "Why would it matter?"

"Because he's trying to eliminate suspects."

"The FDIC case wasn't his. It was ours. He didn't need to know about our operation."

"Then did you notice anyone acting strange the day Cade was killed?"

"No. If I had, I would have said so."

I gestured to Cade's note. "He said he needed someone he could trust. Why didn't he trust *you*?"

"He did."

"Then why didn't he leave that component for you at the dead drop?"

"I have no idea. Maybe he thought he was being watched. Or the dead drop was being watched. I don't know. We do know he wanted to talk to you. This has been about you all along. If I were you, I'd go back through that journal of yours and read it in light of Cade's note. Can you get it? We could do it now."

"I don't have it."

"Don't have what?"

"I don't have the journal. I haven't been able to find it since I emptied the storage unit."

"If you're saying it was stolen during the storage unit switch, I would have liked to know before now." Agent Beyer picked up the items Cade had sent and started toward the door. "If Hartwell Thorpe contacts you, please let me know."

▸▸▸◂◂◂

I told Leo about Cade's note when he came home that night for dinner.

"What was it? That part he sent?"

"I don't know. Some sort of computer component."

"Wow." He shook his head. "This puts everything in a different light."

"It must have been Hartwell all along. He must have killed Cade. And he must have tried to kill me too." I still couldn't picture it, but it was the only thing that made sense. "I just can't see Hartwell killing someone."

"He might have killed you if you'd stayed with him."

"I know. But domestic violence is specific. It's directed at controlling specific people."

"Cade wasn't a random person. He was someone who discovered something about HARTAN's technology. He was as big a threat to Thorpe as you were. If Cade found what he thought he had, then Thorpe killed someone who could have called into question the premise of his whole company."

"Then why did Cade need me?"

"What do you mean?"

"If he had that component, if it was some sort of smoking gun, then why did he need, so badly, to talk to me?" And what conversation had he been referencing in the voicemail he'd left? The only time I remember him mentioning Hartwell was when he was urging me to be cautious about our relationship. He'd made his thoughts about my ex very clear.

Leo shrugged.

"He could have just turned that part over to Agent Beyer. But he didn't. Why not?"

"He had to think you'd add to his evidence. You must know something about Hartwell that proved his point."

"If that component is evidence, if it's so damning that he wanted me to protect it, then whatever I mentioned to him must be even worse."

Leo reached out and stacked my empty plate on top of his. "Something else I want to understand: How did Hartwell know he'd been discovered?"

That's what I'd been wondering too.

After dinner, Leo was called away to work on something. "Hoping

I'll be home later tonight, but if not, you have Detective Sims's number. And there are agents around. If you need anything, just call her. Or call Beyer."

That evening as I was studying, I became aware of sounds coming from the sunroom. I turned away from my books, toward the room. Cocked an ear to the noise. Something was rustling around out there.

Mice? Or a squirrel?

Mrs. Harper said she had a squirrel come down her chimney once; she chased it all over the house. I hoped it wasn't a squirrel.

Whatever it was stopped.

But then it started again.

A door in the sunroom led into the fenced backyard and, from there, to the garage. Was Leo home?

"Leo?"

I got up from the dining room table and took a few steps into the living room so I could take a closer look. All I could see was a circle of streetlight that had puddled on the floor.

But something was in the sunroom. I could hear it.

"Hello?" If it was a critter, maybe my voice would scare it away.

There was a moment of silence. One of those moments when I could actually hear myself listening.

And then a figure emerged from the gloom and stood silhouetted between the light of the living room and the dark of the night beyond the sunroom's glass.

Not Leo.

▸▸ CHAPTER 47 ◂◂

I ran into the kitchen.

Footsteps pounded across the floor behind me.

I threw the switch for the kitchen light and then reached for the disposal.

Something buzzed and the house went dark.

In the sudden loss of light, my vision went blank for several seconds before it adjusted. But that didn't keep me from moving. I took two more steps to the back door. I flung it open and sprinted across the deck. "Help! FBI!"

I could still hear footsteps behind me.

Where to hide?

I raced toward the gate in the fence that enclosed the backyard. "Help! FBI!"

A light sliced through the night. It rested on my face for a moment. Then it veered off to the darkness behind me.

One voice. Then two. "He's gone around the other way."

A hand grabbed my elbow.

I shook it off. Recoiled.

"It's me. It's Detective Sims. It's just me. You're safe."

▸▸▸◂◂◂

Safe.

An hour later, I was sitting inside on the couch. Leo sat beside me, arm wrapped around my shoulders. But I couldn't stop shivering.

I turned to him, brought my knees up to my chest, and curled into a ball.

He pulled me close.

An agent was in the sunroom, investigating how the intruder had accessed the house. Several agents had spread out through the neighborhood, trying to see if they could track him down.

I was safe inside Leo's house. For now. But what about the next time he went to work? What about the next time I was alone?

I wasn't safe at Mrs. Harper's.

I wasn't safe at work.

I wasn't safe at the library.

And now I wasn't safe at Leo's house.

My phone rang.

I let it.

Leo's hold on me loosened. "You're not going to answer that?"

"It's my d-d-dad." Just this once, I would call him back later.

"Have you told him what's going on?"

I tried to shake my head, but my shivers wouldn't let me. "He doesn't need to worry about me." I clenched my jaw to keep my teeth from chattering. "He has enough to w-w-worry about."

"And you think that, what? You've been protecting him by not telling him the truth?"

I tried to shake my head. "K-k-keeping him from worrying."

"That's not your call."

I uncurled my legs, sat up, and tamed my shivers enough to answer. "Y-yes. It is."

The agent came out of the sunroom, several plastic bags in hand. "I'm done here."

Leo rose and walked him to the door, locking it behind him. Then he returned to the couch. And the conversation.

"How long have you been protecting him?"

"End of my freshman year." That's when my scholarships ended and I had to start taking out loans.

"So basically, you've been lying to him for . . . what? Ten years now?"

My shivers were gone. "I haven't lied to him. I just haven't told him the truth."

"So if you think about him, sitting at home, thinking of you, what do you think he's thinking? When he imagines a typical day for you, what do you think he sees?"

I knew exactly what he saw. I didn't answer.

"I'm betting his typical day for you doesn't include you working at the coffee shop or coaching high school students or shoveling all your money into paying off loans."

"It would break his heart if he knew any of that. It would kill him. He's so proud of me. He wanted more for me than he had."

"So basically, everything he thinks he knows about you is a lie."

"I know what I'm doing."

"But *he* doesn't know what you're doing. Essentially, he thinks you're the same person you were ten years ago."

I pressed into the corner of the couch, trying to buttress myself against his unexpected onslaught. "I don't want him to know who I am, okay? After I've passed the bar, after I land a job at one of those law firms in the city, that's when I'll catch him up and—"

"You mean that's when you'll just skip over the last ten years of your life."

"And what would I tell him? 'Guess what, Dad—know how you're so proud of me? For going to an Ivy? And then law school? Well, guess what I did with all that education? I buried myself in a mountain of debt and I'm working in a coffee shop and coaching kids and trying really hard not to get murdered. So yeah." I flashed two "rock on" signs. "Rock star."

"He'd be proud of you if you were living under a bridge. That's what my grandmother used to say about me."

"Well, you're a police detective! And with the way things are going, let's not jinx me, okay? Besides, it won't even matter. It will be like fast-forwarding to the good part. And then he'll be all caught up and he'll never have to know."

"All I'm seeing is that you're keeping people who love you best at arm's length at exactly the time when you need them the most."

"He needs me to be the person he thinks I am."

"What he needs is the truth."

"And how do you know?" I was practically yelling. "You don't know anything about this at all! So just—stop trying to tell me what to do."

"Listen. I'm sorry. You're right: I overstepped. I'm just making a suggestion. I'm not trying to force you to do anything."

He wasn't. I knew he wasn't. Because he was the exact opposite of Hartwell. I held the pillow up to my face. "I am screwed up, Leo. I am so messed up."

"Everyone is messed up."

"Not like I am. I can't even tell my father the truth about my life. I am a first-in-class student who wasn't smart enough to realize what all these degrees would cost. And I am a twenty-eight-year-old woman who thought I knew what love was. If I were you, I would just stay away."

"Well, here's the thing." He leaned close, put an elbow on the back of the couch, then reached over to pull the pillow away. "You're not me."

"I could get you killed."

"Or maybe even fired."

I felt myself frown.

"It was a joke."

"I'm not funny."

"But you are fierce."

I voiced my deepest fear. "What if I don't get to be saved?"

"Is that a question? Or an answer?"

I couldn't tell.

"If it's an answer, then I don't think you understand the question." He kissed me and then he enfolded me in his arms.

Maybe Leo was right. Maybe it was time to tell my dad the truth. I was an adult. I shouldn't have to hide it from him anymore. I picked up my phone and called him.

"Whitney! I'm so glad you called."

"I've been wanting to talk to you."

"This is perfect timing. I just asked Frankie to marry me."

Um, what?

"You still there?"

"Yes. Wow." What was I supposed to say? "Did she say yes?"

"Yes. Yeah. She said yes."

Did I hear beer bottles clinking in the background? "Congratulations, Dad. I'm really happy for you."

"Thanks. But what was it you wanted to say?"

"What?"

"You said you'd been wanting to talk to me."

"Oh. Yes. Just wanted to hear your voice. That's all."

"Is everything okay?"

"Fine. Everything's fine."

After I hung up, Leo took my phone from me and then took my hand.

"I couldn't tell him. He just got engaged to his girlfriend. There's really nothing to say."

I sat there on the couch for a long time with my head on Leo's shoulder. We stared into the fireplace where a fire should have been.

▶▶▶◀◀◀

Eventually, when the agents were done outside, Leo woke me up. Together, we went upstairs. He reached inside my room and turned on the light for me.

When he turned to leave, I grabbed his sleeve. "Sleep with me."

He came back. Squatted in front of me. Captured a stray lock of hair and tucked it behind my ear. "I don't think you're in any condition to make a decision like that."

"Just sleep. That's all. Please."

He cupped the back of my head. Pressed his forehead to mine. And then, shaking his head, he stood and slid his shoes off. "Just for the record? I don't think this is a good idea."

"Please, Leo." I lifted the covers and scooted so I could feel the wall at my back.

He slid in. After a moment I threw an arm around his waist.

He caught my hand and tugged it up toward his chest. For a long time, I lay there in the dark, listening. And then I let my cheek fall forward to the warm skin of his back and I slept.

▸▸ CHAPTER 48 ◂◂

The next morning, I gave Mrs. Harper a call to see how she was doing.

"Whitney Garrison!" she sighed. "I have to be truthful. Loudoun County isn't Arlington. But I'm fine."

She told me about the trials of life in a cast. And how much she missed the club. And Heidelberg Pastry Shoppe.

"And how about you? Did you get that package?"

"Yes. Thank you so much for sending it."

After chatting for a few more minutes, she said good-bye. "You take care of yourself, Whitney."

I was trying.

As I was getting set up to study, I got an email from one of my professors passing along a job opportunity. One of the big tech firms had a philanthropic arm that was looking to set up a cryptocurrency model that could be used to send aid to developing countries.

I thought of you.

Use me as a reference.

The big tech firms were all trying to figure out a way into cryptocurrencies. They all wanted to try to harness the power of the blockchain. But in many ways, they were late to the game. It was nice of her to think of me though. I visited their career portal. Shot them a copy of my résumé. What could it hurt?

As I got out my study guide, Leo called.

"I checked in with the team, just to see what they could tell me. Rumor is Hartwell does have an alibi for the storage unit."

"Really?" How could that be?

"That's what they say."

"An honest-to-goodness alibi?"

"Beyer checked it out."

"Then who switched my unit? And who took my journal? I'm confused. All the evidence points toward Hartwell."

"When there's a conflict between what you want to be true and what's actually true? You have to go with what can be proved."

"I know. I just . . . Now I don't know what to think."

After studying for a while, I made a peanut butter sandwich for lunch. Reviewed the topic of secured transactions as I ate.

A news alert pinged my phone.

Housing Market Tips into Slump in FL, TX, CA, NYC, MA.

Florida, Texas, and California?

That group of states sounded familiar. I clicked through to the article. It was a standard news report citing statistics from the current year as contrasted with the year before along with the five-year trend in the housing market. There was a rapidly growing glut of prestigious properties for sale in the major cities in the US. What had begun as a blip in the Northeast had turned into a trend across the country.

Developers overbuilt when foreigners like the Chinese had been investing in real estate. But since we'd become less-than-reliable trading partners and friends, the US had become a less desirable place to live. And people from some of the foreign countries who had previously invested could no longer obtain visas to enter the country. In Boston in particular, there had been a sharp uptick in real estate coming on the market.

And that brought to mind a long-ago conversation. Who had been speaking? I wished I could remember.

"*. . . My sister's a real estate agent up in Boston. Says it's crazy up* *there. Chinese nationals, all those foreign students, showing up at her office, dropping off their keys. Signing their power of attorney over to her so she can handle the sales. It's nuts. They're leaving everything! TVs, stereo systems. Those fancy exercise bikes. Cars in the garage."*

"What's she supposed to do with all that?"

"Whatever she wants, I guess. Some pretty hot properties are on the market. Lots to choose from. She wants me to come up and take a look at a couple."

I'd stuck my head into Congressman Thorpe's office to drop off a file. When the congressman waved me off, I turned around and went back out. I ran into Cade at lunch. Told him I had a real estate tip—we were always talking about what we'd do after we finally made our millions. So I told him there was a buyers' market up in Boston. And then, if I remembered right, I contrasted the life of the average starving American graduate student and the apparently fabulous life of the average Chinese graduate student.

"Wonder why they're leaving all of a sudden like that?" he'd asked.

I remember thinking *Who cares?* and then wondering who would be lucky enough to get a hold of what they'd left behind.

But Cade had asked the million-dollar question. *Why were they leaving all of a sudden like that?*

Could be that China wanted tighter control over the students they sent overseas. Could be they were worried those students might be turning into dissidents. But they'd recalled their students in such big numbers that at least one real estate agent had taken notice.

If China had sent graduate students to America to do a job—to see what they could learn from us and about us—then it stood to reason that they would pull them back when they had all the information they needed. When there was no more left to learn and nothing more for them to do.

What did Boston have?

Harvard, MIT, Northeastern, Boston College, Tufts, and several dozen other universities.

It was difficult for me to believe there was nothing more for any of those students to learn at those schools. So why was it more advantageous for them to be back in China than it was for them to be here?

As I thought about that, everything finally clicked.

Leo had told me I should focus on the things I could do, not the things I couldn't.

I couldn't remember a face.

I'd been looking over my shoulder for a killer and I'd focused on not being able to recognize his face.

I should have been looking instead for a pattern.

I was excellent at putting together an argument, at discerning patterns. I lived my life by patterns. The way people wore their hair. The way they walked. The way they talked. It was the details that counted.

Details.

Details created patterns.

I'd been overlooking some details, but now I'd figured out the pattern.

Cade had discovered something at the FDIC.

The FDIC was meant to ensure the stability of the American economy. So I had to assume China was making a play to destabilize it.

The 2010 hack gave China access to data on millions of people. They could use it to access existing accounts. They could also use it to create new, fake accounts in the name of actual American citizens.

China had also hacked the verification mechanisms for the new stablecoin launch. The system was supposed to verify that all the users of the system had FDIC-backed accounts. They could also make the system accept accounts that wouldn't have normally been backed by the FDIC. There could be thousands of accounts now in FDIC-backed banks that belonged not to American citizens but to Chinese citizens. Or even to the Chinese government, hiding behind proxies.

But that wasn't, perhaps, the worst scenario. Our economy worked because people trusted that when they deposited money into a bank account, it would be there, no matter what. If China controlled access to those accounts, they could do anything.

They could drain them.

They could block access to them.

Even worse than that, by establishing and funding fake accounts, if the economy did tip into recession, they could push it into depression by using all of those accounts to overreact to the markets.

They could also use those fake accounts to route money to politicians in exchange for votes to weaken our banking laws. I thought about all of the congressmen who had inexplicably changed their votes on the financial systems bill in between the committee vote and the House floor. Maybe China had already used those accounts to route money to politicians.

They had already isolated us in the world markets. If they decided to dump all the government debt they owned, the standard assumption was that we could lean on our allies to help us by buying it up. That was the assumption I'd used in my project for Congressman Thorpe.

But we didn't have many friends anymore.

Due to the trade wars, due to the fact that we had unceremoniously pulled out of most of the major international treaties and alliances, no one owed us any favors. No nation with the reserves to do so would feel compelled to rescue us.

So if our economy tanked, what nation wouldn't question why the dollar was still the world's reserve currency? Why should the dollar be given that honor when the nation's citizens didn't seem to trust their own country? Why should the dollar be given that honor when that nation had encouraged bad behavior on the world's stage? When that nation increasingly demonstrated that it stood for nothing but its own self-interests?

Even more—and this is what I had missed—why should *any* nation's currency be used as the reserve? Didn't that imply favoritism?

If the United States of America could fall prey to misguided policies and economic forces, then couldn't any country?

How could China completely destroy our economy?

By using market chaos as an opportunity to offer up a new cryptocurrency as the solution to all of the world's problems as the world's reserve currency. It was a genius move. Why should the world's reserve currency be shackled to any one nation's interests? Why shouldn't it be so stable that it wouldn't be subject to market downturns, global pandemics, or regional conflicts? If China could offer a new cryptocurrency and have it accepted as the reserve, then that would be a coup.

A generation ago, no one would have trusted China with a cryptocurrency. Now? After they'd spent billions on public aid projects in Africa? After they'd become the biggest trading partner in Asia? They had a solid UN voting bloc and global goodwill on their side.

As I'd told my interviewer at the law firm, they could set the rules. All of them. Or change them at any time.

And Cade had implicated HARTAN in a possible new attempt to hack the FDIC's systems.

It wasn't difficult for hardware and software developers to leave back doors in their products that would allow hackers to slip into systems from the outside. Cade's find seemed to support that. Maybe that's why HARTAN swapped American parts for Chinese during the manufacturing or installation process.

The thing I didn't understand was why. Why had Hartwell done it? The value of HARTAN was that they didn't have to rely on Chinese parts.

In fact, when he'd first started his company, no one believed he could do it. China supplied most of the rare earth minerals required for advanced technology. They had cheap labor. They had less restrictive environmental laws. The idea that HARTAN could produce the same components at a competitive price was laughable. The company had almost gone under.

At the eleventh hour, an angel investor had supplied the boost that was needed. And then he'd won the federal contract, and now he was Wall Street's darling.

The killer had to be Hartwell. He'd killed Cade to keep him from reporting what he'd found.

I called Leo.

▶▶▶◀◀◀

"So it's an attempt at world domination by China? Is that what you're saying?"

"Yes."

"That's not breaking news."

"I think it is. I think all the pieces are in place now."

"Okay." He paused for a moment. "Let's say they are. Let's assume that they're going to do everything you just told me. So what?"

So what? "Do you not understand? Economy tanks. Country in chaos. China becomes the dominant world power."

"But what does that have to do with the hacks back in 2010?"

Had he not been listening? "That's when it all started. That's when they got access to—"

"No. I get all that. But what does that computer part Cade gave you, what does HARTAN have to do with that hack ten years ago?"

"It's stepping-stones. They did that first hack, then they hack something else. They put all that information together. It's an accumulation of actions over time."

"Yes. Right. But didn't Beyer say Cade discovered a mole?"

"Yeah."

"The implication was the mole had been there from the beginning. That can't be Hartwell."

No. It couldn't.

"So while I'm happy Beyer can nail your ex for something and throw him in jail, I don't think Thorpe is the whole ball game. We're still missing something."

"In the big scheme of things, if our economy is about to be pushed over the edge, is whatever we're missing really so important?"

"I'm going to make a few calls, okay? See if I can get someone to follow up on this. I'll get back to you."

He hung up before I could say anything else.

▸▸ CHAPTER 49 ◂◂

I called Agent Beyer and told him what I remembered. He joined me at Leo's house an hour later. "Sorry for the delay," he said as he came through the door. "There were some things I needed to set up."

I sat down at the dining room table.

He put a hand to the table as he stood in front of it. "You remember the conversation. Are you sure?"

"I'm positive."

He told me we might as well go downtown to the agency.

I scooped up my backpack. If I had to be there for a while, at least I could study. I told him about my conversation with Cade as he drove.

"*That's* what Cade wanted to talk to you about? Real estate in Boston? Are you sure?" He picked up a thermal cup from the holder in the console between us and took a sip.

"I'm positive."

"Why? I don't get it."

I led him through my reasoning, step by step.

"So what are you saying?"

"I'm saying that China is getting ready to tank our economy. Sooner rather than later."

"You got to that from some Chinese students up in Boston leaving town in a hurry?"

"I got that from a lot of things."

"And you expect me to take that to my boss?"

I unzipped my backpack, pulled a note card from my stack, and wrote down a list of names. Handed it to him.

He took it, held it up above his steering wheel so he could see it. "What's this?"

"These congressmen should be investigated for accepting foreign campaign money. And I'm sure they have counterparts over in the Senate who should be investigated too."

"Why? I can't just request an investigation like this without any evidence."

"These are all representatives who sit on the Financial Services Committee and supported a bill in committee and then voted against it once it reached the floor. If you look into their finances, I'm sure you'll find illegal contributions routed through American bank accounts that are actually owned and funded by China."

"That's not possible. Foreign campaign donations are illegal."

"The Chinese hacked the FDIC back in 2010 and then hacked the verification system for the new stablecoin. It gave them access to Americans' accounts as well as the ability to create new ones."

He bent the index card and deposited it into one of the cup holders. "Okay. So what about that conversation was so important to Cade?"

"The fact that the Chinese are pulling their people out of the US. Something's going to happen. Soon. They want their people out of our country when it all falls apart."

"And you expect me to connect point A to point B through points F, G, and Q?"

"You asked me to call you if I remembered the conversation. I have."

"Fair enough." He pulled out his phone. As we sat in traffic on the interstate near the Pentagon, he opened it. Thumbed a message. "In that note he wrote to you, though, he wanted to talk to you about your ex. The conversation you just told me about had nothing to do with Mr. Thorpe."

I bit my lip. I knew it didn't. That's what had bothered Leo too.

"I don't know what else to tell you. Except HARTAN is Hartwell's company. China hacked the FDIC back in 2010 and now they're apparently hacking the security system put in place to ensure it's never hacked again."

"You never spoke with Cade about your ex?"

"We did. He didn't like Hartwell."

"I can see why. Did Mr. Thorpe ever talk to you about his business?"

"Not in any detail. Although he loved to repeat the legend that had built up around it."

The interstate was officially jammed. We could see the flashing lights of a police car up ahead. Agent Beyer maneuvered into the left lane as we approached the Fourteenth Street Bridge. "What legend is that?"

"He couldn't get any backers at first. Nobody believed in him enough to invest. They believed in the idea, but everybody, all the big tech companies, were trying to do the same thing. So he put his own money into the company. Took out loans. He reached a point where he thought he'd have to give up, and then an angel investor appeared. That's when everything turned around for him. He got his investor. Developed, then secured, his supply chain. Within a year he was bidding on the contract with the FDIC. A year after that, he was installing the system and taking the company public."

"Did you and Cade ever talk about that?"

"He joked around about it." In a bitter sort of way. *What are the chances*, he'd say, *of every single thing lining up so you can take your company from zero dollars to a record-breaking public offering on Wall Street in under two years? And why can't I get a chance like that! Perfect guy with the perfect company. No wonder he got the perfect girl.* It made things a little awkward. I could ignore how I knew Cade felt about me until he said things like that. When he did, I changed the subject. Maybe that's why we'd talked so much about economics.

We drove north on the parkway with the river on our right. Joggers in bright running shorts and tank tops crowded the paths. Motorboats shredded the Potomac, leaving white stripes of wake behind them. My thoughts turned back to Cade. He'd been so interested in the concept of angel investors. *"You mean they just drop money into your lap? Out of the clear blue sky?"*

Basically? "Yeah."

"You mean there's people out there who just look for ways to give other folks a hand? In the form of giant investments?"

"Yeah. I mean, they're looking to make a return on that investment. There are detailed agreements. Usually you give them part ownership in the company and guarantee them a percentage of the profits."

"How do you find them? I mean, if someone had this really great idea for a hot sauce that's kind of a cross between Tabasco and sriracha, for instance, and everybody who's ever tried it really likes it, how do you get an angel investor interested?"

"I have no idea."

"How did Hartwell find his?"

"I don't know. Some connection through his dad, I think."

I heard myself gasp.

Agent Beyer jerked his head in my direction, which caused him to swerve.

"Sorry," I said.

"You okay?"

"I figured it out." I told him what I'd just remembered. "I'm almost positive that's what Cade wanted to talk to me about. It connects everything. Hartwell's angel investor came through his father. Congressman Thorpe is one of the names on the list I gave you. I think his father's already been influenced by the Chinese."

"So make it easy for me. Just give it to me straight. What's the connection?"

"China is the angel investor. I think the money that saved Hartwell and his company is Chinese. I'll bet they have a controlling interest in the company."

"I was really hoping you had some kind of smoking gun."

"I do. Do you think his company could keep their security clearances if the government knew it was owned by the Chinese? Do you think the contract would have been awarded to HARTAN if they knew the parts would come from China? That's the missing piece. It's not that Hartwell used Chinese components. I think it's that he was *forced* to use them. I think he's been compromised. And so has his company."

"Well. That's just perfect."

"If by perfect you mean treasonous."

"It provides a context for Cade's death. If people wonder why, now they'll know."

As we passed Rosslyn, Agent Beyer pulled his phone out. Made a call. Asked for Hartwell to be brought in. When he was done, he dropped it into the cup holder in the center console.

Our view across the river was now blocked by trees. We'd left the city behind for a forest.

The car slowed noticeably. Agent Beyer signaled and then pulled into the right lane. "I've got a warning light on the engine. Just came on. I'm going to look for someplace to pull over. You want to open the glove box for me? Pull out the manual? Find the warning lights section?"

I pulled it out. Flipped it open.

"What's the one for engine temperature?"

I scanned the chart. "The thermometer that looks like it's floating?"

He sighed. "That's the one. What does it say to do?"

"Pull over immediately and wait for the engine to cool down."

He pulled off at Fort Marcy. It was one of myriad historical sites in the region marked with signs to invite the curious. As we left the parkway, the road climbed a hill. We followed it to the right and then disappeared from civilization. He pulled into the long, narrow parking lot. It was ringed by tufts of grasses and a profusion of weeds. He stopped the car at the very end.

We were surrounded by trees. The parking was situated on a sort of plateau. On the rise above us, a trail meandered up into the woods. Just in front of us was the sign for a trailhead that led down, away from us, into the forest. Agent Beyer turned off the engine. "I need to take a look under the hood."

There weren't any other cars. The park was deserted.

"Maybe one of the caps came loose. Have I got some gloves in there?" He pointed to the glove box.

I opened it back up. Rummaged around. He had a couple pens and a flashlight rattling around. No gloves.

He opened the door. Bent down over the seat. "I always pop the hood when I want the gas and the gas when I want the hood." A moment later the hood released. "Can you look in that center console? Maybe that's where I put them."

He put a foot to the ground.

I found a pair of sterile gloves. They wouldn't do anything to protect him from heat, but they might keep his fingers from getting greasy. I handed them to him.

He went out and raised the hood.

As he tinkered around, he started talking to himself.

The car got hot fast. Sweat was forming on the agent's cup. The scent of green tea began to permeate the air.

Green tea.

Iced green tea.

There were only two people I knew who drank their green tea iced. Mustache Man and Agent Beyer.

Mustache Man was a suspect in the case.

Agent Beyer had admitted he was a regular at the Blue Dog.

Leo's words came back to me. *Dang—a handlebar mustache. Have to hand it to the guy. Cheesy, but effective. Pull off the mustache, throw it away, and you're a totally different man.*

Why wouldn't Agent Beyer have told the team—told Leo—that he was the man with the mustache? *Because Mustache Man was the killer.*

Agent Beyer was the killer.

Agent Beyer had killed Cade.

And now, I was alone with him in a deserted park.

I opened the door a crack. His words became clear.

"I can't trust you to do anything, can I? It's not about her—didn't I tell you that?"

What was he talking about?

"What I don't understand is why you had to take that journal. Why you had to mess around with that storage unit in the first place! You'd better hope no one finds out that I had to make up your alibi."

I felt my mouth drop open. And then I heard another voice.

"You know what happened when she pressed charges after the library? They put me in jail. I spent the night there! You can't do that to someone and get away with it. Besides, there might have been something about me in that book. She wrote down everything!"

Was that—? Agent Beyer slammed the hood down and I was able to see through the windshield again.

Hartwell was standing there right beside him.

▶▶ CHAPTER 50 ◀◀

I pushed the door open, intending to flee.

But Hartwell was quicker than I was.

He made a grab for me.

“No!” I retreated from him. Releasing my seat belt, I moved toward the driver’s seat and grabbed hold of the steering wheel.

Hartwell caught hold of my ankle.

I kicked out at him with my other foot as I fumbled for the door on the driver’s side.

But Agent Beyer opened the door and then just stood there, blocking my exit.

Hartwell dragged me back across the front seat and grabbed my arm as he pulled me out. He slapped me.

I raised my forearm to protect myself.

“Thanks to you, thanks to the restraining order, I’ll be losing my security clearance!”

He gave me a shove, slamming me against the car. “The owner of the FDIC’s contractor for cybersecurity can’t not have a security clearance! Because how am I going to explain that?”

I ricocheted off the car and stumbled. Pitched forward. “Then maybe you shouldn’t have hit me!”

He kicked me in the ribs as I fell to the pavement.

My breath left me as I jackknifed on the ground in pain.

"I knew Cade was trouble. I saw you two talking at the coffee shop. We saw our system had been tampered with. The thing is? I can't afford an investigation. Literally. If the contract gets canceled, if Wall Street hears about any of this, HARTAN's stock tanks. If the bottom falls out, I can't pay the Chinese back. If I can't pay the Chinese back, then they'll find some way to tell the feds everything." He swore. Ran his hands through his hair, paced down to the end of the car.

Tears slipped down my cheeks. I pushed to my knees as I watched Hartwell. He paused for a moment as he reached the trunk. Then he pivoted and started back toward me.

I dropped back to the pavement. Curled into a ball.

"Hey—!" It was Agent Beyer.

He pushed Hartwell away. And then he knelt beside me.

He put a hand to my back.

"I'm sorry. I don't condone this sort of thing. If I could have left you out of this, I would have."

Hartwell protested. "This isn't your business, Beyer."

Hartwell tried to charge him, but the agent grabbed him by the arm. He yanked him forward, off balance, and then pulled a gun from his waistband and cracked him on the side of the head with the butt.

It felled Hartwell in his tracks.

Seizing the opportunity, I pushed to my feet. If I could make it into the forest, down one of the trails, maybe I could hide. Holding on to my side, I made it three steps. Four. Then I heard the report of a pistol as a bullet nicked the ground in front of me.

I froze.

Lifted trembling hands.

"Turn around."

I turned. Slowly, carefully.

"Let's do this the easy way, okay?"

I said nothing.

He raised the gun.

I spread my hands wider. "Okay."

I took an experimental breath, trying to see how much damage that kick to my ribs had done. A lot.

I lowered a hand to my cheek. Felt the contours of a hand-shaped welt.

"He got you good."

Hartwell was still sprawled on the ground at Beyer's feet. "Is he— Did you— Is he dead?"

"No. But he will be soon."

Beyer prodded him with his foot.

No response.

"Might have been better if I hadn't hit him so hard, but things happen. Want to give him a kick?"

"What?"

"Might make you feel better."

"I don't think—"

"Right here." He pointed out Hartwell's side with his toe.

I shook my head.

"Turnabout is fair play."

I shook my head again and then winced at the movement.

"Think it makes any difference? Scum like him? Go ahead."

"No."

"Then I'm going to need you to do some work. You're a smart girl. You wouldn't leave a body lying around in the open like this."

What was he talking about?

"Way I see it, you're going to want to drag him to that ditch down there." He nodded somewhere out behind me into the trees.

"I—I can't."

He cocked the gun. "It's amazing the things you find you can do when you don't have a choice."

I glanced behind me. The ditch was about ten feet away. I bent.

Gasped from the pain in my ribs.

"I'd hurry if I were you."

I picked up Hartwell's hand. Tugged on it.

It slipped from my grasp.

"You're going to have to put your back into it."

I raised my head and looked over at him.

He was leaning against the hood of his car, still pointing his gun at me.

I reached out with both hands and took hold of Hartwell's forearms. I planted my feet and leaned back with everything I had. Cried out in pain. I tried my best but I only moved him about a foot. I had to drop his arms and pause for a moment, hands on my knees, to catch my breath.

A bullet clipped the grass beside me.

I jumped.

"I need you to take this seriously."

I took up Hartwell's arms again and gave another tug. And then another. I got him past the fringe of weeds. My hands slipped. I dug my fingers into his arms and tugged again. My breath was ragged, my pain acute. As I tugged again, I tripped and fell, jarring my ribs on the way down.

Fear had seized my throat, but as I gasped again in pain, a sob broke free.

"I need you to work faster."

I rolled to my knees and took up his arms to try again.

"You'll do better if you stand up."

"If you want him down there so badly, then you do it!"

He cocked his gun.

"Why are you doing this?" The words tore from my throat on the heels of a sob.

"Because I have to. He was too stupid and you were making too many connections." He went silent as he watched me for a moment. "Just a suggestion: maybe you could roll him."

"What?"

"Roll him. Might be easier."

It should have been. I tried. But his arms kept flying out, stopping the momentum.

I took off my cardigan, threaded it underneath him, and tied it in a knot. Rolling got him to the edge of the ditch much faster. With one last push, he rolled down the slope. When I got up and turned around to leave, I saw that Beyer was right behind me.

He gestured down into the ditch with his gun. "You too."

▸▸ CHAPTER 51 ◂◂

After I gingerly slid into the ditch, he scrambled down beside me. Then he reached out around my ribcage and pulled me to his side.

I gasped with pain.

He spoke into my ear as he grabbed my arm. "I just need to borrow your hand for a minute." I tried to pull it from his grasp, but he slid behind me, securing one arm to my side. Then he fit the fingers of the other around the gun. He pressed them to the stock. Released them, regripped my fingers around the stock again, and pressed.

"What are you doing?"

"It's not what I'm doing. It's what you're doing. You're getting ready to shoot your ex-boyfriend."

I twisted, trying to free myself from his embrace.

He held me fast.

"But this is your gun. They'll know it wasn't me."

"I've already reported it missing."

"They'll figure it out."

"I don't think so. It's going to look like a murder-suicide."

"I'm not murdering anyone. And I'm not committing suicide."

"They'll see the bruises on your arm. They'll see the lump on his head. The gun will have his hair on it. Maybe some of his scalp if I'm lucky. And they'll see your fingerprints all over the place. The trail you made as you dragged him to the ditch. No one will doubt what happened here."

"They'll find your fingerprints too."

"That's to be expected. It's my gun. But you stole it. And you stole my car. I could have arranged this either way. Didn't matter to me. But I figure this way, in the end? You get even. Everyone will think you killed him before you killed yourself. And don't worry, I'll make sure everyone knows you had a restraining order. You're going to be a very sympathetic victim of domestic violence."

"I won't do it." I tried to bend, tried to slip away.

He held me fast. "It's the least you owe me. I was all set to poke around for Cade's killer for a while and then declare it unsolvable." He released me, but as he stepped away, he kept his gun trained on me. "And then you put two and two together. So give me your shoe."

"What?"

"Your sneaker. Just take it off."

"My shoe?" I couldn't understand what he was asking, but he was the one with the gun. I used the heel of my other foot to lever it off.

He eased the front of his foot into it and then used my shoe to kick Hartwell in the ribs.

Hartwell groaned.

"I think he should be awake to see this, don't you? So he can live the full experience before he dies?"

"You killed Cade, didn't you?"

He didn't answer, but he didn't have to. He was planning to kill Hartwell and me too. There was only one reason for him to do that. "You're the mole."

He gave Hartwell another kick.

"Did you do it for money?"

He scoffed. "Money? No. I did it for the best of reasons. I did it for love. I fell in love with a Chinese national. She asked me to overlook something that I should have reported. It wasn't anything significant. And I was in love with her so I did it. I didn't even feel bad about it. But that one thing led to a second thing. And then a third thing."

"You're a traitor."

"In a sense. But she wasn't asking me to do those things because she wanted to compromise me. It's because someone had already compromised her. Her family was back in China. If she hadn't been able to get me to do those things for her, then the Chinese would have hurt them. She loved them. I loved her."

"It's treason."

"Maybe to you. It's not that I hate my country. It's that I loved her. I love her. That's my whole argument. The problem isn't that I'm a bad guy, Ms. Garrison. It's that I'm such a good one."

"You're going to be caught. They'll figure it out."

"Maybe. But I'm not the only one. That's the genius of the Chinese. That's what's going on here. There's me. There's Hartwell. And there are others. Multiple actors, all playing their roles for their own reasons, all disconnected from one another. Sometimes at night, I lie awake and wonder just how many of us there are."

My heart stuttered.

He gave Hartwell one more vicious kick.

Hartwell writhed on the ground and then came to, swearing.

"Watch your mouth. There's a lady present." He gestured with his gun. "Your turn."

"My turn to what?"

"To do whatever you want. Punch him. Kick him. Bite him. I don't care."

Hartwell tried to push to his feet. He swayed for a moment and then gave up, sinking to his knees.

I shook my head. Regretted it instantly when it began to throb. "No."

"I'd think it would give you a sense of closure."

"I'm not like that."

"We're all like that." He used my shoe to kick Hartwell. "Sure you don't want to try?"

I did. I *did* want to try. I *did* want to see what it would feel like to be the one punching Hartwell, kicking him, instead of him kicking me.

"Just once?"

I shook my head, both tempted and repulsed by the possibility.

"Your loss." He took my hand and fit it to the stock of the gun again. Aimed it at Hartwell.

Hartwell protested. Raised a hand as if to stop us. "What are you doing?"

Agent Beyer responded. "What somebody should have done to you long ago. You're not a good person."

"Whitney—wait! Please!" Hartwell reached out, pleading, with both hands. "I swear I'll never follow you. I'll never contact you. I'll never touch you again. I swear it. I *swear it*! I'll do anything. Just tell me what to do."

My skin crawled. The hair at the back of my neck stood on end. I couldn't control my trembling.

"I'm sorry! I'm so, so sorry! Just-just-just—"

I clenched my jaw. Tried to make the trembling stop. "Just let him go." I spoke the words through my teeth.

"Can't."

"Whitney! *Help me!*"

I squeezed my eyes shut. I just wanted it all to stop.

Hartwell was crying. "Do you want money? Is that what you want, Beyer? My father will pay you. He'll pay you whatever you want."

"Shut up!"

The crack of a shot rang out as the agent's hands squeezed around mine.

▶▶ CHAPTER 52 ◀◀

The agent released the gun and collapsed behind me.

The sudden freedom caused me to stumble forward and I dropped the gun.

Hartwell rolled up into a ball and lay there shrieking.

And then people appeared like ghosts from the woods. Down from the trail above us. Up from the trees below us.

And all I could do was nothing.

Absolutely nothing.

Leo came up to me. He took me by the elbow and turned me away from the agent.

I pointed to the gun that was on the ground. Tried to tell him what had happened, but no words came out of my mouth. And no breath came out of my lungs.

My vision narrowed, turning everything gray and fuzzy.

I put my hands to my knees, then bent and lowered my head between them.

Vomited.

Leo put a hand to the back of my neck, then twisted to shelter me, fitting his body to mine.

I turned into him. Held on to him as my body convulsed in one long, wrenching sob.

He took me by the hand, led me to a low earthen wall, and had me sit down. He sat with me, held my hand, while I told one of the FBI agents what had happened.

I told them what I'd figured out and what I knew of Agent Beyer's involvement. I told them where to find the index card with names I'd written down and why they needed to start asking questions.

Quickly.

While there was still time.

An ambulance came.

They treated me.

They treated Hartwell before they put him into a squad car and took him away. And then they put Agent Beyer on a stretcher. Just like Cade, he'd died with a hole in his head.

One of the other police officers drove Leo and me home. Leo sat with me in the back seat.

"I thought he was going to make me pull the trigger. I really did." I shivered in spite of the heat.

Leo took hold of my hand. Guided the ice pack I was holding back to the welt on my cheek.

"I don't know how he was planning on getting away with all of it. How did he think he wouldn't be suspected?" I asked.

"Everyone on the team knew your story. Knowing the background of your relationship with Hartwell, he probably thought no one would be suspicious of a murder-suicide. And when you don't have suspicions, you don't look for alternate explanations."

"But how was he going to get away? Was he going to hike out?"

"He'd rented a car. He'd parked down at the end of one of the trails."

I looked out the window as the car turned off the parkway and onto Arlington Boulevard, climbing the hill from Rosslyn to Courthouse. "What about Hartwell?"

"He won't be bothering you anymore. Espionage comes with a pretty big jail sentence."

"What if he tries to blame it on me? What if he tries to say I was going to shoot him?"

"You'd have all of us as witnesses."

I turned to him. "How did you find me?"

"What you said at the house about stepping-stones gave me an idea. It seemed like Cade was made to believe the mole was left over from the 2010 hacks. But what if the mole hadn't been in the agency before that? What if he'd come on the scene *during* the hacks? I asked some questions about the FBI investigation back then. Got confirmation that Beyer was the one who signed off on everything. He was the one who worked with the FDIC to ensure that the suggested countermeasures were actually taken. And after that case, he got called in to a lot more hacking cases. The FDIC had seven big hacks in 2015 and 2016. He was given those investigations too."

"But we already knew that. We knew he led that first investigation. And didn't some commercial company analyze it too?"

"They did. But who verifies the verifiers? No one. We just accept what they say without proof that it's true. I called Detective Sims, but she said you'd already left with him. I may have officially been off your team, but I never really left. I could still track your phone. I saw when you headed toward the parkway. Thought that seemed odd. I wasn't that far away, so I decided to follow you."

"You were there the whole time."

"Right behind you."

I hadn't been alone.

Through all of that, I had never been alone.

▸▸▸◂◂◂

It didn't take long for the story to explode. Someone must have helped reporters find it because before the afternoon was over, it blew up in the media.

That evening, Congressman Thorpe came over to Leo's house. He tried to tell me that there must have been a misunderstanding. That his son couldn't have done the things he was being accused of.

I pointed to my blackened eye.

Showed him my arm.

I even pulled up my shirt so he could see my ribs. As he left Leo's house, one of the FBI agents pulled him aside to talk.

It didn't surprise me. His name was on my list.

Even out on the West Coast, my father heard the news. It made all the national media outlets. The story had everything: politics, corruption, espionage, hacking. It even had a bonus villain. And since that person was a congressman's son, it was a big deal.

My father called me that evening. "Are you okay? Why didn't you tell me any of this?"

"I didn't want you to worry."

"I would have wanted to know. I would have gladly worried!"

"You couldn't have done anything about it. And with the house and everything—"

"Even with the house and everything, you're still my favorite kid."

I was his only kid. "You have enough going on."

"I still want you to be honest with me. And you never answered the question."

"What question?"

"Are you okay?"

"I don't have to worry about being killed anymore."

"You still didn't answer the question." If I ever wondered where my cross-examination skills came from, I only had to look to my father. "What *do* you have to worry about?"

"The bar exam. A place to live. The one I was in didn't work out."

"But you're living somewhere, aren't you?"

"I'm staying with a friend."

▸▸ CHAPTER 53 ◂◂

It took a while to unravel what had happened, what Hartwell was responsible for and what Agent Beyer had done. The FBI wouldn't tell me everything.

Here's what I was able to piece together: Agent Beyer was on the team that investigated the original Chinese hacks. Cade found whatever it was that Beyer left in the FDIC's systems. It was Cade's tragedy that he was assigned back to Agent Beyer himself. The mole he was looking for was his FBI handler.

The agent was placed in the precarious situation of wanting to know all the information Cade had found but not wanting to reveal himself. He was able to convince Cade they were looking for a mole, an FDIC insider. Unfortunately, Beyer let the investigation go on for one question too long.

It was pure coincidence that Hartwell had been corrupted by the Chinese as well. And it was fate that put Cade at the nexus of both schemes.

Despite the fact that Hartwell was tightly connected to political and social power, despite the fact that he knew what to do, what to wear, what to say in any situation, none of that helped him in the end. As he liked to say, details mattered. The fact that he'd lied about his company's financing and let China into the FDIC's secure systems made his fall from the moneyed elite all the more stunning.

I suspected investigators would eventually discover that millions of dollars in illegal contributions had been injected into our politics. China had been in our financial system for twelve years. For some congressmen—like Representative Thorpe—that was six congressional campaigns. Over the years, with China's prompting, politicians had hollowed out the financial reforms that had been enacted after the Great Recession of 2008. To Congressman Thorpe's credit, he had tried to do the right thing with his bill. But little wonder that when China began to pull strings, all those congressmen changed their minds and voted against it.

All across the country, Chinese citizens had been quietly but quickly leaving the properties they'd purchased. What had been viewed as a boon to the real estate market should have been seen as a massive attempt to get the heck out of Dodge.

As the trade wars were happening, China's objective wasn't to normalize trade relations with us. It was to unbalance our relations with everyone else. We were worried about them manipulating *their* currency? We should have been worried about how they were manipulating *ours.*

The Chinese economy had taken a beating for several years during the trade wars. But they knew we'd be paying for those few years of trade wars for the rest of a generation. By letting us do the hard work of harming ourselves, they were able to simply watch as we punished our own allies, pushing away all of our friends.

I wouldn't be surprised if, someday soon, the FDIC quietly tells the almost five thousand banks they insure to closely examine the credentials of their account holders. I wouldn't be surprised if, in the next year, more laws are put in place to make it more difficult for foreigners to purchase real estate. And I would be shocked if a dozen or more politicians don't suddenly quit campaigning for reelection and decide to resign instead.

▸▸▸◂◂◂

I stayed with Leo until I took the bar exam. But after that, things started to get complicated. We decided that I needed to move out in order for us to figure out if we could move on, into the future, together.

A friend of his had a nanny apartment that they weren't using anymore. Their children had graduated from high school and gone on to college. It was a haven of peace and quiet built above their detached garage. Situated at the back of their woodsy lot, it had all the charms of a tree house.

And multiple layers of security.

▸▸▸◂◂◂

The job lead that was forwarded to me by my professor turned into something big. One of the tech billionaires had chosen cryptocurrency as his pet project. He wanted to save the world—literally—by ensuring that disaster aid for developing countries actually made it into the hands of the disaster's victims. He wanted guarantees that if there were any stipulations—like rebuilding outside of flood plains or replanting fields with environmentally appropriate crops—they were encoded on the currency's blockchain.

The team he was putting together was small, but it was mighty. The day I interviewed with them, we sat around the conference table and debated the merits of the basic concept of a stablecoin. Was it just delaying the inevitable, wholesale move to cryptocurrency, or was it a worthy first step? Most of the team was wearing jeans that day. And part of the compensation package was assistance with paying off student debt.

I signed on to start work at the end of October, even though a permanent position was contingent on passing the bar and being sworn in. That wouldn't happen until after my character and fitness review was completed. I was told that would be in December.

I still had to work at the Blue Dog in the meantime, of course. But now I had the added difficulty of complete strangers recognizing me from the news.

Corrine told me it was a good thing. "Guys like girls who can kick a little you-know-what."

"I can never tell if I know them or not."

"You just stick with me. You never know what might happen. Like that guy right over there." She pointed him out as he walked into the shop. He came to the counter in a roundabout way, nearly tripping over a chair that had been left askew at one of the tables. We'd discovered that was standard for the guy who'd first come to our attention because he was wearing a sling.

She leaned over the counter as he approached. Kissed him. And then she slipped a cup from the stack and marked it for his standard order: an iced coffee with coconut milk.

His approach hid the presence of another man. Now I saw he was heading straight for the counter. Straight for me.

He raised a hand. "Hey, Whitney. It's me. Leo."

But I already knew it was him. I could tell by the way he walked. I could tell by his jacket. I could tell by his hair and by the way he was holding his phone. For me, it was all in the details. And I loved every last one of them about him.

I marked a cup for his order.

He kept pace with me, talking about our upcoming trip at Christmas to visit my dad, as I moved to the espresso machine, pulled the shot, and steamed the milk for it.

When I finished he took it from me, nodding toward a table over by the windows. "I'll just hang out, finish up some emails, while I wait for your shift to end."

As he settled in at the table, I took the next order.

It used to be that I was always the one waiting.

Waiting to pay off my debt.

Waiting to pass the bar.

Waiting for my life to start.

But that was before I met Leo.

Now I knew that life doesn't have a Pause button. It doesn't wait until you're ready for it. It continues in spite of trauma and tragedy. Even when you don't think you have anything to offer. It was Leo who helped me see that in spite of not being able to recognize anyone's face, I was actually pretty good at recognizing most people's souls.

And Leo's was unforgettable. At least to me.

About ten minutes later, when my shift was over, I stiff-armed the swinging door that led to the back room. Then I drew the apron off over my head and looped it over a hook on the wall. After opening my locker, I grabbed my backpack and then headed out to the floor to find Leo.

I walked up and stood beside his table. "Ready?"

He slipped his phone into his pocket and tilted his head up toward me. "Hey. You know something? It's strange. For a person with face blindness, somehow you always seem to find me."

I bent and pressed a kiss to his lips. "You're right where I left you."

"Hmm. Should have changed my jacket, huh?"

"There still would have been your shoes." He always wore brown leather lace-ups when he was working.

He stood. Took my hand in his. "What if I had a beard?"

I stood on tiptoe and nuzzled his neck. "There still would have been your cologne."

"You like it?"

I smiled. "I like it."

He held the door for me as I walked through.

I waited on the sidewalk for him to catch up.

"Hey—what if I cut my hair?"

I reached up to pull at a lock of hair that had slipped onto his forehead. "Don't. I like it just like this."

"I'm going to have to work harder on perfecting my disguise then."

"No." I looped my arm through his. "You need to give it up, Leo. You're going to have to face it: there's just nowhere to hide. Not from me."

AUTHOR'S NOTE

This book almost killed me. Figuratively speaking, of course. As an author who writes from the first-person point-of-view, I experience my stories through my characters' eyes. Whitney Garrison is a driven, intelligent woman. She can't, however, remember faces. As I wrote this story from her perspective, I found I couldn't recognize faces either. My normal method of describing character interactions relies to an extraordinary extent on eye contact and facial expressions. As I placed myself in Whitney's shoes, I was disoriented. It was challenging to depict characters' relationships and emotions with no reference to facial features. More challenging still was the rather late realization that I had two villains instead of just one.

Surprise!

I wrote this story and then rewrote it several times. And just when I started to think I had figured out the plot, I realized I didn't understand it at all. But thanks to the patience and encouragement of my agent and editors, we figured this story out.

Face blindness is a condition that affects about 2.5 percent of the population. It exists on a spectrum. A person can be born with this condition or it can be acquired from a head injury. Some people who think they have trouble remembering names actually have trouble remembering faces. Face blindness can also lead to difficulty in mapping geography, noting differences in skin color, and distinguishing between similar objects, such as cars. The idea of a face-blind person witnessing a crime is not unique to me. I found reference to at least one movie and a Vimeo video that use this premise too. In order to keep their influence from my writing, I didn't watch either of them. I did, however, listen to an NPR interview about face blindness and read many articles written by those who have this condition.

There is no Blue Dog|RINO Coffee Shop. But it is a reference to politics. Blue Dog refers to a Democratic politician who tries to work across the aisle with Republican colleagues. RINO (Republican in Name Only) refers to a Republican politician who is often found voting in favor of Democratic policies. In previous political climates there have always been Blue Dogs and RINOs on Capitol Hill. Currently, in our polarized political environment, the terms are considered to be an insult. In fact there are no longer any Blue Dogs or RINOs on the Hill. Hence the coffee shop's motto, ". . . and other fantastical creatures."

The Italian Store, Punch Bowl Social, and Heidelberg Pastry Shoppe are real, and I encourage you to visit them if you're ever in Arlington.

China did indeed hack the FDIC in 2010. The hacks may have continued into 2012. There were also at least seven major cybersecurity incidents at the FDIC between 2015 and 2016. The FDIC is not the only federal agency that China has hacked. China is also responsible for hacks at the OPM, DISA, DOE, NASA, NSA, DOD, USGS, DOL, USAID, and other government agencies. They've stolen security-clearance information, sets of fingerprints, and "all personnel data . . . for every federal employee, every federal retiree, and up to one million former federal employees," according to the American Federation of Government Employees. The information China has stolen includes military records, addresses, dates of birth, job and pay histories, health insurance and life insurance information, pension information, and data on age, gender, and race for over twenty-one million Americans. What are they doing with all that data?

No one knows for sure.

China is not the only perpetrator of state-sponsored cyberattacks. Russia, North Korea, and Iran often make headlines for hacking other governments.

I imagined the hack of the stablecoin verification system. In the course of writing this story, however, the following events either occurred or came to light:

- The CIA's ownership of Crypto AG allowed the agency to spy on the "secure" communications of both enemies and allies for decades.
- Two Chinese nationals laundered over $100 million in cryptocurrency.
- In 2018 North Koreans gained access to a digital currency exchange and stole hundreds of millions of dollars' worth of the currency. In 2019 North Korea also ran a cryptojacking scheme that diverted crypto coins to servers in North Korea.
- Ivy League schools have been accused of accepting hundreds of millions of dollars in foreign money from countries, including China, without properly reporting the funds.

I almost gave up this story entirely when I realized cryptocurrency was central to the plot. It's not a concept that's easy to grasp. I tried my best to provide enough information to advance the plot without overwhelming it. I hope I succeeded. If not, I think the swift pace at which the technology is developing will probably lead to global comprehension very soon. The next generation will probably make national currencies obsolete.

Street Sense Media publishes a biweekly newspaper and creates content on a variety of media platforms to give a voice and purpose to those who are experiencing homelessness. It provides economic opportunities through its newspaper vendor program and case management services to help people like Ruth find permanent housing and gain access to the services they need in the Washington, DC, area.

The way Whitney grasped China's scheme, by pulling together seemingly unrelated information, echoes the rise of curatorial journalism. In a world that is all data all the time, traditional journalism hasn't yet adapted to the abundance of available information. Current news cycles don't allow journalists to stick with stories long enough to follow them to completion. And they don't allow journalists the time to probe issues deeply. A new sort of journalism is developing that pulls together—or curates—news from many sources and from many different directions.

In our society, it often seems that having money is the ultimate measure of success. Where this is the case, not having money can be interpreted as a character flaw. The pandemic of 2020 has revealed the catastrophic failings of a system in which money has been equated with morality. A system which was designed to reward those who have it instead of protecting those who don't.

As I came up with discussion questions for this book, I thought a lot about the themes of this story and about Whitney's experience. I also spent a lot of time weighing my words. This book is not meant to be an economic screed or a political statement any more than Jesus's words were when someone asked him to choose the most important of his religion's requirements. It's striking to me that when he answered, he didn't choose one of the Ten Commandments. He didn't say, "You shall not commit murder." He didn't remind his listeners not to lie. His highest value had nothing to do with personal freedom or material success. Instead, he made us responsible to each other. He asked us to lift our own sights higher. He asked us to love others as we love ourselves.

This pandemic has, in a way, allowed all of us to examine the beliefs to which we have pledged ourselves, both as individuals and as a society. When we're finally able to start putting things back together, we will have an opportunity to recalibrate. To turn toward each other rather than away. I have no doubt that we can do better. We can do more. For our children, for the class of 2020, and for those students coming along behind them. Because it is not us against everyone else. It is all of us for each other. Our success or failure as a society will depend upon it.

DISCUSSION QUESTIONS

1. Do you consider yourself to be a good judge of character? Do you judge people based on what you observe, or do you rely on your instincts? Have you ever been wrong?
2. Hartwell exhibited some of the classic traits of narcissism. Whitney is a smart person. Why was it so difficult for her to leave Hartwell?
3. In chapter 37 Whitney states her belief that people who have money aren't necessarily better or smarter than everyone else; they're just luckier. Do you agree?
4. Earning a college degree has long been a milestone on the road to the American dream. Like many students of her generation, Whitney went into great debt in order to finance her education, and she finds that instead of opening doors for her, it has limited her options considerably. How did you find yourself reacting to her situation? Did your reaction surprise you?
5. What is the relationship between the two jobs Whitney holds? Do you think her hopes for cryptocurrencies are realistic?
6. Part of the plot in this story revolves around cryptocurrency. How much do you know about this technology? Does the idea of cryptocurrency excite you or terrify you? Why?

7. In chapter 39 Whitney notes that when she was growing up it seemed like her father always knew everything. "And he was always right. I didn't know how to let him be wrong." When you know someone is taking the wrong path or making the wrong choice, what is your responsibility to them?
8. Due to her face blindness, Whitney has lived her life with the daily disappointment of failing at things she can never be good at. Leo challenged Whitney to focus on the things she can do instead of those she can't. When have you been tempted to focus on your weaknesses instead of your strengths? In what ways would your life change if, instead of trying to compensate for what you're not good at, you commit to the things that you are?
9. In the last chapter of the story, Whitney reflected that she was always waiting: "Waiting to pay off my debt. Waiting to pass the bar. Waiting for my life to start." By the end of the story, she realizes that life doesn't have a Pause button and that it continues even when you don't think you have anything to offer. What are you waiting for in your own life? What would it take for you to get on with living?

ACKNOWLEDGMENTS

I owe so much to the team of people who made this book possible. My agent, Natasha Kern, once again came through with exactly the right words exactly when I needed to hear them. My editor, Jocelyn Bailey, gave me much more grace than I deserved. And Erin Healy raised my spirits about this story with her enthusiasm at a point when they were flagging, and then she helped me polish it to a shine.

Writing a book requires vast reserves of mental and emotional energy. It also requires distancing from regular life. Once again, my family generously shared me with my characters during the months it took to write this story. I could not continue to do this without their love and support.

Sarah Reidy explained cryptocurrency to me in a way I could understand. The blame for any mistakes about the concept and how it's portrayed in this story lies with me. Finally, Allison Wolf provided the inspiration for a critical conversation between my characters.

ABOUT THE AUTHOR

Photo by Tim Coburn

Siri Mitchell is the author of sixteen novels. She has also written two novels under the pseudonym of Iris Anthony. She graduated from the University of Washington with a business degree and has worked in various levels of government. As a military spouse, she has lived all over the world, including Paris and Tokyo.

▶▶▶◀◀◀

SiriMitchell.com
Instagram: @siri.mitchell
Facebook: @SiriMitchell
Twitter: @SiriMitchell